The EXchange

The EXchange

Nikki Rashan

www.urbanbooks.net

Urban Books, LLC
78 East Industry Court
Deer Park, NY 11729

The EXchange Copyright © 2013 Nikki Rashan

ISBN 13: 978-1-60162-388-1
ISBN 10: 1-60162-388-7

First Trade Paperback Printing July 2013
Printed in the United States of America

10 9 8 7 6 5 4 3 2 1

This is a work of fiction. Any references or similarities to actual events, real people, living or dead, or to real locales are intended to give the novel a sense of reality. Any similarity in other names, characters, places, and incidents is entirely coincidental.

Distributed by Kensington Publishing Corp.
Submit Wholesale Orders to:
Kensington Publishing Corp.
C/O Penguin Group (USA) Inc.
Attention: Order Processing
405 Murray Hill Parkway
East Rutherford, NJ 07073-2316
Phone: 1-800-526-0275
Fax: 1-800-227-9604

The EXchange

Nikki Rashan

ex-change [iks-cheynj] to give up something for something else; to change for another

Prologue

Kyla

Maybe I wasn't relationship material, after all. After going to sleep and waking up next to Asia for nearly nine years, the monotony of our day-to-day lives had gotten the best of me. From the moment we rolled over to say "Good morning" to the last "Good night," every move felt robotic. I would have even accepted a charming "Bonjour" or *"Buenos días"* from Asia, anything to alter our uniform days, which I could have mimicked in my sleep. Even though some days I wanted to set my hair on fire just to create some excitement in our lives, I didn't intend to leave Asia. I just wanted to shake us out of the relationship coma we remained in. We were alive with beating hearts, but we were otherwise lifeless.

I hadn't felt that way for very long. For eight years, Asia and I had marveled at the beauty of our relationship. The ease with which we interacted, the level of respect we had for one another, and the trust we shared between us. Asia was still my truest, deepest love. Right?

It hit me about a year ago. We had woken on a Monday morning, after a weekend spent lounging around the house together. Every movement we made from the shower to bedtime was a carbon copy of the day before. Before work, we had stood side by side, applied makeup, and prepared our hair together. Inside the walk-in closet, I had reached for a dark-colored business suit, while Asia had grabbed a comfortable pair of jeans and a long-sleeve cotton shirt. I had put on four-inch heels; she had put on walking shoes.

Downstairs we had filled our individual thermoses with black coffee, grabbed our workbags (mine a briefcase, hers a duffel), kissed lightly on the lips, and headed to the garage. Asia had backed out first and tooted her horn before driving off, and I had left next. That was our morning routine every single workday.

In the evenings, we would relax in the family room with carryout dinner or the latest recipe one of us had tried to make, and watch a blur of reality television shows Asia loved. The shows we watched weren't dependent upon the season like a sitcom or drama. Reality TV had no preference for sunshine or snow; reality shows dominated television all year round, and Asia loved them all, from celebrity competitions to shows about backstabbing, two-faced women forced to fake friendships. Later, after we had watched the round of shows that appealed to Asia, we would go upstairs and perform most of the morning routine, but in reverse.

Most nights we would change into comfortable pajamas, but it seemed that approximately every four days we would make love, and that particular Monday evening we were on our fourth day. So that night we emerged from the closet naked and hopped into bed. Asia promptly settled on top of me and swiftly performed her routine: She spent a few minutes kissing my lips, my ears, my neck, and my breasts. She stroked each nipple for about a minute each before her fingertips trailed down to my middle. She caressed me "there" the way she knew I loved, and didn't stop until I was ready. I knew this because she always told me. With one final rub to my lower lips, she looked at me, grinned, and said, "She's ready." Then she lowered herself and proceeded to please me.

Afterward, we swapped spots, and I pleased Asia in the ways in which she loved. As she approached orgasm, she whispered, "Yes, Kyla." A few moments later, she repeated herself. "Yes, Kyla." A longer gap followed. Her body tensed and tightened; her breathing halted. And in one exhale and release, she said it again. "Yessss, Kyla." This, too, happened every time.

I said all that not to suggest there was anything wrong with my and Asia's relationship. We had yet to encounter any major disruptions since we had been together. We loved one another, and the love we had was good. It flowed effortlessly. It was comfortable. It was really comfortable. Maybe a bit *too* comfortable, as my ex-best friend Tori warned would happen with any long-term relationship. We certainly had our moments of spontaneity and new experiences. Occasionally, we'd go out at the last minute on a Friday night and dance until our thirtysomething bodies could no longer bend, shake, and sway. We treated ourselves to twice-a-year vacations, one to a place we both longed to go, usually to a Caribbean island, and another to one of our hometowns. We alternated between Wisconsin and Texas. And sometimes we'd make love from the moment we dropped our briefcase and duffel bag in the foyer, and ran into the family room, up the stairs, and into our bedroom, until the early morning hours. However, 9.5 days out of ten we stuck to our routine.

The replication of each day had suddenly pinched me like a random twitching nerve on that particular Monday. With each repetitive day, the intensity had increased, until I had become a full-blown, walking, emotionally agitated funny bone, one filled with strange sensations that would not subside no matter how strongly I willed them to. What was a girl to do?

***
Asia

Nine years was a long time to be in a relationship, and I was proud of the fact that Kyla and I had succeeded in this feat. I had to admit that in the beginning, and even after we had moved in together, I was not always certain we would make it that far. Sure, I had faith we would last, and from the moment I fell in love with Kyla, I prayed we would grow together into little old women with canes. But based on Kyla's previous hit-and-run track record, I didn't know if she would have the stamina to maintain a long-term partnership. Her lengthiest relationship, four years, had been with Jeff, and in the end she . . . what? She cheated on him with Stephanie.

Many days I had to remind myself that if it were not for their affair and Kyla's revelation of her love for women, I wouldn't have been able to have her. On those same days, I also hoped her cheating days, along with the "love 'em and leave 'em" habit she formed once she got to Atlanta, were over. Kyla had been intimate with more women than she could count, and I, like them, fell in love with her despite her seeming inability to settle. As time passed, Kyla had proven that I was the only one she wanted and desired. "You make me want to be a better me," she once told me, and a better Kyla she had been. I was human, though, and every so often I had to rein in my doubtful thoughts and reaffirm to myself that our relationship was not about who she was in the past, but who she was with me.

It had only been recently, in the past year or so, that I had had to remind myself of that more frequently. While Kyla had been every bit the woman I had hoped she would be, it seemed that one day there was a sudden shift in her temperament. Although we continued to maneuver through our days as usual, underneath her complacent behavior I felt her discontentment. She hadn't done or said anything to make me feel that way. She didn't have to. I could see it in her weary smile when we said good-bye each morning, and after twelve months of that familiar expression, still she had not opened up about the gloom that surrounded her. It seemed she had reverted to the reluctant Kyla I first met, afraid to share her truest emotions.

In the evenings, when we reunited and I was greeted by the same smile, I tried to imagine the thoughts in her mind. On occasion, I attempted to talk to her and find out why she seemed so detached. But I got nowhere. About six months ago, we were sitting on the couch in the family room, our usual spot for dinner, and faced again with her reserved disposition, I had the urge to ask her if something was the matter.

"You've been extra quiet lately, honey. Something been bothering you?"

Kyla looked at me thoughtfully. Behind her still expression I could see a swirl of emotions and thoughts running through her mind. As in the past, no words found their way out of her mouth. She was determined to hold them in.

"No, not really. Same stuff."

"Stuff like what?" I asked, pressing.

She shrugged.

"If something is wrong, I wish you'd talk to me." I tried to conceal my agitation, but her unwillingness to share her feelings aggravated me more than whatever she had to say. Kyla could tell me she wanted to go live on the moon for a year, and while I would certainly tell her not only that she was crazy but also that it was impossible, at least I would know she trusted me with her feelings. I had to believe that whatever she was concealing made it too difficult for her to endure the invasion of her private thoughts.

I only hoped she would be able to resolve whatever was causing her uneasiness in a manner that was conducive to us and the longevity of our relationship. And that she'd do so as soon as possible. The hazy state of our relationship couldn't go on much longer.

The Offer
One
Kyla

"We broke up."

"You broke up?" I repeated and immediately stood to close my office door. I sat back down in my chair. "What happened?"

"She said I was too much."

"Too much what?"

"Too much everything. Too loving, too helpful, too willing to sacrifice myself for her."

"Angie . . ." I paused, uncertain what to say next. "That doesn't make sense. Who says that?"

"Deidra, apparently. She said I was too involved in every aspect of her life and she had no independence."

"Well, you've been together a long time. Of course, you're supposed to be involved in her life. Asia and I involve each other in everything we do."

Angie sighed. "She told me she feels suffocated. That she has no room to breathe and be herself. She said I'm just too much." She sighed again.

Angie was my ex-girlfriend. Well, let me correct that statement. Angie and I used to "spend time" together, which meant we shared a fiercely intense intimate relationship. But we were never an official couple. We met shortly after my move to Atlanta, just as I was embarking on a year-plus-long deep voyage into Atlanta's sea of gay women. I had laid my head on pillows across

metro Atlanta, from Kennesaw to Morrow and every
suburb in between. During that stage, Angie had been
my only constant lover. Most of my interactions had
been one-night stands or short-lived trysts. It was only
when I had grown weary of my own behavior and had
met Asia that I ended my extended fling with Angie.

Ironically, Deidra just happened to be Asia's ex. We
ran into each other over eight years ago, and after an
awkward reunion, the four of us became fast friends.
Although it took a while for Asia to warm up to of a
friendship with Deidra—she had learned that Deidra
was seeing Angie before she and Asia officially broke
up—they had grown to tolerate each other's company
again in a cool, platonic manner. We were an odd
bunch: a foursome who had all directly and indirectly
slept together. We had survived the "ex-to-friend"
transition and had maintained trusting connections
ever since.

From what I knew about Angie, she was indeed a
giver, a pleaser. She wanted nothing more than to see
to it that her woman was happy. In fact, the more I silently thought about it, the more I realized that was part
of the reason I didn't settle with her myself. She wanted
to "take care of me," and I wasn't the right woman to
fill that need for her. I could imagine that after a while
I would lose my independence owing to her protective
nature. She wasn't controlling, but she did want to be
active in all areas of her woman's life, from the sim-
plest gesture of opening a car door to supporting her
woman's every need, emotionally and financially. Who
wouldn't want that? I didn't. In the end, Deidra didn't,
either, despite the love she had exhibited toward Angie
over the years I had witnessed their relationship.

"I'm sorry, Angie. I never would have seen this coming."

"I think I did," she confessed, to my surprise. "Ever since we got her beauty shop up and running, she's been extra busy, spending more and more time at work or hanging out with the other stylists. Her wallet got thick, and her friends expanded. She didn't need me anymore." The way Angie spoke with such clarity and indifference, it was almost as if she were opining about the end of someone else's relationship and not her own.

I thought about the number of engagements we were supposed to attend as a group over the past several months but didn't. Angie backed out because Deidra could not attend. We hadn't realized those were signs of the beginning of the end.

"Why don't you come over tonight? Asia and I will be having an *American Idol* evening. Join us."

"You know I don't watch TV," she replied. I knew that as true. Before Deidra, Angie had one unplugged television in her apartment. When Angie wasn't giving her attention to work, she was giving it to her woman. Why should she waste time gazing at a television when she could gaze at her woman? Damn, maybe she was too much. When Deidra moved in, two new televisions were added to their space, with cable channels and all.

"One night of tube watching won't kill those nerdy computer brain cells of yours," I joked.

She acquiesced with a slight chuckle. "Okay, I'll come over."

"I should call Deidra." Asia closed the cabinet door harder than necessary and opened the box of noodles she had retrieved from inside. She was making spaghetti. Again. It was a quick and easy dish and her favorite to make when we had guests. Only, she made it far more often than that.

"You should," I urged her. Asia hated to "not know" something, and already she had become irritated that Deidra hadn't mentioned her veered feelings about Angie.

"I can't believe she didn't tell me."

"Why would she tell you?" I asked. "She knows you'll just tell me."

Asia placed the noodles in the pot of boiling water. "Say she did, and I told you. You would have told Angie, right?"

"I doubt it."

"See, she could have told me, then," she concluded.

"That would have put us all in a weird position, so I'm glad she didn't."

Asia squinted at me with her dark, beautiful eyes. She still handled me with calm aggression. She was always direct and to the point and didn't allow me to shuffle my thoughts and feelings under the rug when we were in conversation. That was the main reason I hadn't mentioned my boredom to her; she would eat me alive. I had already played the conversation in my mind.

"You're bored because what, Kyla?" She would ask, speaking in a cynical but gentle motherly tone.

"Because we do the same thing every day."

"What do you want to do differently?"

"I don't know."

"Have you tried to do anything differently?"

"Not really."

"We have jobs, so we really can't change that," she would state.

"I know."

"We have to eat, and we've already been to nearly every restaurant in the city."

"I know."

"Do you want a new car?"

"I just got one last year."

*"Yes, I'm aware of that. You just seem to need to
liven things up a bit. I didn't know if that would help."*
Her eyes would look at me quizzically. *"New house?"*

"Come on, Asia. No," I would answer with a grateful look around our four-bedroom home.

"New clothes? More money?"

"No and no."

*"Do you miss your family? Want to see your niece
and nephew?"*

Years ago, my sister, Yvonne, had gifted me a niece,
Gladyce, now ten. Since then she had had another
child, James, who was six.

"My trip home is already booked for the spring."

*"So you're happy with your house, car, job, clothes,
and family. That leaves me."*

Another stare standoff while she awaited a response
to a question she didn't ask. Of course I was happy
with her, I would think. I just wanted something—anything—exciting.

"I'm more than happy with you."

"I see. So the problem is what, then, Kyla?"

The imaginary conversation always ended with that
question because there was no way to explain the antsiness I felt inside and, worse, to cure it.

Asia acquiesced with a soft sigh. "You're right, it'll be
awkward because one of our couple friends has broken
up and now we're friends in the middle." She paused
for a second. "Let's see if it's really over first. Maybe
there's still hope for them."

"Sure," I agreed.

Asia stirred the boiling noodles and dismissed the
subject. "How was your day?"

And so we began our nightly rundown of what had happened during our day. Asia's home health care business had expanded over the years, and to handle the increased patient count, she had hired a growing list of nurses and case managers. Asia's love for personal care hadn't diminished, and she still assigned a few special patients to herself.

I actually held the position of my former boss, Gary, and was the purchasing manager at the department store I had worked at since my move to Atlanta. Gary's love for young music sensations had eventually benefitted us both. Gary had jumped at the chance to leave his position five years ago, after his daughter, Missy, joined a girls' singing group, A-LIVE, and experienced local fame. Gary became the group's manager, and when I last spoke with him, A-LIVE was still performing at various small venues in metro Atlanta.

Oddly, now I understood why Gary had always been so relaxed and easygoing in the office, while his buyers stayed frazzled. Most of the work he delegated, and those underneath him worked harder than he ever chose to. I, however, empathized with the buyers in my department and took on certain tasks Gary never did. I still took advantage of the less strenuous hours and left the store no later than 5:30 P.M. most days.

Most of the buyers I worked with were wonderful, particularly Andrea, my former assistant, who filled my position after my promotion. Andrea had married her love, Santino, and Asia and I were frequent guests at their family's events, including the *quinceañera* of Andrea's niece and the wedding of Santino's cousin. Andrea remained wise beyond her years, and I continued to rely on her natural instincts in times of need.

It was Erika, a sassy, brassy East Coast know-it-all, who got under every inch of my skin. She was an arrogant young thing who thought Manhattan was the Garden of Eden and Atlanta the devil's paradise. So why didn't she move back to New York? I had asked her that very question on a number of occasions. She had no real explanation, other than she had moved here with a guy friend and didn't want to leave him by going back home.

On top of her relentless arrogant attitude, Erika hated two things: black people and gay people. I found that insanely amusing, considering the city in which she lived. Her expression became pinched like a pug-nosed dog when I was introduced as her boss. She looked at my skin as if she hoped someone had played a cruel joke on her and in just one minute I would reveal myself as a blue-eyed, fair-skinned woman dressed in black face. Our relationship never had a chance to develop and only went downhill from there.

Every day I would have at least one Erika episode that I shared with Asia. But now the stories, though at times slightly varied, had begun to sound uninteresting.

"Erika rolled her eyes at me today, when she thought I wasn't looking."

"Erika made a snide comment about lesbians when she knew I was within earshot."

"Erika asked to be reassigned to another department so she wouldn't have to work under me anymore."

Asia's responses had gone from "Girl, she needs a good slap upside her head" to "Same old stuff, huh?" to the reaction she gave me after that day's story—a simple "Mmm-hmm" that screamed, "I've heard this before."

We silently waited for Angie.

***

With the spaghetti we drank wine, and with the wine came giggles. By the end of the first hour of *American Idol,* we were a slurring threesome. Angie's demeanor was so light and carefree, I had begun to wonder if she had fallen out of love with Deidra herself. She smiled when she told us that she and Deidra hadn't been intimate in three months. She laughed as she said Deidra would be moving out in a couple weeks. And she nearly fell on the floor in amusement, unable to catch her breath, when she stated that Deidra planned to reimburse Angie for all the money she had put into Deidra's shop, Beautiful You, and that she wanted back Angie's keys to the salon.

Asia and I laughed nervously with her, confused by Angie's joyful state. But not for long. When Angie came up for air, her giggles turned to whimpers, and her tears of laughter transformed into tears. Her usually cool demeanor shattered, and she broke into a shoulder-shaking cry. I looked at Asia and she at me, until our natural instincts kicked in a few seconds late. Asia lifted Angie's chin and placed a hand on her back and another on Angie's chest when it seemed Angie was unable to exhale and breathe properly. I ran for tissues from the guest bathroom and returned to wipe Angie's eyes and wet nose. I sat in front of Angie, with Asia to her side, and we remained in that position while Angie released the suppressed hurt from within.

We consoled her simultaneously.

"It's going to be okay, Angie," I softly told her.

"These things take time," Asia added.

"We're here if you need us," I assured her.

"Are you sure it's really over?" Asia asked.

I pinched Asia's ankle. I couldn't believe she had asked that question while we sat together and observed the anguish Angie suffered.

"Yes," Angie breathed heavily. Then sniffed. "It's really"—double sniff, then whining exhale—"over."

Asia and I caught each other's eye again, and though she gave me an apologetic look, clearly she was satisfied to confirm the demise of the relationship. For several more minutes we consoled Angie in the way most friends do: we took her side.

"It's Deidra's loss," Asia said bitterly, seemingly still perturbed by the way Deidra had abruptly ended their relationship.

"If she doesn't appreciate all you have to offer, you're better off without her," I declared. It was odd, though, considering that Angie had offered me all of her and I had declined as well. I began to feel hypocritical bestowing worthiness praises upon Angie when I had not wanted her in a relationship capacity, either.

Angie accepted our encouragement with nods of her head and soft "mmm-hmm" moans of acknowledgment and agreement. Eventually, her tears slowed, and she regained her typical relaxed composure. As that happened, her expression swiftly switched from one of sorrow to one of red-faced discomfort. She seemed embarrassed to have lost control and revealed her vulnerability. I knew Angie to be sensitive, although I had witnessed her sensitivity only when she was trying to be nurturing, not when she felt injured.

Angie wiped dry the tears on her crimson skin and let out an awkward chuckle. "Damn wine." She half smirked. "I think I'm going to go."

"You don't have to leave," I quickly told her. I didn't want her to feel like she wasn't welcome to express herself in any way she needed.

"No, really. I think I've ruined your *American Idol* party." She looked at Asia, knowing the *American Idol* show wasn't necessarily my idea.

"It's okay. There are seven more weeks of the show." Asia gave Angie a small smile.

Angie stood, anyway. We stood too.

"Let me go on and get out of here," Angie repeated.

"Well, come by anytime, okay?" Asia requested.

"Sure, I'll do that."

Asia tilted her head at me, a slight gesture that advised me to walk Angie out.

"I'll go with you to your car," I told Angie.

Asia and Angie exchanged a hug before Angie dragged herself solemnly toward the front door. I grabbed a jacket from the hall closet and followed. The late February night had lowered the temperature into the unwelcome twenties. Outside we stood next to Angie's car.

"You sure you're all right?" I asked her.

"I'll be okay. Guess I didn't realize I had such deep feelings about all of this." She stared at me, and in her eyes I caught a glimpse of something I hadn't seen in years. "More than you really know, Kyla."

"Breakups are never easy," I offered.

"No, they're not. Not when you really love someone." She didn't blink when she spoke those words to me. I knew exactly what she was implying, and I chose to ignore it and assumed her heightened emotions had got the best of her. There was no way Angie could seriously flirt with me on the day of her breakup, and right outside of my house.

"We're good?" she asked after I disregarded her statement.

"What do you mean?"

"We can still be friends even with me and Deidra not being together, right?"

"I don't see why not."

"Good." Though Angie's tears had dried, her face reddened again. "Don't leave me hanging, you hear?"

"Why would I do that?"

"Because you did before. I don't want to lose you again."

I raised my eyebrows at her but avoided responding to that statement as well. "Get home safely. Text me, and let me know you made it." I reached for a hug. She wrapped her arms around me tightly.

"Thank you," she whispered. "I'm so glad I have you."

When we released each other from the embrace, I looked directly into her eyes. "That's what friends are for."

Two

Asia

It seemed every time I turned around, Kyla was on the phone with Angie. If I called her while I was driving, she would have to put me on hold while she ended her conversation with Angie. When she walked in the house from work, her cell phone was to her ear. She would hold up her finger to me and delay our interaction until they finished their exchange. In the evenings, as we watched television, she would excuse herself to have periodic five- and ten-minute conversations with Angie. I respected her willingness to aid in Angie's healing, though at times it was excessive. Didn't Angie have any other friends to lean on during the breakup?

"How's she doing?" I asked Kyla several nights after Angie's visit.

"She seems to be okay. In some ways, she's okay with the relationship being over. But it also seems like she doesn't trust Deidra's reason for wanting to end it."

"What? She doesn't believe that Deidra felt suffocated?"

"Right. I mean, she admits she wanted to be a part of everything Deidra did, but she won't accept that as the sole reason for the breakup."

"Does it even matter?" I asked. "If someone doesn't want to be with you, does it matter the reason why?"

"Of course it matters," Kyla countered.

"I disagree. What matters is that the person doesn't want you. The reason why . . . who cares?"

Kyla laughed. "So if I told you I wanted to end our relationship, you wouldn't care to know the reason why?" she teased.

I smiled. "Don't go turning this into something personal."

"Just asking. Hypothetically speaking, you wouldn't care what the reason is?"

I turned down the TV volume. "Well, of course I'd be curious about why. What happened? Did I do something wrong? But if the fact is that you want to leave me, I guess that's all I need to know."

"I could walk away from our relationship after nine years without you so much as asking why?" she challenged. Her playful mood had vanished.

"Probably. If the end result is the same—you don't want to be with me—I'm not going to pester you for reasons why," I explained to her.

"From my standpoint I would think you didn't care. Maybe you even wanted the relationship to end too but didn't say it."

My expression turned thoughtful. "Yeah, I guess I didn't think about that. I can see that. You're right. There's always two ways to view the exact same situation. It just depends upon the person's position and perspective."

"You're right about that. Two people can be in the exact same place and still feel differently about it," she replied, pensive.

We were quiet again after I turned the TV volume back up. I saw the lips moving on the famous host's face, but I heard no words. There was something about Kyla's statement that had me unsettled. It was as if I could feel that she really meant something by those words, and this underscored my observation that something had been bothering her but she wouldn't say what.

I laid my head on Kyla's lap, and instinctively, as always, she began to stroke her fingers through my hair and against my scalp. She looked down at me with sad, distant eyes.

"What are you thinking?" I asked, probing, and turned the volume down again.

"What makes you ask?"

"Don't answer my question with a question. You know I hate that."

She stared at the TV. "Nothing's wrong," she told me.

"You bothered by what I just said about breakups?"

"Not really."

"Not really doesn't mean no, so what's wrong?"

She contemplated her words. "I guess it bothers me that it seems like you wouldn't care if we broke up. After all this time, how can you not care?"

"I didn't say I wouldn't care," I replied, clarifying the issue. "If you broke up with me, I'm not going to dwell on the reason why. If you didn't give me a reason, why would I sit back, biting my nails, trying to figure it out?"

We turned our attention back to the television but only for a second.

"I don't want to know after the fact. Be woman enough to tell me if there's a problem before the breakup even happens," I continued.

She didn't say anything, but the twitch in her lip told me that my words had pinched a nerve.

"What is it?" I asked, hoping she might finally reveal what had her troubled recently.

Kyla's hesitation spoke volumes; her reluctance confirmed that there was without a doubt something she wanted to share. She surrendered to the weight of her secret.

"Nothing, Asia," she lied to me.

I sat up abruptly, irritated, so Kyla couldn't run her fingers through my hair anymore.

"What?" she asked, confused.

With the remote in hand, I ended my seesawing with the volume and turned it back up for the last time.

"Nothing."

We were quiet less than thirty seconds before Kyla's cell phone vibrated on the coffee table in front of us. Neither of us had to guess who it was. Kyla answered, our conversation suddenly forgotten and her spirit lightened once again. She and her cell phone left the room and went into the kitchen, from where I soon heard laughter. I turned the volume on the TV up higher.

Three

Kyla

I was so happy Asia and I had decided not to adopt a child. That moment of gratitude surfaced while I waited in McDonald's on a Sunday morning and sipped on cheap, but delicious coffee. Around me were a number of red-eyed, frazzled moms who tended to toddlers who stood in their seats, got grape jelly between their fingers, and demanded to go to Playland. Over the years, Asia and I had babysat my godson Aidyn, the son of my friend Nakia, and had experienced such traumatic outings ourselves. Asia and I realized the level of patience and devotion required to raise children full-time was more than we possessed.

For some time we felt guilty about our decision. What woman didn't want to procreate and bring life into this world? We believed ourselves to be so selfish. It took one additional crying episode from Aidyn when we had to leave a candy store against his will for us to confirm and accept that kids would not be a part of our future. *Hallelujah,* I thought as I continued to watch the struggling moms, while the dads read the newspaper, oblivious to, or ignoring, the chaos around them.

I checked the time on my cell phone. Angie was ten minutes late. Over the past week and a half I had talked to Angie every day, more than we had during the course of our friendship. Even when she and I had dated casually, we'd enjoyed only once-a-week calls. Most of our conversations involved me reminding Angie of the common adage that people come into our lives for reasons, seasons, or lifetimes, and even though Deidra was only for a season, she was for a reason too, and it was up to Angie to figure that out. Angie received my consolations graciously, with little disputing or questioning. In most breakups, the dumped tended to dwell on what she could have done differently or how she could have changed to satisfy the dumper's needs. Instead, Angie had concluded that if Deidra wanted out, that was on Deidra; she took no responsibility for the end of their relationship. And she gave me the impression that she was over the relationship already. Her indifference confused me, and I quietly questioned the sincerity of her outburst at my house.

While discussing those who had transitioned in and out of our lives for reasons or seasons, Angie had concluded that I was in hers for a lifetime. She had decided that there must be something special about our connection, especially when she considered she had not maintained friendships with any of the other women she had dated in the past.

"You're unique," she'd told me. "I always felt that about you."

I responded that her current crisis was not about me, and definitely not what we once had, to ensure that she healed from the breakup with Deidra and emerged with a healthy state of mind. Although it was my plan to focus solely on Angie's happiness, as I talked with her on a regular basis, I became aware of the beautiful qualities she possessed, some which I hadn't recognized over the years. When she was with Deidra, we talked, but mostly about the day-to-day "surface" topics in life: her IT business, my work, and our relationships. When we went out as a foursome, our interactions were light and fun. Angie and Deidra were the couple we hung with for a good time, not to exchange viewpoints on politics, spirituality, or any subject of a deep, personal nature.

The more I talked with Angie, the more I learned things about her that I had not been receptive to during our moments of pillow talk. Well, Angie and I hadn't really engaged in pillow talk. In the bedroom, the only words spoken were explicit, and when we went out on random dates, Angie spent that time wooing me and attempting to convince me to be her woman. In hindsight, I realized I hadn't actually known many details about Angie. I knew she was good in bed. She was the best, if I had to be honest. Although I had not one complaint about my sex life with Asia, even she hadn't brought me to the sexual heights Angie had. Occasionally, I would involuntarily slip into a fantasy about my and Angie's bedtime experiences. Once in a while we would be out and I would catch Angie kissing Deidra on the ear, and I could almost feel the kiss myself. Angie's smooth lips were some of the softest I had ever felt. Sometimes Angie would look at me after the kiss, and I'd have to rush and look away. In those instances I was reminded of the delicious ways she had tantalized every section of my body.

I felt like it was only after Angie and Deidra's breakup that I got to know who Angie really was beyond her sexual abilities. I learned why she loved women the way she did. Growing up, Angie had idolized her father, and from him she had learned the treasures of a woman. She had observed, and later mimicked, the way in which her father freely showered her mother with affection. He complimented her mother's every new outfit and hairstyle. He praised her cooking, helped with cleaning, and pampered her with sporadic visits to the spa for massages and manicures. His eyes would light up when her mother walked into a room, whether she had just awoken and entered the kitchen, disheveled and sleepy-eyed, or had spent hours doing her hair and makeup before an evening of fine dining. He ensured that Angie's mom never had to work too hard and still made sure all her needs were met. Angie had taken note of her father's silent and overt gestures of adoration and had pledged to show her woman the same appreciation.

Angie had said she couldn't figure out why she had been unable to maintain a relationship with a woman who welcomed such devotion. When Angie explained her father's history of loving and how it had influenced her, my thoughts temporarily betrayed me and I wondered, had I taken the time to learn about Angie in the past, would our future have been different? Could we have been more than just friends with benefits? Could my present be with her and not Asia? I had to shake off those thoughts. Although I wanted to be the support Angie needed, I couldn't allow her breakup to break into my thought processes in a destructive way. I had to regain the control I had so easily begun to lose.

"Hey," Angie said and slid into the booth opposite me.

"Morning, Angie." I looked at her empty hands. "Where's your coffee?"

"I was going to check and see what you wanted first, but I see you already got yours." She seemed disappointed. I had cheated her, deprived her of the opportunity to do something for me. "Need anything else?" she asked, hopeful.

"Sure. How about an order of hash browns?"

Angie jumped back up. "Be right back."

She returned a few minutes later with a large coffee and two hash browns. "I didn't know if maybe you wanted two," she told me as she passed them to me.

I recalled saying, "An order of hash browns," as in one, but took them both graciously. "So how are you doing today?" I asked her.

She sipped on her coffee and stared past me as she determined what the appropriate response should be. I used that moment of hesitation to take in her physical appearance. I remembered why I had been so attracted to her. She was still such a cutie. Angie had never been a girlie woman; I had never seen her in a dress and heels or with heavily applied makeup. She was, however, aware of her femininity and enhanced it with silver hoop earrings, light eyeliner, and fitted jeans. Across from me, she had on a snug pair of dark jeans and a black T-shirt with a cream-colored thermal top underneath. She had allowed her normally short, curly hair to grow out over the past few years and wore it smoothed back in a long ponytail. Her skin had aged ever so slightly, and only when she smiled did the gentle crinkles around the corners of her eyes reveal that she was nearing her fortieth birthday.

"I'm doing just fine," Angie finally announced.

"What's the temperature like at home?" I asked, considering that Angie and Deidra had another week of living together before Deidra moved out.

"I haven't seen much of her. I've been taking on extra work orders, trying to stay away from the house. She seems to be working a lot too, and when I hear her come in at night, it's well past midnight." Angie stared off again. "I don't know what's keeping her out so late."

Angie and I had already discussed whether she thought Deidra had already found companionship in someone else. As well known as Angie was in the lesbian community, we thought that if Deidra was indeed involved with someone new, it would have gotten back to Angie. But to our knowledge, Deidra didn't have anyone else. If she did, she kept it top secret and out of Angie's eyeshot and earshot.

"She's probably just trying to stay away too."

"Right," Angie agreed, though her tone hinted at uncertainty.

"I'm actually surprised you're not working today. Isn't that one of your staples? Being available twenty-four-seven? I thought for sure you'd get some early morning hours in."

Angie smiled genuinely. "I thought I'd spend the day with you," she told me.

My eyebrows crinkled. "What? All day?"

"Yeah. There's a small-business owners' conference at the Omni Hotel. It's the last day, and there are a couple sessions I registered to attend. I hoped you'd join me."

I was confused. Why did Angie think I would be open to spending my entire Sunday with her? She hadn't even asked if I had plans, but had just assumed I would clear my calendar to spend more time with her. "Angie, no, I'm sorry. I can't."

"Oh, do you and Asia have plans already?" Her tone suggested she was confident that we didn't.

I groaned on the inside. Asia was out on her usual day off, making what looked like one of her final visits with an ailing patient. That was part of the reason I had agreed to meet Angie versus sleep in comfortably next to Asia. I didn't know how long Asia would be unavailable, and sadly, whenever she did return home, we had no plans. It was likely that we would spend another Sunday evening indoors watching a rented movie or catching up on the remaining string of reality shows we had recorded on DVR during the week. If I went with Angie to the conference, surely I would be home by early evening and would have the rest of the night with Asia. I supposed it wouldn't be a big deal to attend with her.

"What time are the sessions?" I asked Angie.

Angie grinned behind her Styrofoam cup, an obvious indication that she was pleased I had considered her offer.

"Noon and two o'clock."

"Okay. Let me text Asia and let her know."

Angie waited while I sent a short message to Asia: Headed to the Omni Hotel with Angie. I hit the back button to correct that. Headed to a small-business conference at the Omni with Angie. She needs company. See you later.

"Should I drive?" Angie asked. "Then we don't have to look for and pay for two parking spots."

I wished I had an explanation for the unexpected uneasiness I felt about riding in Angie's car. I felt silly for being uncomfortable and even sillier that I acted as if she were some random stranger I had just picked up in McDonald's, like it was a nightclub. She was Angie, my friend of ten years, so what was there to be fidgety about? I grabbed my purse.

"Sure, I'll ride with you."

We left with our half-filled cups and got inside Angie's luxury sedan. I hadn't been inside Angie's new Porsche Panamera, an upgrade from the Lexus she had driven when we dated. The smell was strangely familiar, a mixture of Angie's signature perfume and coconut-scented car freshener.

We rode quietly, and not surprisingly, we listened to a CD of contemporary jazz. That was all I had ever known Angie to play in her car, and in her bedroom too. It was relaxing and seductive, just like Angie's natural aura and charm. Suddenly I became shyly aware of her presence and took a long gulp of coffee to swallow the rising tickle from my belly. Angie brought forth a feeling of excitement and newness I hadn't known in quite some time. Although I knew Angie sexually, having learned about her on a deeper emotional level, combined with the physical closeness, was surprisingly thrilling. I sighed inside. That wasn't the type of stimulation I had hoped for in my life. I wanted it from Asia, but I got it with Angie.

"So what's going on with you, Kyla? We've been talking incessantly about me, and that's not my style. Talk to me about you. What's on your mind?"

I was not going to tell Angie my thoughts at that moment. Not because I felt she would be dismayed by my straying thoughts. I already recognized the yearning in her eyes when she looked at me. She didn't attempt to conceal her desire. I didn't tell her, because an admission of such thoughts would betray Asia and feed into Angie's energy. I questioned my actions and myself. How had I become so quickly tempted to surrender to my feelings for Angie? It had been only a little over a week since she and Deidra broke up, and only then did she and I begin to relate on another level. However, for an entire year I had been craving some relief from boredom. Next to Angie, bored I was not. Still, I was not prepared to give in to rationalizing unfaithfulness, so I talked about the only subject that would set Angie and me straight.

"Asia and I are doing great," I told her, even though she had asked only about me. "Work is going really well for both of us."

"That's good," Angie responded as she took a turn onto the freeway and headed downtown. "I've noticed you don't work quite the long hours you used to," she added.

"No, not so much."

"That must be nice. Now you have time to do more things together."

"True."

"Hey, did you two check out that play that was here recently?" Angie was referring to a soulful musical, one that Asia and I had heard about on the radio but had opted not to attend.

"No, we didn't go."

"Have you seen Leonardo DiCaprio's latest movie? I heard it's really good."

I looked out the window. "No, we haven't seen it."

She tried again. "I bet you've checked out the latest exhibit at the art museum. I know how much you love museums."

My stomach cringed. I knew of the exhibit, though I had not made the effort to go. So much of my and Asia's "free" time was spent catching up on household chores, like laundry, and tending to necessities, such as car servicing and grocery shopping. Or we simply relaxed after busy workdays, mostly vegging in front of the television.

"Nope, we haven't been to the museum."

"Damn, you two sound like me and Deidra toward the end . . . not doing anything together."

Her words were a verbal slap. How dare she insinuate that my and Asia's relationship was showing signs of impending demise? Maybe I was just extra sensitive about the fact that someone else had noticed its lackluster state.

"We are *not* like you and Deidra," I insisted, irritated by Angie's suggestion.

Her right hand met my left thigh. She rubbed it. I liked it. "I'm sorry. I wasn't trying to upset you. It's just that the Kyla I know likes to have fun. You've always known how to have a good time."

"All that fun I used to have wasn't always good for me," I reminded her, even though fun was exactly what I craved.

Angie nodded and removed her hand. We rode silently the rest of the way to the hotel. Angie had to catch herself when she headed over to open my car door for me. She was the only woman I had ever permitted to do such a kind gesture for me on some of our dates, and though I had always told her I was capable of opening doors and exiting on my own, she had insisted. I opened my door just as she was rounding the back end of the car to do it for me.

"Oh, right," she said, but she still grabbed the handle before I could and closed the door behind me.

"You sure we're dressed okay for this?" I eyed her weekend attire and my own pair of jeans.

"Yeah, it's a casual thing."

She was right. Inside we were greeted by men and women dressed in a similar fashion making their way to various small conference rooms. Angie signed in at the registration table and picked up the guide that identified the sessions and room numbers. We entered a room to hear a lecture offering guidance to CEOs of one-man businesses and took a seat in the back row. Angie pulled a small notepad and pen from the leather hip bag around her waist. She jotted down a few pointers while the speaker shared tools for time management. I half listened, my mind mostly focused on the way Angie's knee tilted outward when she leaned forward to write and how it had rested gently against my knee. I assumed that the move was accidental, and though it was innocent enough, the denim-to-denim touch felt like fire. I readjusted myself, crossing my leg so that it pointed in the opposite direction. Angie noticed and shook her head at me with a playful smirk. I was grateful when the hour-long session concluded.

"I really appreciate you coming with me," Angie stated as we roamed the busy hotel and waited for the next session.

"No problem. I just want to make sure you're all right." We stopped outside the hotel gift shop. "You seem to be okay," I added.

"There's nothing I can do to change the situation. If Deidra wants to leave, Deidra can leave. I won't beg anybody to be with me. I'm just glad I still have you." Angie grinned and then walked inside the shop.

We perused the trinkets inside the shop, especially the key chains, mugs, and postcards adorned with images of some of Atlanta's famous and historic sites, including the Georgia Aquarium, Centennial Olympic Park, and the Martin Luther King, Jr., National Historic Site. As I held a postcard with a picture of Stone Mountain, Angie positioned herself behind me, so close that her hips and thighs touched the back of my jeans.

"That's cute," she said as she admired the scenic view on the postcard I held. Her hand rested on my shoulder, and her index finger subtly caressed my neck.

I exhaled. This had to stop.

"Angie." I turned around. Her face was so close: only two inches separated her lips from mine. She looked into my eyes, down to my lips, and back up to my eyes. I smelled the cinnamon gum she chewed, and felt the warmth of her breath on my mouth. My lips tingled.

"Angie," I whispered again. I needed to tell her to back up, to stop with her subtle flirtations, and to respect my place in her life as a friend and only a friend. If only I didn't like the way it felt.

"Angie!"

Angie and I, alarmed, jumped back from one another.

"Deidra." Angie's tone was flat, but angry.

Just outside the gift shop stood Deidra and Sanford, one of the stylists in her beauty shop. In their arms were boxes of hair tools and accessories. I swiftly recalled a radio commercial I had heard while we drove to the Omni. A commercial that advertised a local hair show that weekend at none other than the hotel in which we stood.

My face burned. I could only imagine how Angie and I must have appeared in their eyes. Friends that were exes—one of them fresh out of a breakup—standing so close and perhaps moments away from a kiss. No one said a word. Angie sneered at Deidra while I awaited Deidra's next move. She looked at Sanford.

"See?" she said to him. "This is why."

Sanford uttered a sassy "Humph" before hustling Deidra away.

"Unbelievable," Angie finally said.

"Please tell me you didn't know she'd be here." I prayed she hadn't placed us purposely in a location where we would be seen by Deidra. Why would she?

"Of course I didn't. We haven't said one word to each other in over a week. I don't know where she's at."

"You know this doesn't look good." I returned the postcard to the twirling stand and caught sight of the security camera in the corner above us. I was exposed. Had it seen what I felt?

"What? We're two friends standing in a gift shop, looking at a postcard. What's so wrong with that?" Angie asked, a weak attempt at innocence.

"You did say friends, right?"

"I did."

"So you know that's what we are, then?" Truly, I had geared this question toward both of us. I didn't tell her I had begun to feel more than friendship for her again.

"I know we're friends, Kyla."

"Then what's up with all this? All this . . . all this closeness."

"I was just looking at the picture with you."

"Stop playing dumb, Angie. I see it all over your face."

Angie crossed her arms over her chest. Her expression was perplexed. "You see what?"

Oh, shit. Had I imagined the desire in her eyes? Had I mistaken her words for something other than friendly gratitude? Was it only me, and not Angie, who felt that our connection had begun to deepen beyond friendship? I was embarrassed. My chest warmed, and heat flushed my cheeks.

Before I could respond, Angie broke into laughter. "God, Kyla, you're still so easy." She grabbed me by the elbow, led me out of the store, and reached for her keys. I nervously looked around for Deidra.

"Let's go. It's okay if I miss the other session."

I didn't argue with her, only followed her out of the hotel. She spoke again as we approached her car.

"You don't have to keep reminding me that we're friends."

"I don't?" I asked sarcastically.

"No, trust me, I know we're friends, Kyla, and really, I truly appreciate you supporting me since the breakup. I'm sorry if I'm making you feel some kind of way. It's not fair." Angie paused while we got in the car. "But I can't lie," she continued after we drove out of the hotel parking lot. "I've never fully gotten over you. When we broke up—"

"We were never together, Angie," I said, correcting her.

"Really? It's like that?" Her tone was edgy. "Okay, well, when you ended whatever we had, I let you go because that's what you wanted. It's not what I wanted. Yeah, I know I entertained other women, but none of them were any competition to you. All these years we've been friends have been easy and hard. Easy because I was happy to at least have you back in my life in some way. Hard because I know how much you love Asia."

"What about you and Deidra? Didn't you love her?"

"Sure I did," she answered casually. "Deidra was what I needed when I needed it. I gave her every symbol of love I could. A place to live, vacations, jewelry, a luxury car to drive, and it was all from the heart. But did I love her the way I should have? No. There was never a moment during our relationship when I couldn't imagine my life without her. I was okay with the end, whenever it came."

"So what about the crying episode at my house? What was that about?"

She was amused. "My tears were unexpected. I think it was the wine. You know I don't drink that shit."

"That's not a good excuse," I told her. "What was that about? You had me and Asia thinking you were really hurt by the breakup. But from the looks of things, it's almost like you wanted to break up, anyway."

"On the real, losing the relationship had me scared."

"Why?"

"Straight up?"

"Of course."

"I was scared I would lose you. I sat there talking about Deidra with you and Asia, and it hit me that I didn't know if that would be the last time I'd see you. If the breakup would be the end of me and you."

"There was no me and you," I told her again.

"The end of seeing you," she said, clarifying. "I didn't know if Asia would still be okay with us kicking it without Deidra around. It's one thing for all of us to double-date, but to kick it with me as a third wheel or without her at all . . . I didn't know if she would trip on me and you, with our past and all."

"She has known about our past all this time and hasn't had a problem."

"The difference is I had a woman then."

"So that's how you felt at the house? That's what prompted all those tears?"

Angie sucked in her next breath. "Yes," she confessed and exhaled.

"And now?"

"Now I need you. Like I said, I don't want to lose you."

"Angie, whatever you're looking for from me, I can't fill that role," I said in an attempt to convince us both.

"You say that right now, and that's cool. For now we can continue to be friends."

"Just friends?"

"Yep. Like we've been all this time."

"That might be hard now that you've told me how you feel." *And given how you're making me feel . . .*

"Seriously, all this time did you have any idea how I felt? I never let it show. I respected your relationship then, and aside from a few slips this week, I swear I'll continue to respect your relationship going forward."

"Promise?"

"Nope." Angie laughed. "For real, though, you've never felt anything for me? You've never missed anything about us?" She took her eyes off the road to look at me. She licked her lips sensually, rolling her lips inward and sliding her tongue outward. The move was performed slowly, but it seemed to happen quickly. I felt the tickle in my belly again.

"Just drive," I advised her, while I avoided telling a lie and confessing the truth—that all I had been thinking about was her.

Although we rode without words, everything inside me was the opposite. My feet twitched nervously and screamed at me to run from the situation. My thighs ached and yelled at me to keep them closed. My heart pounded loudly, which reminded me of the anxiety I felt as I sat next to Angie. And my brain shouted, *What's wrong with you? Stop being silly. You have a beautiful woman in your life. Stop being a fool.* I tried to listen to each blaring warning, but most of my focus was on the way Angie's hands glided across the steering wheel when she made a turn. The smoothness and slenderness of her fingers as she tapped against the leather to the beat of the soothing music. Those fingers used to perform magical and delicious tricks on my body in ways no one else had. Finally, I turned my head to the window, shut out visions of Angie, and turned up the volume on the screeching alarms ringing throughout my body.

When we reached my car, I rushed to get out of hers. I had to get away from her.

"What? No hug?" Angie asked after I opened my car door.

"Angie, please don't," I begged. I was drawn to the memory of the last time I sat next to Angie in a car years ago, right after I ended our fling. Then, too, I was weak for her, but I had stayed strong. I attempted to gather my strength again.

"Go on," she said but got out of her car at the same time. We stood outside my car. "I won't pressure you, Kyla. I swear, I won't. It's just that while I was with Deidra, I was able to hide the way I feel about you. Now that I don't have her or anyone to distract me, all I can think about is you. Don't leave me, though, okay? I really need you in my life."

"You've made this complicated, and I'm kind of mad at you for it. I wish you had just kept it to yourself."

She stepped forward, again coming closer than she should. I leaned on my car, angry with myself. I needed to push her away and tell her to get out of my face. That was what I should have done, regardless of her sensitive state. But I didn't. Instead, I welcomed the contrasting heat from her body against the cool winter air.

"I'll be to you only what you want me to be," she told me, her body pressed against mine. "If you say we're just friends, I'll stay in my lane. I've been backseat riding for years, and I can keep doing it." Discreetly, she stroked my waist, and then she whispered in my ear. "But if ever you want me to drive, say the word and I'll take you for a ride."

My cell phone rang. When I held the phone up, I saw Asia's name appear on the screen.

"I have to go now."

Angie stepped away, and I turned my back to her, got in my car, and drove off without looking back.

Four

Asia

It had been a week that daily I either left a voice-mail message for Deidra or sent a text message to her with no reply. My respect level for Deidra had never been 100 percent, and with each day that she ignored me, it declined even further. The least she could do after years of friendship was return my call. Finally, on Sunday, just after I left one of the two patients I had kept on my schedule, she sent a text: We need to talk. Call me.

"What's up, Deidra? About time you responded back," I scolded as soon as she answered the phone.

"Wait. Hold on, Asia. I need some privacy."

Against the background noise I heard her rattle off directions to Sanford, whom I had met on a few occasions when Kyla and I met Deidra and Angie at the shop. His voice was an easily identifiable shrill. I then heard scuffles and shuffles and figured she must have left the room.

"Okay, I'm back."

"So what's going on, girl?"

"Right now I'm about to get ready for a hair show. What's up with you?" she inquired anxiously.

"Same old stuff. I heard about the breakup with Angie." I didn't feel like small talk with her.

"Is that right? I should have known. Who'd you hear it from?"

"Kyla, of course. And Angie. She came over last week. Why didn't you tell me about it?" I questioned. Surely, we hadn't been the best of friends, but I still thought she would have confided in me that there had been a problem.

"What's there to tell? I fell out of love with her," she explained, free of any hint of remorse.

"It's that easy for you, huh? Just casually tossing someone aside, like they don't even matter?" Even though I was no longer upset about the ease with which she had ended the relationship I had with her, I knew I still sounded like it.

"Okay, don't get me wrong. It's not as if I just woke up one day and realized I was unhappy and decided to leave. It was gradual. More and more, I felt like all Angie wanted to do was suck up my independence and leave me helpless to her."

"I don't get that. From what I've seen, Angie has given you everything you've desired. Only now that she has got your shop up and running, she's done *too* much?" Deidra's selfishness was infuriating.

"I don't have to explain it to you, Asia. All I can say is our time is over."

"She was so heartbroken when she was over. She was crying and all."

"Yeah, whatever. Trust me, Angie's all right," Deidra replied.

"You sure about that? When she left, I made sure Kyla walked her out to make sure she was calm enough to drive."

Deidra snorted. "She did, huh? That's exactly why Angie is all right. Did you watch those two from the window?"

"What? Of course not. Why would I do that?"

"Because you should be keeping an eye on them. We both should have been keeping an eye on them this whole time." She paused. "Do you know where Kyla is now?"

"I do. She's with Angie at some conference at the Omni," I told her confidently, recalling the text message Kyla had sent me earlier.

"Mmm-hmm. I just ran into them in the hotel, and they looked more than cozy."

"What does that mean?"

"Let me just say they seemed very comfortable in each other's presence. Trust me, Angie's fine without me so long as she's got Kyla."

"You know what, Deidra? I don't know where this is coming from. I don't know if you're trying to get back at Angie for something or what, but keep Kyla out of it."

"How can I keep her out of it when she's the reason for all of this? She's always been the reason."

"The reason for what?"

"Angie may have blessed me with everything I've ever wanted, but none of that matters if I'm not the one *she* really wanted. She's suffocated me, trying to prove a love for me that wasn't really meant for me."

"What are you suggesting?"

"I think you'll find out. Kyla will find out too. Angie isn't who she presents herself to be. Look, Asia, I have to get back to work. Thanks for checking up on me. I appreciate it, but I'm just fine." She paused a moment. "Me and you, we're not Angie and Kyla, so I have a feeling we won't be talking much more. I never really believed in that friends-who-are-exes shit, anyway. I did it for Angie because I was crazy about her and knew how much Kyla meant to her. But all of us hanging out, like that shit was normal? Please."

Deidra had a point there. Deidra had never been on my favorite persons' list, but because I had accommodated Kyla's friendship with Angie, I had welcomed both Angie and Deidra back into our lives. Did I agree with it? Not necessarily. It wasn't because of Deidra. I didn't give a shit about my dating relationship with her. My history with her was a forgettable, irrelevant part of my past. But it hadn't always been the easiest to pretend that nothing had happened between Kyla and Angie. Whenever we were out, I couldn't erase the knowledge I had of their past sexual interactions.

"I hear you, Deidra, and I'm cool with that. I trust you'll be well."

"Thank you."

I heard her footsteps once again, and the background noise resumed once she reentered the busy room.

"All right, Asia," she said. There really was nothing else to add. No "I'll talk to you later" or "Call me back."

"Yep. Bye."

Angrily, I threw the phone onto the passenger seat. How dare she suggest any interaction between Kyla and Angie went beyond friendship? Regardless of their history, I had perceived them to be nothing but friends, and I hadn't witnessed them being anything but that. I had assumed the attraction switch between the two of them had been turned off a long time ago. It had to be, since there was no way they would have been able to hide that. Not from me at least. I reached for my phone again and called Kyla.

"Hey," Kyla answered. I heard a car door close.

"Hey, honey. I'm headed home." I tried to sound casual. Her car started in the background. I was familiar with its low, feminine growl. "You still with Angie at the conference?"

"No, just left her."

"Okay. How was it?"

"It was all right," she answered quickly, her voice a monotone.

"Lots of people there?"

"Seemed so."

I frowned. Her answers were too bland, too short. She was nervous.

"Did Angie enjoy it? Learn anything?"

"I think so. But . . ." She stopped.

"But what?" I asked, prodding.

"We didn't stay for the second session."

"Oh no? Why is that?"

She cleared her throat. "Angie said she didn't want to."

"I see." I waited. I wanted to see if she would mention Deidra.

If she and Angie had run into Deidra, then she would tell me. She would tell me the story since it was fresh gossip. She would tell me about how she had been at the conference to support her heartbroken friend through a breakup, and lo and behold, who did they just happen to bump into in the midst of it all? Of course, she'd rush to tell me that story. But if she didn't, there was something to hide, and she'd keep it to herself. Kyla remained silent, and I prayed her lack of words meant Deidra had invented the entire scenario.

"So where was the conference again?"

She didn't answer right away. It was only half a second, but her silences were easily interpretable unspoken words.

"Omni Hotel," she finally answered. "So I'm headed home too. Want me to grab anything?"

I was instantly pissed. "Really, Kyla?"

"Really what?" She tried to sound confused.

I sighed. "Did you run into Deidra today?"

"Deidra?" she asked, as if she hadn't heard me. Another giveaway. She was stalling.

"Yes, Kyla. Deidra," I repeated.

"Um, yep, yes, we did. She was at the hotel for a hair show."

Shit. Exactly what I didn't want to hear. Deidra had told the truth.

"That's interesting. So what happened?" I wished Kyla wouldn't act dumb with me. We had been together too long to play silly, childish games.

"Nothing. Nothing, really."

"Let me rephrase my question then. What were you doing when you saw her?"

"Oh, I was in the gift shop."

"The gift shop. Okay, so I know *where* you were. What were you *doing?*" I stressed.

She continued to speak in choppy sentences. "Looking at a postcard. I was looking at a postcard, and then I saw her. Her and Sanford."

"Did she say anything to you?"

"No . . . no." Her pitch was too high. She might not have been lying, but she certainly wasn't being truthful.

"So she saw you, you saw her, and she kept walking? Come on, Kyla, I know you know how to tell a story. You tell me stories about Erika every damn day. So what happened? What *exactly* were you doing when you saw Deidra?"

She was quiet for a moment, and all I heard was the click of her blinker.

"I was looking at a postcard, and—"

I cut her off. "Where was Angie?"

"She was in the gift shop too."

"Doing?"

"I think she was looking at the postcard too."

She thought? Such a damn lie. She knew good and
well if Angie looked at the postcard too. And even if
she had, who cared? I didn't think twice about shit like
that. What concerned me was the reticent way in which
she told the story. There was something she hadn't
shared.

"What did Deidra say to you?"

"Nothing to me." She paused again. "She called Angie's name, we looked up and saw her, and then she
walked away."

"That's it?"

"Yep, mmm-hmm, that's it."

"Then what?"

"Then we left."

They left after seeing Deidra. Because of guilt?
Again, I waited. Everything she hadn't said and hadn't
asked seemed to support Deidra's accusation. I wasn't
going to accept Deidra's words wholeheartedly yet and
fret that there was something other than friendship
between Kyla and Angie. However, Kyla's terse and
matter-of-fact responses proved she was not being
forthcoming. And she hadn't even questioned why I
specifically asked about Deidra. She had to know I already knew, yet she was too afraid to ask my purpose in
bringing up the topic.

A couple of facts Kyla knew about me were that I
didn't accept bullshit and I didn't like being played
like a fool. I had been patient with her while she wal-
lowed in whatever had been on her mind for a year.
If she wanted to choose Angie over me to resolve her
problem, then her problem was about to become bigger
than she had ever imagined.

"I'll see you at home." I hung up before she could
respond.

Five

Kyla

I believed every person had four major life choices that would dictate the course of life for many years into the future: what college to attend, whether or not to have children, where to buy a house, and whom to marry and settle down with for life. At the opposite end of each decision was the path left unchosen, unseen, and unknown. Sure, we could change our mind later and go back to school, have a child in our forties, move to another city, or divorce our spouse, but the altered course had already been paved. Angie was the choice I had bypassed, and now I wanted to reconsider.

If only we could all have a personal guardian angel at our side, one that hovered quietly in the background and ensured that we stayed true to the path that was meant for us. The angel wouldn't interfere unless we veered from our pre-written story; the one that was meant for us and all those we encountered. Because if one person changed course, it would affect the lives of others in great ways and even in the slightest ways.

I reflected on the Valentine's Day party over eight years prior, when Asia and I bumped into Angie and Deidra. Had Asia and I opted to stay home, or had we chosen a different party, the four of us wouldn't have rekindled our friendship. If I hadn't been friends with Angie, I wouldn't have known about their current breakup. The question was, how different would all of our lives have been had we not bumped into each other that critical night years ago? Were Angie and I meant to run into each other, interweave our lives for several years, and then find ourselves at a crossroads, uncertain if we should have been together all along? I couldn't grasp the concept that Asia and I had spent all those years together, only to fall apart. I needed my guardian angel. I needed her to stop me from trying to find the right in what I knew was wrong.

Incessant questions ran through my mind while I drove home, but one question in particular had an answer. Did I want to leave Asia for flighty feelings for Angie? That was all they were, right? The answer was no. I couldn't allow my irresponsible response to Angie's affections to cause confusion and controversy in my relationship with Asia. I reflected on the many short and bumpy road trips I had had with various women until I found my smooth, traffic-free highway: Asia. Even though I had driven toward a tempting exit with Angie, I had remained strapped in my seat and had stay on course. That was what I told myself.

Asia was waiting for me in the family room. The television was off, and no music played. She simply sat on the oversize couch in the quiet. That was when I got nervous. I could sense that even though I wanted to remain on our highway, she was about to put up a roadblock.

"Come sit," she instructed.

I didn't bother to remove my coat or gloves or the purse strapped over my shoulder. I sat next to her. Her eyes, those penetrating eyes, looked into mine.

"What's going on, Kyla?"

I didn't want to respond with "What do you mean?" because I knew exactly what she meant. How to begin my explanation was my quandary. I had played the beginning of this conversation so many times in my head. Should I recite that beginning? *I'm bored, Asia.* Only now, the rehearsed conversation had evolved. *And Angie seems to be helping to cure my boredom.* Although that was the truth, I didn't believe that was the appropriate beginning. I thought of a new one. *You've probably sensed something is wrong, and I'm sorry. I'm prepared to work on being better and getting back to my usual self.* That was the truth too, but I knew the conversation would quickly swerve to Angie and the day's events. I knew Asia knew something about Deidra, or she wouldn't have asked specifically about her. I just hadn't been able to react naturally when she called, my mind and body too deliciously frazzled by the heat of Angie's body and her words.

"First, let me apologize for not coming to you sooner," I began. "I know I should have." I paused. "For a while I have felt our relationship hasn't been as exciting as it used to be."

She stared and waited. Her expression blared that all she wanted to know was what was up with Angie.

"I'm also sorry about Angie. I, um, I don't want her to become a problem in our relationship."

"Tell me, Kyla, why is it that you're apologizing for Angie? Exactly what happened that brought about this apology?"

I squirmed inside, though I was determined not to shrivel under pressure and stammer over my words, the way I used to. Hell, the way I had when I talked to her just an hour ago. The less honest I was, the more of Asia's respect I would lose. I wanted to "be a woman," something she had mentioned the other night, and tell the truth, in hopes that she would accept it and grant me forgiveness.

"As you know, Angie and I have been talking a lot more since she and Deidra broke up. I really only wanted to be a good friend to her, help her through a hard time. It seemed right away Angie hinted that she had never really got over the relationship we had, and, well, I have to admit that I started to wonder myself what might have happened if I hadn't ended it."

"So now you and Angie would like to call what you had a relationship? I didn't realize that was what it was," she stated condescendingly.

I sighed. "We don't need to debate that again. You know what I mean."

"I just want to be clear on all the facts, that's all," she responded smartly. "You're apologizing because you and Angie regret not pursuing a relationship?"

"I didn't say that."

"Then what are you saying?"

"That talking to her and spending one-on-one time with her made me wonder a little bit about what it might have been like . . . had we tried to be together."

Asia sat back, cool. "That's normal, Kyla. I'm not suggesting I like what you just said, but it's only normal to sometimes wonder what life might be like if you had made another decision. That doesn't bother me. It would only bother me if you're dwelling on that missed opportunity and regretting the choice you did make. Is that the case?"

I had told half the truth. I *was* dwelling on it, but I hadn't reached the point of regret for the choice I made to end my intimate relationship with Angie after I met Asia. "No, that's not the case."

She tapped her fingers against her thigh and squinted at me while she constructed her next question.

"You said our relationship hasn't been exciting. I would agree. Is this your answer for that? Angie? Your friend? Your ex–fuck buddy? The woman you've had in my face for the past nine years? She's what it's come to?"

"I wasn't looking for this to happen," I explained. "For Angie and Deidra to break up and cause some kind of . . . kind of spark in my life. I'd rather it be with you."

"Spark?" She snickered. "That's what Angie is creating for you? Did you do anything to create a spark for us, Kyla?"

And so the imagined conversation begins. . . . "I didn't. But I want to."

"You want to what? Make up for feeling guilty about Angie and make it better with us?"

I couldn't stand her powers of perception sometimes. "Yes."

"I wish you had come to me . . . come to me before it became so easy for something like this to happen. I realize we haven't been the Kyla and Asia we were years ago. Some days are more eventful than others. I get that. But that's how relationships work, Kyla, and either you stay dedicated and faithful through those times or you don't," she scolded.

"I have been faithful. Nothing has happened between me and Angie."

"Oh no?"

"No. Why do you suggest that? Did Deidra say something?"

She laughed. "Funny you ask if Deidra said anything. That makes me think she did see something."

"Nothing has happened," I repeated. Even though Deidra interrupted what might have been a kiss, the fact was, we hadn't kissed.

"Deidra gave me the impression that she caught you two in a compromising position. Is that true?"

I warmed again, as if Angie's body still rested against mine. I didn't answer.

"That's what I thought." She sat quietly for a moment, her temperature rising as well. She was angry, and her cheeks were flushed under her dark skin. She snapped her fingers. "I have an idea. Why don't I give you a little time to think about how you feel? Let you figure out if you made the right decision with Angie."

She had begun to stack the barricades. I panicked. "What do you mean?"

"I mean just what I said. Go on and be sure it's not Angie that you want."

"I don't want Angie. I already told you that."

"No, you didn't say that. But I don't believe you, anyway. I can tell you really don't know what you want."

Before I could respond, she leaned forward, ran her fingertips across my face, and then placed her hand behind my head. She brought my face toward her and kissed me. She kissed me deeply and passionately, more intensely than she had in a long time. It was as if she was asking, "Is it me or her?" taunting me with her tongue wrapped around mine.

"I'm going upstairs. *Alone,*" she announced. "You can stay down here or in one of the guest bedrooms."

"What if I want to stay in my own room?" I asked, pushing back.

"Then I'll stay in a guest room. Good night, Kyla." She walked toward the hall.

I looked at my watch. "It's five o'clock."

"Yep. Good night," she said without turning back to me. I heard her run up the stairs, and several seconds later the door to our bedroom closed.

I sat back on the couch and exhaled. That hadn't gone quite like I thought it would. My plan was to explain my feelings, to let Asia know I would get past this temporary infatuation with Angie, and to remind her that my life with her was all I wanted. Instead, she had left the matter unresolved. Actually, she had left it open, as if I was seriously contemplating leaving her for Angie. If I were in her position, and she had confessed feeling temptation with another woman, I might have given her the same option. What person wanted to know that her partner was attracted to someone else? Not just physically attracted, but emotionally connected as well. It was hard to know which was worse: the desire to just fuck someone or actually allowing someone to have a piece of your heart.

Finally, I took my coat off, removed my shoes, and lay on the couch. Thoughts danced through my mind as I considered how I might proceed. I had accomplished part of my mission by admitting that I felt a lost spark in our relationship. I wasn't sure what to do next. I could take Asia up on her offer, whether she meant it or not, and test the waters with Angie. Maybe I should spend more time with Angie to see if what I felt was real, to determine if the flame I felt for Angie was a growing fire I couldn't put out. Or if it would extinguish on its own as swiftly as it ignited.

If I explored Angie and spent more time with her, I would risk losing Asia forever. Surely, she wouldn't take me back if I suddenly attempted to return upon discovering that Angie was only a phase. Asia would slant those beautiful eyes at me in retribution and say to herself, *How dare you think you can come back to me now, Kyla?* The more I thought about it, the more I couldn't imagine that Asia was serious about me exploring my feelings for Angie. She must have wanted me to run behind her and plead my love for her, not date someone else. Then again, Asia had always been no-nonsense. Would she really have suggested I entertain the thought of a romantic relationship with Angie if she didn't mean it?

I curled into a tight ball, like a captured fish, as if the weight of my thoughts was crushing me in a net. My mind struggled, flopping back and forth between Asia and Angie, until finally it grew tired and slowly succumbed to rest. When I woke up, it was 9:00 P.M. and dark. The house was quiet. I figured Asia must have fallen asleep too.

My cell phone buzzed. I picked it up and learned I had missed two calls, both from Angie. She had also sent one text. Please call me. I rolled back over, stretched, and quickly made up my mind to call and see what Angie had to say.

"Are you all right?" she asked upon answering the phone.

"Not really," I confessed. I spoke low into the phone. "What's up?"

"I wanted to make sure you were okay. You drove off so fast."

"Asia was calling, and I had to get home," I told her. "Plus . . . I really needed to go. Things were kind of intense."

"I know." I felt I could hear her smile through the phone.

I was quiet and angry again that I hadn't already put a final stop to this. Something selfish inside me wouldn't let it go. I liked the thrill Angie gave me. I acted like that bored housewife in the movie *Unfaithful*. She had no reason to cheat on Richard Gere. She just did it, and her one decision caused injury to many.

We remained silent, and our silence, as it tended to, spoke the words we were contemplating whether or not to share.

"Asia home with you?" she finally asked.

"Yes."

"Let me guess. Deidra told Asia she saw us, didn't she?"

"She sure did. And it's not good."

"Well, nothing happened yet, so you should be good, right?"

My chest tightened. "No, it's not good. I, um, I told her how I've been feeling lately."

"Oh?" She was intrigued. "And how is that?"

I sighed. "I'm not sure if it's a good idea to share that with you. I need to deal with this on my own."

"I'd really like to know, Kyla, how you feel. . . ." Her voice trailed off. "Will you tell me?"

Before I could answer Angie, an irate voice startled me in the darkness. "Who are you talking to?"

Asia turned on the hallway light and revealed her presence. I squinted at the sudden light; then nervously and cowardly I hung up the phone and set it to my side. I didn't answer Asia, only met her gaze. I was guilty. She stared back at me for a moment, and I heard every angry thought she didn't speak. Finally, she shook her head, turned off the light, and went back upstairs. I wished I had heard her come down.

My guardian angel, whether she was real or imagined, quietly tiptoed away and left me to continue the fateful decision-making process on my own. I picked my phone back up and replied to Angie's question via text. Yes, I'll tell you. Meet me tomorrow.

Six

Asia

She was like the leopard that never changed its spots. No matter how much she willed them to disappear, underneath they were always there. I should have known Kyla couldn't stay faithful to me. What angered me most, why I was more pissed off than hurt, was I felt like a fool for having allowed it to happen. For being silly enough to trust Kyla, a woman who had had her face between the legs of half of Atlanta's gay women. On occasion I had even been embarrassed to be seen with her. I preferred not to go out with Kyla often not just because we had gotten older and didn't need to be in the club every weekend. It was also because we'd run into all these women with whom she had slept. We both would lower our heads in shame. Still, sometimes I would suck it up and go out with her confidently, proud to be the woman who had changed her. I guess I really hadn't, after all.

Kyla knew I didn't take kindly to mistreatment in a relationship. I had shared that with her during one of the very first conversations we had, the one in which I told her my ex-girlfriend took all my money to support her other woman and her children. Was this any different? Taking my heart and then, after all these years, considering giving her own to someone else? That angered me more than if she had taken my money too. That was more personal.

I had given Kyla the open door to explore the confused feelings she was experiencing right now, and I meant it. But had I expected her to be hiding out in the dark, cuddling with a pillow on the couch, whispering on the phone with Angie already? No. I had expected her to follow me to the bedroom and demand forgiveness. I had expected her to prove her love for me. I had given her almost four hours, and when she hadn't come up to see me, I'd gone down to her, only to find her snuggled up, with Angie's voice cooing in her ear.

Fuck what I told her about being a woman and talking to me about her feelings. Had she come to me and told me she was bored in our relationship, I would have been willing to help find ways to solve the problem. Instead, she'd come to me with boredom as her problem and Angie as the solution.

I needed to talk to a friend. Someone I could share Kyla's shenanigans with. I wanted to call Tracy, my girl from Dallas, but Tracy was on a ten-day European cruise that had departed only a couple days ago. The best person next to Tracy was Melanie. Melanie was a friend of ours. We met her several years prior, while she and her girlfriend were visiting during Atlanta's notoriously popular Labor Day Pride weekend. Kyla and I met them while we sat in a bookstore and watched all the excited out-of-town passersby headed toward Piedmont Park. Melanie and her girlfriend, Jovanna, introduced themselves to us, and the next day Kyla and I requested their online friendship via Myspace. Shortly after we met, we all deleted those accounts and moved on to Facebook, where we kept in touch.

Melanie and I gravitated toward one another the most, and within months our friendship escalated from just an online interaction to telephone conversations. I liked Melanie's style, and we easily vibed. She was smart and dedicated to her work, and I enjoyed the direct, open, meaningful philosophical conversations we had about politics, religion, and relationships. Honestly, we had had deeper conversations than Kyla and I had had over the years. But had I wanted to get with her just because I had got to know her well? Had I considered leaving Kyla to pursue intimacy with Melanie? No. Even if she'd been single, I wouldn't have. And that was the difference between Kyla and me. I knew what a true friend was, and I knew how to be a loyal mate. It seemed, no matter how hard Kyla tried, she couldn't succeed in the partnership arena. I gave her credit. She had lasted nine years without incident. Nine years wasn't the forever she had promised, though.

"Melanie, are you busy?" I asked when she picked up my call. I hoped she wasn't. I knew Melanie would give me the honest, straightforward feedback I needed. She wasn't a fake friend who would pacify me with dishonest sentiments.

"Not too busy. Going over some paperwork. What's up?"

"Jovanna home?"

"No, she's out with Ali. Everything all right?"

"I'm pissed right now. I'm really angry at Kyla, and I don't know what to do about it."

She shuffled some papers around in the background. "What happened?"

"Today Kyla was hanging out with Angie while I was working, and—"

"Angie, the ex?" Melanie said.

"Yep." During one of our earlier conversations I had told Melanie that Kyla and I had been out with Angie and Deidra. I had mentioned that Deidra was my ex, and had added that Angie was Kyla's. Melanie found the situation odd, as most would.

"Okay." She sighed. I could tell her lawyer brain was already in motion.

"Deidra and Angie broke up a few weeks ago, okay? Angie came by the house and put on a sad act, but now I'm not sure if that was for my benefit or what. I got a call from Deidra, telling me she had just spotted Kyla and Angie in a hotel gift shop. She insinuated that they appeared close. So after I talked to Deidra, I called Kyla, and she was being real short in her responses to questions about her and Angie. I could tell she was holding something back. Then she comes home and has the nerve to tell me she's been feeling a little something for Angie now that they've been talking more since Angie broke up with Deidra."

Melanie was quiet for a moment. I knew Melanie had issues with third-party relationship interference. She and Jovanna had experienced a relationship hiccup a few years back, when one of Melanie's clients, Sunday, began to stalk both her and Jovanna online. Jovanna took matters into her own hands and conned Sunday in such a manner that she vanished from their lives as swiftly as she'd entered. Melanie had once admitted to me that she was flattered that someone as beautiful as Sunday took interest in her, but not once did she allow Sunday to come between her and Jovanna, no matter what Jovanna thought. What bothered her most was that Jovanna hadn't trusted her and had seemed paranoid and jealous. In the end, she realized Sunday really had been toying with Jovanna, which was what had caused Jovanna's unusual behavior.

"Let me make sure I have this clear. Your friends, who are also both of your exes, have broken up with each other. Kyla, in consoling Angie throughout the breakup, has developed feelings for Angie. Now what?"

"Well, I did something I'm not sure I should have done. I told Kyla she should explore her feelings for Angie."

"Why did you say that?"

"For a couple reasons. One, I was really upset, even though I didn't let her see it. Two, I really don't want to be with someone who doesn't know if she wants to be with me. I love her. Of course I do. But am I supposed to chase after someone whose heart is betraying us?"

"You've been together so long, Asia. Every relationship has its trial. From what I understand, it's been pretty smooth between you two until now, right? If I were you, I wouldn't make any drastic moves or go putting her out of the bed just yet."

I was quiet.

"You did that already, didn't you?" She chuckled.

I laughed sadly. "I did. But I went downstairs a little while ago to talk to her, and guess what? She was on the phone with Angie. Can you believe that shit?"

"Damn, okay. Still. Wait it out. Just wait it out. In the big scheme of things, she hasn't actually crossed any lines with Angie, right? Well, not recently, correct?"

"No, it doesn't seem that she has."

"Give it some time. I know it doesn't feel good to know she's confused about some other chick right now, but I don't think this is worth trashing your relationship over. She'll realize that too."

I wanted to trust Melanie's words and accept the confidence she placed in Kyla. Melanie wasn't aware of the details of Kyla's promiscuous past, other than what I had shared about Kyla and Angie. I wanted Melanie and Jovanna to like Kyla for the person she had become, not the person she was back then. Now I questioned if she had ever really changed.

"I'm mad at her, Melanie."

"You have every right to be," she replied. "Still, all these years of trust can't be shot down by one fleeting emotion."

"Is it really fleeting? I don't think she would have said anything if she thought it would just pass. I know Kyla, and she would have kept it to herself."

"That's possible. Or maybe she wanted to be honest with you and move on."

"Maybe." I replayed Kyla's words in my mind. She did tell me she was sorry and she wanted to move past whatever she had begun with Angie. "Anyway, I'm way too stubborn to back down now, not after I just caught her on the phone with Angie. She's going to have to prove herself now."

"I agree with you on that. But don't expect her to come knocking on the bedroom door tonight. I'm sure she feels too guilty to do so."

"Probably." Angrily, I buried my head in the pillow and spoke muffled words into the phone. "This is so silly. I'm too grown to be mad that my woman was on the phone with another woman. I feel like I'm in high school."

"It's not silly, because it's not just any woman. It's her ex. And it's not just that they were on the phone. They were talking after she just admitted some feelings for her. This isn't childish, if that's what you're thinking. You have every reason to feel concerned. Hold on and see what happens. She'll come around."

"I'm glad you have faith in her."

"You don't?"

I wanted to. However, I was fifty-fifty on which direction Kyla would take. "Only time will tell."

"Talk to me whenever you need me."

"Thanks. I will. I'll let you get back to work."

"Okay. Talk to you soon."

After we ended our call, I almost opened the bedroom door to listen for Kyla's voice downstairs. I was curious if she had gotten back on the phone with Angie. Instead, I pulled the covers over my head, and even though I was furious at Kyla, I prayed she would be at my side when I awoke in the morning.

Seven

Kyla

I was embarrassed to call my cousin and confidant, David. There was no way I could explain to him my thoughts of straying with Angie and get his perspective on why I had become more and more tempted to cheat on Asia. David, in his firm but feminine voice, would scold me and slay me to pieces. He would remind me of the elated feelings I had had when I first met Asia. He would tell me about the ease with which I had transitioned from bed-hopping to monogamy, because that was how deeply I had felt about Asia. He would remind me about Asia's support when I traveled back home to Jeff's wedding. She was the solid reinforcement I needed to face family and friends for the first time after I came out and then left home.

And finally, he would prop my eyes open and force me to look around. Asia and I had a good life, a beautiful home, great jobs, loving friends. We had comfort and security. Then David would have me close my eyes and listen to my heart. He'd ask me to recall all the special moments Asia and I had shared, and to remember the sweet murmurs my heart had spoken to me instantly, as it knew even before my mind that she and I were meant to be together.

I should have called David. To hear the brutal truth from him was exactly what I needed while I drove to meet Angie for lunch at her apartment. She had called just after I arrived at work to confirm our meeting.

"We're still getting together, right?" she'd asked anxiously.

"Yes. Where are you working? I'll meet you nearby."

"Come to my place," she'd suggested.

"You know that's not a good idea. Is Deidra there? What if she comes home?"

"Deidra's gone," she'd told me.

During a fight that morning about what Deidra had witnessed between me and Angie at the Omni, Deidra had thrown the apartment keys at Angie and had left, and supposedly she was not expected to return. Without her keys, Deidra could no longer get in the apartment on her own. She would have to be buzzed in by Angie. Meeting Angie at her apartment was still a bad idea and an unwise move overall, I knew. Yet I avoided placing a call to David and continued to drive with my cell phone tucked in my purse.

Finally, after years of the same drill, Asia and I had veered from our morning routine. We hadn't showered one after the other, gotten dressed together, grabbed our coffee, or kissed good-bye. Asia was out of the house before I opened my eyes. It was the sound of the garage door opening that awoke me. I had sat up quickly, still on the couch, only to hear her truck start and the garage door close a moment later. I ran upstairs, curious if she had left a note, maybe an affectionate sign that she wasn't mad at me. There was nothing. The room was painfully silent, and it felt like I had walked onto a stage that wasn't my own. The bed was made to perfection, each pillow placed in its proper vertical and horizontal position. Light shined through the blinds, illuminating the rings and necklaces in the jewelry case on the dresser and causing them to sparkle. Even each ring sat upright and rigid, as if on exhibit. I undressed and tossed my clothes on the bed to muss the space up a bit, help the room feel lived in, to breathe some life into it.

The bathroom was also spotless. Not one drop of water in the sink, and none in the shower. There was no lingering scent of her perfume in the air. It was as if she hadn't even been there. Perhaps that was her point. Maybe she wanted me to know what it would be like without her. She wanted me to miss her. I did. I missed everything about us, which, ironically, was the reason I headed to Angie's. Would my visit with Angie be the wake-up call I needed to set me straight, or would it reinforce my growing desire to have something new *and* old, to exchange the present for a chance to create a new future with the past?

Inside her apartment building, Angie greeted me at the front door, between stacked boxes that surrounded her feet and trailed into the living room. I hesitated before I stepped inside. My heart tried one more time to speak to me about Asia. I heard it lightly. Softly, it told me that a step into Angie's apartment would alter Asia and me forever. Was it worth the risk? I closed my eyes and took a step backward.

"I'm sorry," I told Angie and ran back toward the elevator that had brought me to her second-floor unit.

She followed. "Kyla, wait." Angie reached for my waist and wrapped her arm around it tightly. "I thought we were going to talk today."

"I can't, Angie. I just can't."

"Come inside, Kyla," she urged and began to lead me back to her apartment. "I don't feel like I'll see you again if you leave right now, and that's not going to happen."

I paused. *You know what to do,* my heart said. I didn't honor its wisdom a second time and took slow steps next to Angie and into the apartment. She grinned after she closed and locked the door behind us.

"I made grilled cheese." I could tell she hoped I thought melted cheese on toasted white bread was cute. "Can I take your coat?"

Fearfully, I removed my coat and regretted the low-cut sweater I had put on with my wool slacks that morning. Angie spotted my cleavage, and instinctively, I placed my hand, palm open, beneath my collarbone.

"Come have a seat." Angie tapped the wooden chair at the small table in the dining area, which adjoined the living room.

I sat down, and Angie placed before me a plate with a warm grilled cheese sandwich, a small stack of Pringles potato chips, and apple slices on the side. I admitted to myself that it was cute, like a kiddie meal in an elementary school cafeteria.

"Drink?"

How I craved a shot of vodka, but I played into the child menu theme. "Juice, please."

Angie returned with grapefruit juice, a plate for herself, and took a seat across from me. I bit into the sandwich, and the gooey cheese oozed across my tongue and out the corner of my mouth. I licked it quickly.

Angie smiled deviously. "Is it good to you?" she asked, the right side of her lips lifting upward. She enjoyed the sight of my tongue.

I ignored her. I had begun to believe there was more to our interaction, and Angie had always insisted there could be, but what if sexual chemistry was our only strong point? I could have sex anytime I chose to. Love wasn't as easy to obtain.

"So will you share with me what's been on your mind?" she began.

"I could tell you, but why should I? What good will it do?"

"I can't tell you whether or not you should—or what good it'll do—since I don't know what it is. Just tell me because you're here and because you said you would."

I loosened the latch on the box that sheltered my fears. I had come to her place for that very reason, to express my confused desires and to see what would happen next.

"I've really been enjoying talking to you," I finally admitted. "I feel like I'm getting to know you in a way I didn't before."

"I'm enjoying talking to you too. I always have," Angie told me.

"It's beginning to make me wonder if I missed out on something between us. I'm wondering if I should have given us a chance back then."

"You never gave us a chance to get to know each other before. We did intimately, of course, but not personally. I have always thought that if you had given us a chance to really get to know each other, maybe we could be more."

I nodded.

"But you were always so quick to put a halt to that whenever I brought it up. I enjoyed every bit of the time we spent together. Maybe it doesn't seem like it, but I'm about much more than sex. We could have it all, Kyla, love and lust. That would be a great combination, wouldn't it? In a lot of relationships there's a little lack in one of those areas. Me and you, we got the sex down. Why won't you let me love you?"

I listened without responding.

"Look. I don't want to overwhelm you and plead my case like the jury is still out. You closed it a long time ago. But if there's any opening, and it seems like there is, I'm here. I've always been here."

"All these years of hanging out together. Me, you, Asia, and Deidra. You're saying the whole time you wanted me?" I asked.

Angie lowered her head and pinched her eyebrows between her thumbs. "I know it wasn't right. It wasn't fair to any of us, especially Deidra. But yes, there wasn't a moment you couldn't have had me. If that chance is now, I'll take it."

I didn't know what to think or what to feel. I was torn between my love for Asia and the temptation I felt with Angie. Last time I was in the same position, I was in love with Jeff and felt tempted by Stephanie, and my final decision proved to be the best I had ever made. It eventually led me to Asia. So how could this ambiguity be right if Asia was my supposed destiny?

"What have you said to Asia?" Angie asked, able to penetrate my thoughts.

"I was honest with her yesterday," I answered. "I told her how I've been feeling about you but assured her the feelings would pass."

Angie flinched slightly.

"I thought she'd accept it, appreciate my honesty, and we'd move forward. Instead, she told me to explore my feelings with you."

Angie snorted. "She didn't mean that shit."

"She shouldn't have said it, then."

"Kyla, she said it just to see how you would respond. Take her up on it or beg to be with her. You know that game. You're not new to this."

I shrugged my shoulders. Angie quickly interpreted my presence as a sign that I really favored her over Asia.

"You know what? To me, that means you're here because you really want to be here. Not just because Asia said, 'Go ahead.' Because you didn't have to take advantage of the opening she gave you. Say it. Say you want to be here with me and not with her," she urged firmly.

Angie was up and next to me. She turned my chair away from the table and got on her knees. She ran her hands across my thighs and gave them a squeeze. She looked up to me.

"Tell me you want to know what it's like to be with me," she whispered, her voice transitioning to low and husky as the longing inside her grew.

She caressed my skin through my slacks, and I was instantly aroused. She felt my heat. She rubbed deeper into my muscles and eased the tension in my legs. My chest heaved, and I exhaled. Her touch excited me such that even I was surprised. Angie laid her head in my lap and kissed me. Her breath I could feel through the wool material. I wanted to protest, but I couldn't.

"I can love your body, love your mind, and love your heart, Kyla, if you let me."

I closed my eyes to cool the sting from my tears.

"Will you let me do that?"

I stroked Angie's soft curls for a moment, until she raised her head to me. "I can't answer that right now," I replied honestly. "I can't say I'm ready to let go of what I have with Asia to have an opportunity with you. I believe every word you've said. I do. Something tells me you sincerely mean it. But I've done too much hurting in my past. I swore I wouldn't hurt anyone else again, especially someone as undeserving of hurt as Asia."

"Being here right now is already hurting her. Imagine how she'd feel if she knew. I'm not telling you what to do, but you're halfway here already. Come on. One more step," she coaxed smoothly.

"I know," I agreed. "One more move and I won't be able to get her back, anyway."

I spoke the words and fully understood my next actions would initiate steps backward, down the path I had become overwhelmingly anxious to travel. I bent to meet the kiss Angie leaned in to give me. It was good. It was more than good, and it was only a moment before her tongue was in my mouth. We kissed, and my tears began to fall. I cried because I loved the way it felt. I cried because I didn't want it to stop. I cried because for the first time in nine years I broke my own heart by not standing by the promise I had made to myself and to Asia: to be faithful to her. I was a cheater, willing and suddenly ready.

Angie seized the opportunity without hesitation. She stood up and led me to the couch, her face buried in my neck before she laid me down. She kissed, she licked, she nibbled, and she whispered, "I've always wanted you." She removed my sweater and my bra. My pants were off, and my panties down, in one swift gesture. I was lost in the moment and cried tears of pleasure and distress. Angie reached my delicateness without hesitation and took in my most tender place with her mouth. I screamed, delighted and afraid. I writhed on the couch in ecstasy and shame. I cried, and I came over and over, the tears as steady as the rush between my legs. Both exhausted and elated, we finally stopped. Angie rested her head on my shaking stomach.

"This isn't all I want from you, Kyla," she remarked, reiterating what she had said earlier. "I want it all. I can give it all to you. You don't have to tell me right now. Just know there's more to me than this."

She looked up at me, and I down at her. I didn't answer. I only wiped my tears and sat up. Angie watched me dress and walked me to the door.

"Call me later," she instructed.

"Yes," I told her.

She kissed my cheek, and guiltily I turned from her, as if her lips hadn't just left my tender flesh moments before. My tears resumed the moment I stepped onto the elevator, and fell harder once I was outside and was getting into my car. I dug in my purse, and an hour too late I phoned David.

Eight

Asia

They're here.

That was the text message sent by Deidra while I was visiting with Mrs. Johnson, a dying eighty-four-year-old patient. I was surprised to hear from her. I thought we were done talking. Fifteen minutes after receiving it, I was able to step away and respond.

Who is where?

Within seconds she replied.

Kyla & Angie. At the apartment.

My hands began to shake. At twelve thirty in the afternoon on a Monday? Kyla was supposed to be at work.

How do you know?

Because I'm outside and Kyla's car is here.

Go inside! I yelled at Deidra by text. Why was she just sitting there?

Can't. Gave Angie the keys.

Can't you get in?

I could ring the buzzer. Don't need to. I know what's going on in there. Just thought you should know.

I didn't respond. My head began to pound, and my body perspired. How could Kyla betray me like that already? While I had waited for her to knock on our bedroom door last night, she had gone knocking on Angie's today.

I'm telling you, you need to let Kyla go. If you decide to keep her, you better keep Angie away from her.

Still I didn't reply.

I'm leaving. Angie can keep the rest of my shit. I don't give a fuck anymore. She'll get hers.

My teeth clenched, and I squeezed my phone in my sweaty hands. I calmed myself before I returned to finish my appointment with Mrs. Johnson. I smiled, but she sensed my stress. I guessed my hands weren't as delicate as they should have been when I drew her blood.

"What's wrong, baby?"

"Nothing. I'm great, Mrs. Johnson," I lied.

"Don't lie to me, young lady," she scolded, her tiny voice firm, but weak in volume.

"Just a little tension at home, that's all," I told her.

"Mmm-hmm, I knew it. What did he do?"

I laughed genuinely. "Not a he, Mrs. Johnson. She," I said, correcting her.

"Who? Your momma? No wonder you're so sweet. Your momma lives with you?" She gave me a gum-filled smile.

"No, no. My mom is in Dallas with my dad."

"Well, who then?" Her wrinkled skin crinkled further, like balled-up paper.

"My partner. My girlfriend. We're going through a rough moment."

Mrs. Johnson grew silent. Her eyes, which had astigmatism, scrutinized mine.

Finally, she said, "I never would have thought. Well, hot damn. Honey, I could have told you dealing with women is emotional. Child, I had one after my Herbert cheated on me back in the sixties. That was a free-spirited, free-loving time, you see." She coughed, but her eyes twinkled. "Yes, yes. I met Miss Virginia Grace, let's see, when I was thirty-six. I loved some Virginia Grace, I tell you."

As furious and flustered as I was, I was graciously receptive to Mrs. Johnson's shocking trip down memory lane. Just the distraction I needed to squelch the impulse to go toss bricks through Kyla's car windows and Angie's apartment windows. So unladylike, but being cheated on could bring out the worst in anyone.

"I can tell you some stories, honey, believe me," Mrs. Johnson continued. "But let me tell you this. I fell so in love with Miss Virginia Grace that I packed my bags and kids and left my cheating husband behind. She became Auntie Grace to the kids, and my best friend to anyone who asked. We lived the perfect secret life, and I was never happier. I would have given anything for her. I did." Mrs. Johnson's shaky hand reached for a tissue to dab her eyes.

"About five years later Virginia Grace told me it was too much for her. Being locked down in a relationship. It was too much responsibility." She shook her head. "Said it was a responsibility like a job, and to me, it was nothing but pleasure. Like a five-year vacation at my favorite beach. I couldn't wait to wake up to her every morning. She was like a beautiful sunrise." Mrs. Johnson coughed.

"She told me she needed to be free, and next thing I knew, she was gone." Mrs. Johnson's glossy eyes looked into mine. "People say when you love someone, never let them go. I say there's no choice but to let them go if that's what they want. What we want with someone might not be what they want. Don't fight it. Don't force it. Let them follow what they need to do. It was hard, honey. It was hard. My heart hurt worse than when I found out about all the women my Herbert had cheated on me with. But I let her go. I had to. I'd rather she leave and be happy than stay with me and the kids and be miserable. You understand? Sometimes letting go is the greatest gesture of love you can do."

I didn't know how Mrs. Johnson knew her story related to mine, but I supposed in the general terms of relationships she spoke the truth. We couldn't force someone to be with us if he or she didn't want to be there.

"Yes, I understand. Thank you, Mrs. Johnson."

"Now, you go on and handle your business. I'll be just fine."

I smiled, grateful, and began to pack my bag.

"What happened to Mr. Herbert?" I asked before I left.

"Oh, honey, he was right there waiting for me when me and the kids came back. He was real, real sorry and never cheated on me again. And I was okay because I had had a taste of real good love. The kind that no one can take away, even when it's gone. We settled back together, and even though I never loved him the way I loved Miss Virginia Grace, we made it work till he died."

"And Virginia Grace?"

"She went on to have many lovers. That was just her style. I didn't love her any less because of it. You hear me?"

I nodded. "See you next time, Mrs. Johnson."

"Bye, baby."

When I got to my truck, I wasn't sure what to do. I needed to get back to the office, but I wasn't sure how I'd be able to focus with the knowledge that Kyla was inside Angie's apartment, likely doing what came best between them.

While I sat in the leather interior of my truck, I deliberated my next move and tried not to compare myself to Angie and question why Kyla might have chosen her over me. I hated whiny-ass women who cried over a lost love, sobbing, "What does she have that I don't?" I did it anyway.

I considered myself an attractive person and Angie as well, though she had an obvious tomboyish edge. Aside from aesthetics, I noted that we were equally successful business owners. In my opinion, neither of us held the upper hand in either of those areas. What concerned me was intimacy. Out of all the women Kyla had been with, I knew Angie was her best lover. In our early, casual "getting to know one another" conversations, we asked each other "Don't ask if you don't really want to know the answer" questions. In those conversations we confessed secrets, one of which was who our best lover had been. I fully expected Kyla to tell me I was her best, but she admitted that Angie was her favorite, and it was a fact I had never forgotten. Never had I felt inferior to Angie sexually; Kyla had seemingly been pleased with our sex life. Nevertheless, I wondered if Angie could take her to heights of ecstasy that I could not. If that was the sole reason for her resurrected desires for Angie, then in my estimation the whole thing was pathetic.

I put my truck in drive and pulled away from the curb. Where to go next quickly turned into a no-brainer, as I happened to be only fifteen minutes from Angie's place. I turned in that direction. What I would do upon arrival, I wasn't sure. Call Kyla to let her know I was waiting outside? Remain quiet and catch her off guard? Ring the doorbell until they were forced to buzz me inside the building?

After I rounded the corner of Angie's block, I learned none of those scenarios would play out. From a distance I witnessed Kyla exiting Angie's building, red-faced, puffy-eyed, and disheveled. Her eyebrows were wrinkled into a helpless frown, her eyes were wet with running tears, and she'd sucked her bottom lip inward to conceal its trembling. She darted to her car, sped off, and left me stalled in the middle of the street, hurt and angry, certain that she and Angie had crossed the irreversible friendship line that would change my Kyla's future forever.

Nine

Kyla

"I need to come see you," I begged.

"Honey, what is wrong with you?"

David was worried. I was sure it was my near shriek of panic that had alarmed him.

"I just did something I shouldn't have."

"Then why did you do it?" he asked calmly, logically.

"Because at the time I didn't know if I'd regret it."

"And now you do?"

I sighed. "I'm not sure. I'll tell you the details when I get there." I was afraid to hear his berating response if I told him on the phone, while driving, that I had just had sex with Angie. I just might crash.

David echoed my sigh. "Girl, I don't even know what you're talking about, but get your confused ass over here."

"En route." I hung up.

Even though I was in my late thirties, I had no idea what I would do without David. He had been there at my side while I uncovered and revealed my true self as a lesbian after my affair with Stephanie. He had been with me, usually wearing a frown and scolding me, while I explored my sexual freedom after he and I moved to Atlanta. He had been my and Asia's greatest cheerleader throughout our relationship. I felt just as bad sharing what I had done with him as I would if I were confessing my transgressions to Asia. I knew he'd be just as disappointed. But I hoped he could at least help me decide what to do going forward.

My phone rang. I picked it up and saw Asia's name. I was shocked. I didn't expect to hear from her during the workday. I didn't answer. I didn't want to lie to her, but I wasn't prepared to tell the truth yet. I let the call go to voice mail. A moment later I checked for the voice-mail message alert. She hadn't left a message. I was partially disappointed. I would have been able to gauge her mood if I could have heard her voice.

I reached David's townhome in no time. At least the ride seemed quick. In my mind I was still on Angie's couch, my head against the pillow, while she gratified me in the ways I remembered. I had no idea how I drove without incident. I couldn't remember exiting the highway, pausing at stoplights and stop signs, or turning the steering wheel to make right and left turns. I became present only the moment I parked and took the key out of the ignition. Quickly, I buzzed David's unit number and headed inside. From the corner of my eye, just as the glass door closed behind me, I saw a flash of silver, the same shade as Asia's truck. I didn't turn around, but I swore the truck was Asia's. But then again, how many silver trucks were there?

"Get in here, girl. You look a mess," David commanded when I rounded the corner toward his unit. He closed the door behind us.

"What's going on?" His voice was urgent; his eyes concerned.

David hadn't changed over the years. He was still naturally forthright in conversation and had a keen ability to honor others with the truth in a tactful but impactful manner.

His figure had remained slim and he was still really fit, even at the age of forty-four, though his hair apparently counted his age in dog years. His hair had receded and was now a mere strip that circled his otherwise bald head from one ear to the other. Both I and Marlon, his partner, had recommended on numerous occasions that David go ahead and shave the remaining strands sprouting from his scalp, but David had refused adamantly, intent on holding on to the lonely patches of hair. I imagined it was difficult that Marlon, who had nine years on David, still had most of his salt-and-pepper hair.

We moved to the kitchen, where he was packing his dinner for his later shift at work. I leaned against the counter.

"I just did the unforgivable," I told him.

David squealed. There was only one definition for "the unforgivable."

"What in the hell have you gone and done, girl? With who at this hour? Thought all your afternoon indiscretions were in the past?"

I lowered my head, ashamed to tell him the identity of my accomplice. "Angie."

He stopped spreading mayo across his wheat bread. "Hot diggity damn, have you lost your mind or what?"

I started to cry again. "I don't know. Maybe," I whimpered.

"What were you thinking? Angie? Even if it wasn't Angie, what are you thinking, stepping out on Asia like this?" He rubbed his scalp, which he did often.

"I don't know. I don't know. I don't know, David. This has all happened really fast."

"You've always moved fast with women, but, honey, you needed to put the brakes on this. How did this happen?"

"Angie and Deidra broke up a few weeks ago."

"So sad for them. And?" he questioned, his tone warning me I had better have a stronger explanation.

"As a friend, I tried to be there for her."

"Okay . . ."

"Right away she started hinting about us being together. Yesterday she told me she's always wished we could be together."

"All right . . ." He continued to listen to see how I would justify my actions.

"I fell for it. I fell for it hard and quick, and I started contemplating the idea of what if. What if it had been Angie, and not Asia?"

"What if what, honey? Don't be playing them mind tricks on yourself. If it was supposed to be Angie, it would have been Angie. Ain't no walking down memory lane, trying to change the past. Now, what have you gone and done?"

"I just left her house. . . ."

David's eyes stared incredulously at me. "You did the do with Angie. Your ex. Your friend. A woman you've been bringing around Asia for how many years? That's wrong, Kyla. It's wrong any way you might try to make it right. You can't tell me this is just about her and Deidra breaking up, either. What's the real problem?"

"I'm bored," I confessed. "It's not an excuse, I know. It's just that me and Asia seem to have hit a plateau. Every day is just average. Although nothing bad happens, nothing exciting happens anymore, either."

"Well, you just went and shook up both of those now, haven't you? This is not your *average* day, and believe me, Asia will be excited about this, but not the right kind of excited."

"I don't know what to do," I admitted.

"This is like déjà vu, honey child. Back in the day, you were crying about Stephanie and what to do about Jeff." David closed his eyes and shook his head. "Only, then I supported your confused cheating ass and told you to follow your heart. I can't say that this time, baby. I think you messed up, and I think you messed up bad. Asia has never come off as the kind of woman who will forgive and let something like this slide."

"No, she's not," I agreed. "I don't know how I let this happen."

He put his palm in my face and halted my words. "If you say you don't know one more time . . . Yes, you *do* know. You went to Angie's house today and let it happen. Nobody made you. You're too grown not to take responsibility for your actions. The question is, now what?"

I was silent.

"Better figure it out," David continued. "Want my opinion?"

"Of course I do," I answered quickly.

"You got to tell her. This kind of secret will eat you up inside, and Asia's too perceptive not to figure it out on her own. If you don't tell her, best believe it'll come out at some time. What's done in the dark comes to light, baby girl."

I was uneasy and uncomfortable. I knew that telling Asia was the right thing to do and the only way to handle what I had gotten myself into. How simple I would look in her eyes to have so easily failed at honoring the trust she had placed me. Maybe I had never been worthy of that trust.

"I'll tell her. Only God knows how she'll respond."

"Be prepared for it all, honey. She's a classy woman, so I doubt this will result in a nine-one-one call, but you never know how people will respond in a situation 'til it happens. Get your boxing gloves ready, just in case."

I recalled Asia's experience with the ex that stole her money to support the woman she had on the side and her children. They hadn't gotten into a fight or even an argument, and there had been no physical altercation. Asia had merely packed her bags and left. That was different, though. Her ex had seized something tangible, money, which could be replaced. I had stolen her trust, which wasn't easily restored.

"Thanks, David." I wiped my eyes. "Let me do what I have to do."

David hugged me tightly. "I can't lie. I'm disappointed in you. I thought you had settled down for good."

"I did too."

He kissed my forehead and attempted to lighten the mood.

"I'll leave a blanket on the couch in case she kicks you out, but in that big-ass house, you can avoid each other, can't you?"

I almost laughed. "I'll call you later."

Once inside the car, I phoned Asia and left a voice-mail message.

"Asia. It's me. I, um, I was hoping I could catch you. I need to talk to you. Um, since I missed you, I'm going to head home early. I'll see you when you get there."

I exhaled and reached for a napkin in the console. My body was damp from perspiration. The beads of sweat on my forehead, in my armpits, and on my back trailed down to meet with the dampness that still lingered between my legs. I'd have to shower when I got home in an attempt to wash away all remnants of

Angie. Would it even matter? Even if traces of my and Angie's rendezvous ran down the drain, I wouldn't be able to wash away the fact that my relationship with Asia might be over.

Ten

Asia

Kyla wasn't at David's house long. I waited a block away, just to see how long she would hide out there. Within twenty minutes she exited his doors. She must have been so engrossed in the voice mail message she left for me that she didn't realize she drove right past me.

I saw her name as the caller on my phone but chose not to answer. After I witnessed the distressed state in which she left Angie's apartment, I preferred an in-person confrontation. I wouldn't allow her to hide behind her cell phone while she confessed her indiscretions. When I listened to her message, her voice was sad, but not necessarily remorseful, and so I returned to the office for a couple of hours to let her sweat for a while. Then I headed home

Kyla's car was in the garage when I arrived. Recalling Mrs. Johnson's words from earlier in the day, I tried to imitate her cool, understanding demeanor. I couldn't. Kyla was waiting for me in the family room, our usual after-work meeting spot. She had changed out of the rumpled work attire she'd worn earlier, and sat in loose-fitting sweatpants and a sweatshirt, with her hair in a bun. Her face was washed clean and no longer had red splotches from emotion. Casually, her eyes roamed the television, but the absent-minded look on her face indicated that she was not paying attention to what was on the screen. Surely, she was rehearsing our conversation in her mind. The words would come out nervous, though practiced, as they always did when she needed to talk to me.

However, we had never had a conversation like the one we were about to have, and I wished it were as simple as the last time she sat and awaited my arrival. Kyla had accidentally told my mother we had decided against adoption, which my mother had been ecstatic about. Kyla, for some reason, thought I had already shared the news, and she mentioned it one evening when they spoke on the phone. My mother's silent shock instantly proved Kyla had been incorrect in her assumption. She felt terrible and had to reveal the innocent error in judgment to me. At the time I was upset. I had wanted to explain the reasons for our decision when I talked to my mother myself. Instead, I had to listen to my mother's tearful cries for ten minutes before I was allowed to speak. In hindsight, Kyla's confession of that mistake was minor compared to the conversation I knew we were about to have.

"Can I talk to you?" she asked, doleful.

I paused. Her expression was still, but strained. I noticed the tightness through her jawline and her clenched teeth, and though she had spoken her words softly, they were articulate and as rigid as her jaw.

"Of course," I answered. "In a minute." I walked past the room, her eyes following me, and I went upstairs. My insides hurt from brewed anger and aggravation. I needed one additional moment.

The bedroom was not as I had left it that morning. Kyla's clothes from the day before were balled up on the bed, and the work clothes she had taken off lay sprawled across the chaise. In the bathroom she hadn't wiped the sink; dried toothpaste and mouthwash spatter spotted the granite basin. Her toothbrush lay damp at the bottom. She knew I hated that.

Back in the bedroom I picked up Kyla's clothes and unraveled them. I smoothed them out, in search of a trace of anything curious: an out-of-place wrinkle on her shirt, where Angie might have rested her body on Kyla's; or an unfamiliar scent, such as the combination of their sweat, the forbidden stench of betrayal. *Bitches.* I balled up the slacks and sweater again and ran downstairs.

"What's up?" I asked after I took a seat alongside her, so close our thighs touched. Kyla, startled, scooted slightly to her right. I scooted the half inch as well. I wanted to test her courage.

"So what's going on?" I asked again.

Kyla cleared her throat. "How was your day?" she began.

I ignored her question and glared at her. Finally, I answered, "Probably not as eventful as yours. I should probably ask you that question. How was *your* day?"

Kyla seemed instantly frightened, visibly taken aback, like a politician with a broken teleprompter. I had thrown off her well-rehearsed speech, and she didn't know what to say. I continued to watch her. Her taupe skin warmed to a reddish hue. Her clenched jaw tightened further in an effort to conceal her shaking lips. Her eyes began to tear, and mine did too, but out of contempt. Her expression questioned my knowledge. *What does she know?* she wondered.

"You know?" she asked carefully.

My heart throbbed faster than it had in my entire life. Again, her inability to answer a question directly confirmed the answer I feared. A tear fell from my eye. Not from sadness, but from the exhaustion it took to constrain the fury I felt inside.

"I know what? What is it that I know, Kyla? Hmm?" She didn't answer but instead picked at her fingers.

"I didn't mean for this to happen," she said finally. Her voice shook.

"I didn't mean for this to happen," I repeated, mimicking her whiny voice. "Same shit you said to me yesterday, but you went on ahead and carried your ass to Angie's. So what's your excuse?"

"I don't have one. I'm sorry."

"Sorry for what?" I spoke louder. "For fucking Angie? For being weak for some new pussy that you had to fuck up all this? Everything we have? Oh, wait. It's not even new pussy. It's old, worn-out, used-up pussy, so what the hell is wrong with you? I trusted you all these years, thinking you had actually changed. Believing you had actually learned what commitment and fidelity mean." I pointed a finger in her face.

"Well, guess what? You don't. You've mistaken me for one of your old groupies, like you can do this kind of shit to me and I'm supposed to keep running up behind you, kissing your ass. Best believe nobody's pussy is that good to me, not even yours. Fuck you. Fuck this relationship. I don't give a shit what happens from here."

It was all out before I could control it. I meant about half of the words; the rest were just to hurt her. Did I mean she was weak to have messed up our relationship? Yes. Did I mean I didn't care what happened now? No. As much as I wanted her to, inside I was petrified that she would walk out the door.

Kyla cried. She cried a painful, remorseful cry. I had no desire to comfort her for her wrongdoing and make it easy for her to feel sorry for herself and wallow in her own pity. No. I wanted her to feel bad. I wanted her to feel like the same shit she had just trampled into our relationship.

"Tell me what you've done. Admit it. Say it, Kyla. That's what you wanted to tell me, right?"

"I messed up, Asia, I know." She hesitated. "I slept with Angie today."

Though I already knew the truth, I responded as if I had learned it for the first time. I lashed out further, letting her know how it felt to waste nine years of my life on her, and how embarrassed I felt for having fallen for a cheater.

"I knew it. You were a slut then, and you're still a slut now," I growled.

I forgot the words of reason of Mrs. Johnson. I ignored the classy upbringing and the "Always act like a lady" lessons my mother had given me.

"Say it right, Kyla. Don't go trying to soften it up. You fucked Angie today. That's all you two are good for? A piece of ass, right? Is that all I ever should have expected from you? Why waste all these years pretending to be something you never could be? Faithful. You cheated on Jeff, and you fucked half of Atlanta before me. Silly of me to think you knew how to actually love and be committed to somebody. In the end, you always do what pleases Kyla. It's all about you. So what now? You're ready to go be with Angie? I hope she's worth it. Hell, you might not even be worthy of her."

Kyla continued to cry shamefully, her face in her hands. "I don't know what's next. I'm not ready to leave."

"Ha! Really? Don't you think you should have thought about that on your way to Angie's house?"

She nodded.

"Look. I'm going upstairs. Do whatever the hell you want to do, and don't even think about saying shit to me until I talk to you."

I got up, with a sense of déjà vu from the previous night, and walked toward the stairs.

"Wait, Asia," Kyla called after me.

"Fuck you, Kyla," I responded and continued to the bedroom.

I paced around the bedroom in an effort to calm down. I hated the things I said to Kyla as much as I despised the reason behind my words. I was furious at her for disregarding everything we had built together for an experience she thought she had missed and now longed for. As much as I already dreaded the next phase of my life—separating from her, dividing our possessions, and moving on—I knew there was no choice. I would never take her back.

I heard the garage open. I ran to the window. Was she really about to leave? From upstairs I watched her car exit the garage and disappear into the night. I didn't have the energy to worry if she was off to seek refuge at David's or to open her legs for Angie again. Did it even matter?

Eleven

Kyla

"It's over." I sniffed into my sleeve. "I told her what happened, and she went off. She's so pissed, and I don't blame her. I have no idea what to do."

"Where are you?"

"Midtown."

"I'll be there in a minute."

I put my phone down and continued to sit at the bar of the dark corner tavern, a little spot where it mattered not how I appeared. I was frazzled, with swollen, red eyes. The bartender still handed me a drink nearly before I sat down.

"Rough night?" the old server asked me. He seemed tired, his eyes heavy with dark bags, like those of a bruised boxer who lost his fight. He had a glass in hand, ready to pour.

"Yes. Vodka and cranberry please."

He filled the glass with vodka, then added only a few drops of cranberry, enough to turn the libation a sheer light pink. The vodka burned my chest with each swallow. I felt I deserved it. That was my first drink, and I had been there an hour. The two drinks that followed were the same.

I left home because I couldn't sit in that big house with Asia after our argument, if I could even call it an argument. It was more like a one-sided verbal ass whipping. Asia insulted me in ways no one ever had,

not even Jeff, who had been furious when I confessed
to sleeping with Stephanie, but he hadn't been hateful.
I had never seen Asia speak to anyone else like that.
Sure, I knew she had a sharp tongue; it had always
been a quality I admired in her. I didn't know she'd use
that tongue to lash at me so harshly. I appreciated her
knack for speaking candidly. I knew this from previous
conversations we'd had, which I played in my mind.
But the conversation we had just had, I had not envi-
sioned.

Asia's response to my actions with Angie proved
there was no hope for our relationship. Her stance was
clear: we were done. I couldn't find a reason to stay
home, separated from her for another night, while we
tried individually to cope with the new division. I had
made the decision to leave, and I had no excuses and no
justification for it, other than I had found myself at another confusing juncture in life, unsure what decision
was best for me. I probably should have stayed home
and tried to resolve the disturbing discord between us.
What did I do when I was unsure? I continued to dis-
engage, and I chose the alternate plan.

"I'll have a Miller," Angie told the attentive bartender
when she sat on the stool next to me. When I told her
over the phone that I was in Midtown, there was no
need to provide a specific location. We frequented this
spot in the past, before a night of sex at my place or
hers.

"Hey," she said to me. Her eyes softly took in my
distressed appearance and disposition. She reached for
my hand and squeezed.

"How did this happen, Angie?" I asked her, although
I had just answered the question for myself.

"It happened because we're both fools. Fools for
messing up what you have, and fools for not pursuing

us in the past." She paused a moment. "That would make you the only fool, though." She smiled at her poor joke.

A tear dropped from my eye onto the dull, scratched bar counter. I smeared it with my fingertip.

"I'm sorry," she apologized quickly.

"It's all right." I finished my drink and raised my glass to the bartender for another. Angie spied the bartender. He returned her gaze and held up four fingers as he handed me another drink.

"I'll be fine," I told her. "It's just vodka." I gulped half the drink.

Angie sighed. "What's next?"

I laughed and looked at Angie. She was blurry, like the fuzzy little letters on an eye chart during an eye exam.

"You sound like Asia. 'What's next, hmm?' What do you think is next?" My tongue suddenly disobeyed me. My question sounded more like "Wha thoo thi ith neth?" "She said it's over. I guess one of us has to move out, right?"

"You can stay with me," Angie offered, jumping at the opportunity.

"Ha! Stay in the place your ex just moved out of? One out, next one in, huh?"

"It's not like that, and you know it."

"Sure it is. Your revolving door has swung just as many times as mine." I had started to talk louder. The table of three patrons behind us, two male and one female, took notice. I saw them through the mirror behind the bar and whirled around on my stool to face them. I almost lost my balance.

"What are you looking at?" I asked, the words slurred together. They looked at each other and burst into giddy snickers. Angie swiveled my chair back around.

"Let's keep this between us," she instructed.

"Sure, sure." I finished the rest of my drink. The bartender was at the opposite end of the bar, catering to no one but seemingly deaf to my request for another.

"Hey. Hey!" I yelled to him. "Another please." "Unuthu pleath."

He held his finger up to me and disappeared somewhere behind the magical mirror behind the bar.

"What's wrong with him?" I turned back to Angie. The circular movement hurt. My eyes seemed determined to linger on the place behind me where the bartender had stood. I still saw traces of his disappearing act while I struggled to bring Angie into focus.

"You know this is your fault, don't you?" I poked a finger hard into her breast. "If it weren't for you, I'd be home in bed with Asia, sound asleep. No, wait. What day is it? Monday? No, we'd be having sex tonight." I started to laugh so hard and didn't stop until it was difficult to catch my breath. Tears fell. "Yep, tonight would have been our night. That's how predictable we had become." I wiped my eyes with the already damp napkin underneath my perspiring glass.

"But you . . ." I poked Angie again. "You and that good-ass sex of yours."

The table behind us tuned in once again.

"Yeah, yeah, that's right," I yelled to them. "Yep, I'm about to leave my four-bedroom house and my beautiful woman for this one right here." I pointed my finger high above Angie's head, as if she was the grand prize on *The Price Is Right*. "What do you think about that, hmm?"

I stood up. Barely. "Tell me. Should I do it?" I walked over and propped my elbows sloppily on their table. "Should I stay, or should I go?"

They didn't respond.

"Hey!" I slammed a palm against the table. "Don't you hear me?" I sighed. "It doesn't matter, anyway. I think I have to go."

Angie reached for my waist and held me erect just as I was about to stumble sideways. I couldn't see her, though. She was too blurry.

"I think you're right. It's time to go," she said.

"But that's not what I meant," I protested. "I mean, Asia won't let me stay now, will she? I have to go. You all understand, right?" I asked the table, but Angie dragged me toward the exit.

"Come on, Kyla."

We were out the door and in the cold air within seconds. My legs wobbled until they met the front seat of Angie's car. She got in beside me, started the car, and backed out of the small parking lot. The glare of the streetlights we passed was as harsh as direct sunlight. I closed my eyes. When I reopened them, I struggled to control the surge from my belly as we sped down an Atlanta highway. I closed them again.

When I opened my eyes again, I was home, on the family-room couch. My clothes were damp with sweat, and a foul-smelling wastebasket sat on the floor at my side. I attempted to sit up, but the weight of my head forced me back down. "Ouch," I murmured.

"How do you feel?" It was Asia. I squinted through my left eye and found her across from me, in the chair. She was dressed and ready for work, keys in hand.

"Not well," I groaned.

"I see that."

"What happened?" I tried to recall how I got home. Last I remembered, I was lying in the passenger seat of Angie's car. *Oh. Shit.*

"Ask Angie." Her voice was tense. She attempted to control her anger. "Look, Kyla, you have to go. It's one thing that you cheated, but to continue to disrespect me so blatantly is unforgivable." She got up and walked toward the door to the garage. "Be gone by the time I get home." Without another word, she left.

I began to replay in my mind the events from the previous night. The bar. Angie. The funny group at the table. "I have to go," I had told them.

I was right.

Twelve

Asia

It was eleven when I heard the alarm system beep, a sign that the front door had opened. Although I wanted to ignore Kyla's return home, the painful moans and groans and the stubborn protests I heard from the foyer jerked me out of bed.

"Let me go!" Kyla shouted, her words thick and obscure. I reached the landing of the staircase and found Angie attempting to keep Kyla upright, despite Kyla's insistence that she could walk alone. When Angie loosened her grip, Kyla immediately stumbled forward. Angie caught her again.

"I can walk, Angie," Kyla swore.

Angie looked up and saw me. "Don't worry. I got you," she told Kyla but continued to stare smugly at me.

"What the hell is going on here?" I asked, heading down the stairs.

"She had too much to drink," Angie explained.

"That's obvious." I finished my descent down the stairs. "Take her to the family room."

Angie dragged Kyla, who gave in and slid across the floor as Angie pulled. I went to the guest bathroom, grabbed the wastebasket, and followed them. Kyla immediately threw up in it. Together, Angie and I watched Kyla release all the emotions she had tried to swallow with alcohol.

"I'm so sorry," she cried. I didn't know who she was apologizing to, me or Angie. "I didn't mean for this to happen," she said, a repeat of her latest mantra. "I feel like shit. Please forgive me." Again, whose forgiveness did she need?

Eventually, she turned her head to the side and passed out. We stared at her, an awkward, stiff silence between us. Until the reality of what had happened hit me again.

"Why did you bring her here?"

"Because she lives here. I thought she needed to be home," Angie responded.

I snickered. "Is that right? She was pretty damn comfortable at your place earlier. What's the problem now?"

"Yeah, she was. Sorry it all came down to this, Asia," she offered.

I rolled my eyes. "Please. You and Kyla and your tired-ass apologies. It's not necessary, especially when you don't mean it. Yesterday she apologized for having feelings for you, and today she fucked you. So really? That's being sorry?"

"Maybe you shouldn't have given her permission. Do you think maybe this is your fault?" Angie challenged with a confident expression.

I walked up to her slowly and stood in her face. She smelled of alcohol too.

"You want to blame this shit on *me*? This is *you*, Angie, all you. It's been your two-faced ass coming up around here all these years, in my face, the whole time having feelings for Kyla. That's some sneaky-ass shit. A real woman, a respectful woman, would have stopped coming around a long time ago, instead of waiting for an opening to fuck up somebody else's relationship just because hers ended."

Angie stared at Kyla. Her breathing had deepened and was loud and slow. She almost appeared innocent, but everyone in the room knew otherwise.

"I can't help how I feel about her," Angie finally said.

"Bullshit! You should have controlled how you handled it. The same way you didn't say shit about it all these years, you should have kept your mouth quiet now. And if you didn't think you could, you should have walked away. Kyla would have been all right without you, trust me. Now her head is all fucked up and twisted."

Angie looked at me, her brown eyes exuding superiority. "We both know she didn't have to accept any of this, especially my invitation today. She had a choice, Asia. She made it."

I wanted to slap her. "You have some big-ass balls walking in my house, talking to me like this."

"It's Kyla's house too."

"Not for long, it's not."

"That's cool. She's got a place to stay." Angie winked at me.

"You are such a bitch," I told her. "You've been waiting on this, haven't you? This is exactly the reason exes shouldn't be friends. Somebody is usually still holding on to unresolved feelings, and then shit like this happens. Well, you can have her now. How does it feel to get back one of the trampiest women in Atlanta?"

"Come on, you don't mean that."

"Oh, right, I forgot you two are alike, anyway. I hope it works, but really, who's going to be the first to cheat? I can't wait to watch this fiasco."

"Believe it or not, I've never cheated on any woman I've been with, and I would never cheat on Kyla."

"Really? You want to claim that? All this love you claim you've had for Kyla over the years . . . You don't think that was cheating? I bet Deidra did. Maybe I didn't see it, and maybe Kyla didn't know it, either, but trust me, a woman knows if she places second in your heart."

"Deidra knew what was up a long time ago, and she chose to stay." Angie laughed. "You know, Asia, I guess I owe you a double apology. Looks like I took two women from you."

I fought back angry tears. "You better get your lying, backstabbing ass out of my house right now. I don't have time for this shit. I'm going back to bed. By tomorrow night she's all yours."

"Thank you," Angie replied arrogantly and then bent to kiss Kyla's rotten-smelling face. "Good night, Asia." She nodded her head at me and whistled as she headed for the door.

In all my life I hadn't used such restraint to keep from hitting another woman. I wasn't the fighting type of chick and refused to resort to that type of behavior. The more Angie and Kyla pushed me, the more unsure I became that I'd be able to contain myself should they flaunt their affair in my face again.

I hadn't gone back to sleep all night, and I was physically and emotionally fatigued when I got in my truck and left Kyla, confused and baffled, on the couch. When I reached my office suite in East Point, I sat at my desk and considered my next move. The headache of a breakup already overwhelmed me, in addition to the emotional transition I was experiencing trying to fall out of love with Kyla since I found out she slept with Angie. I was disgusted by Kyla's actions and sickened even more by the fact that I still hated to see her go.

I didn't feel like rearranging my life without her. I knew those on the outside looking in always encouraged someone in the midst of a transition with phrases such as "It'll take time" and "You'll be okay without her," just as Kyla and I had with Angie. But what was often forgotten was, no matter the circumstances and no matter the anger, it hurt like hell to have to give up on the dreams and plans of forever a person believed in. Did I think Kyla was the worst person in the world for what she had done? No. I left that space for murderers and child molesters. But did that mean I'd be able to forgive her and keep her in my life? No, I couldn't.

I had to determine how to pass the time. I had never fully understood the nuances of breakup etiquette. What was protocol? Lie in bed for weeks, crying over lost love? Hell, no. Pick up the phone and start calling old friends to see if they wanted to hang out because I was single again? Pathetic. Make myself available for someone new to come into my life? Possibly. Should I really sit back alone while Kyla rekindled her intimacy with Angie?

I sent Melanie a text. It's done. She cheated already. What to do now?

Less than thirty seconds later she called.

"You've got to be kidding me!" she exclaimed, her morning voice cracking a little.

"Not kidding. I wish I was."

"What happened?"

I gave Melanie a short version of the text from Deidra that had informed me that Kyla was at Angie's. I told her how I had waited outside Angie's, had watched Kyla leave, and had followed her to David's. "She came home and confessed they had sex, and then had the audacity to go back out and meet her later on."

"I can't believe it." Melanie sounded disappointed.

"Believe it. Get this. Angie brought her home drunk."

"Oh my God! You didn't kill them both, did you?"

I laughed. "No. Otherwise, I'd be calling you to represent my case."

"What are you going to do now?"

"I don't know. That's why I called you. I need some advice. I've never been this deep into a relationship with so much to sort out."

"It's not easy. I'll tell you that. It took almost a year before my ex and I fully separated. She had too much she needed to get together before she could move out. And you two have a house together. What will you do about that?"

"We'll have to figure that out. Right now I told her she has to be gone by the time I get home tonight."

"You kicked her out of her own house?"

"For now, yes. I don't want to walk around my house all tensed up. And she's the one who messed up, anyway. She should go."

"You know, technically, she doesn't have to go."

"I know, but she will."

"You don't know that. People get to acting crazy when you try telling them what they can and can't do."

"That's true. Kyla won't. She's too ashamed. Plus, I think she's really going to go ahead and see how things go with Angie. Nothing to hold her back now."

"I just can't believe it," Melanie repeated. "How are you doing? For real."

"I'm mad. I'm most pissed off that I have to rearrange my life again."

"You have to keep yourself busy," she suggested.

"I do. What do you suppose I should do? Find some hot little thing to make her jealous?" We laughed.

"Not to make her jealous. We're too old for those games. But if you find somebody in the meantime, well, do what you have to do," she advised.

"How long did you wait to date after your ex?" I wanted to know.

"Not long, but it was different. By the time we officially broke up, the relationship had been over for months. I tried to date Jo while still living with my ex, but Jo wasn't having it. I had to wait until we weren't living together anymore. It was worth it. But don't you go rushing anything. This is still really fresh and sudden. You have to cry and release. I know you want to be tough and all, but this has got to be affecting you."

"I told you I'm mad. What? You expected me to call you, crying? I don't do that kind of shit. Kyla and Angie have me wrong if they think I'm about to sit back in pity-party mode while they move on."

"I got you. Make sure you only do what you really want to, not something in an effort to get back at them."

I smiled. "Don't worry. I won't go shooting up the apartment. I'll call you if I get the impulse, though."

She laughed. "Deal."

"Thanks, Melanie. I appreciate you listening."

"No problem. Anytime. Seriously, let me know if you need anything. I feel bad this has happened. You two have always seemed so happy. It's like this came out of nowhere."

"Honestly, I'm surprised it's come to this too. I can admit that things haven't been as exciting as they used to be, but that's normal. It doesn't mean go out and cheat with a friend because you're bored. Know what I mean? She should have had more restraint and more respect. She should have come to me."

"She did come to you. She told you everything you just told me. You're the one who told her to keep exploring her feelings," Melanie reminded me gently. She was right.

"I didn't expect her to. Not the next damn day. You're saying it's my fault?"

"Not at all. I'm saying you should have communicated truthful feelings to her when she opened up to you. People have to be more careful with what they say in relationships. If in reality you wanted her to ease off Angie and work on your relationship, then you should have said that. Not told her the opposite to see if she'd come chasing after you."

"I wanted her to work on us because that's what *she* wanted. Not because of my urging. She made her choice."

"With your nudge. Still, I hear what you're saying."

"I'll update you later. Go on. I know I just talked your head off before your workday even started."

"No problem. You kept me company on my way in. Catch me up later."

"All right, Melanie."

I leaned back in my chair and extended my arms behind my head. I had intended to spend the entire day in the office, but after the Kyla and Angie episode, I had a new plan. I scrolled through the schedules of my nurses on duty and grinned when I came across the name I was looking for. She had a two-hour lunch break between patients. Perfect. I picked up the phone.

"Sam, it's Asia."

"Oh, good morning, Asia," she replied sweetly.

"I see you have a long lunch today. Do you have plans?"

"I don't."

"Meet me."

"Of course."

"Looks like you're over near West End. Twelve o'clock at Landon's?"

"Yes, okay."

"Great. I'll see you then."

"Bye."

I knew what I was about to do was wrong. However, Kyla wasn't the only one with someone in her back pocket to cushion the fall. Sam was young, free-spirited, and everything I needed to distract me, but not tie me down.

Thirteen

Kyla

"Can I get you anything?"

I settled against the futon in Angie's extra bedroom and looked around. The space was small, but warm, with Deidra's touches throughout. A Buddha statue sat in the corner of the window ledge, though I knew Angie had Christian beliefs. A plant hung on the balcony, but a green thumb, Angie did not have. The pillows Angie gave me were wrapped in lavender pillowcases, Deidra's favorite color.

"I'm all right." It was a lie.

"I'll give you some time. Know I'm right out here."

I nodded, and she closed the door.

After Asia left for work that morning, I lay on the couch for an hour, debating whether or not to oblige her request. The house was just as much mine as hers, and she had no legal right to make me leave. I very well could have stayed, and she couldn't have done a thing about it. I had almost convinced myself to stay; it was only once I became honest with my feelings that I admitted to myself that I didn't want to stay. Not under the current circumstances. There was no reason to delay what I knew would happen, anyway.

I called Angie and told her Asia kicked me out of the house. Angie canceled her appointments for the rest of the day and agreed to pick me up so we could get my

car from the bar in Midtown where I left it, too drunk
to drive. I would then follow her to her apartment.

"Deidra knew you were here yesterday, by the way.
I'm sure she told Asia," Angie also told me. Slowly, I put
it all together. Deidra's big mouth had told Asia about
Angie and me again. I realized that *was* Asia's truck I
had seen outside David's house; she had followed me.
She had known my whereabouts and had made assump-
tions about my actions by the time she got home.

I got up, showered, and swallowed three Tylenol
with black coffee. I packed some personal toiletries and
shoved handfuls of undergarments and comfortable
clothes in a suitcase. Even though I called in to work,
I selected three business suits for the remainder of the
week. I left the house with an understanding that it
wasn't the last time I would be there, yet the moment
was pivotal. Nothing would ever be the same once I
walked out the door.

Angie knocked on the door again. Cautiously, she
stepped inside. "Thought I'd bring you some tea, anyway."

"I don't want any tea, Angie."

"Just take it. It'll help you feel better."

"Okay." I took the warm mug. The burgundy-colored
liquid smelled of raspberry.

"If you get hungry, let me know. I'm about to fix myself something."

"I will. I'm about to make a call and then lie down for
a while."

"How's your head?"

"Better."

"If you need more Tylenol, it's in the hall cabinet. I
can get it for you."

"Thanks."

She backed out of the room and left me alone again. I lay comfortably on the futon and scrolled to David's number on my phone. He answered on the second ring

"Hey, David."

"Hey, baby girl. I've been waiting on your call. What's going on?"

"Well, I'm at Angie's place, with packed bags. That should answer your question."

"What? Honey, tell me what the hell happened."

"After I left you, I went home and waited for Asia. I was all set to tell her what happened with Angie and me. I didn't know then, but I just found out she already knew I had been to Angie's and she followed me to your house. She took over the entire conversation and cursed me out. I left after that."

"Damn, damn, damn. How did she already know?"

"Deidra."

"Aw, shit! So now both of them probably think this has been going on for more than a minute."

"Probably. This morning she told me I had to go."

"Why would you go to Angie's? You know you can come here. It's not right for you to be there," he warned. "What are you thinking?"

"I'm thinking I messed up. I'm thinking there's nothing I can do to fix it. I'm thinking Asia won't take me back even if I beg. So I came here. Angie is what got me to this point, so I'm going to see what happens."

"What happens? You talking about jumping right into a relationship with Angie? Are you crazy?"

"What am I supposed to do?"

"Carry your skinny little ass back home with your tail between your legs and ask for forgiveness. That's what you need to do. This is wrong, baby girl, just wrong."

"I'm already here, David. This is where I'll be for now."

He sighed. "So you've moved in with Angie?"

"Right now I'll stay here. I'll see about going back home once things have calmed down a bit."

"You mean after you see how things are going with Angie, don't you?"

I was quiet. I knew his statement was true. This was not to say I had fallen out of love with Asia and was ready to move on with Angie, but I needed some time apart to see if Angie was all she had proclaimed herself to be.

"I just need a little time, that's all. Asia won't hear a thing I have to say right now, other than letting her know I'm gone."

"You're probably right about that. Probably the only thing you're right about these days. Well, don't go taking too much time, or she won't hear you at all."

"I won't. Anyway, this is where I'll be at least for the rest of the week."

"If you come to your senses, you know our couch is open."

"Thanks. I know."

"I'll check on you later," David told me firmly. "Don't go not answering your phone."

"Okay."

"And stay out of Angie's bed."

"Bye. David." I couldn't promise that.

Just as I hung up the phone and sipped the cooled tea, Angie tapped on the door.

"I made some breakfast for lunch. Come out and join me?"

Inside I moaned. Angie hadn't even given me ten minutes of alone time, and already she was back. I was annoyed but reminded myself why I was there, to sort out my feelings about her. I needed to take advantage of every moment. It seemed she was going to force me to, anyway.

Angie held the door while I stepped out of the room. Apparently, she expected me to say yes, or she would have begged until I did, because she had decorated the dining table and put together a cute candlelit lunch.

"Have a seat." Angie held a chair out for me. I wanted to protest, but instead I accepted her gesture. "I figured you hadn't eaten and probably needed more coffee. How are you feeling?"

"Not too well, but I'm hungry. Thank you. This smells really good."

We ate quietly for a few minutes before I began a conversation.

"What happened last night between you and Asia?"

"That's not important," she answered.

"Yes, it is, Angie. You brought me home drunk the same day I told her we'd slept together. Then she kicked me out. So what happened? I know she had to be pissed off."

"She was mad, you know. I apologized, told her we were real sorry and that none of this was supposed to happen."

"What else?"

"Nothing really. She left you on the couch and went upstairs, so I went home."

"That's it?"

"Yeah."

"You two didn't exchange words or anything?" Given the ease with which Asia cursed me out, I assumed she'd had a few pretty words for Angie too.

Angie put her plate aside. "Forget about last night, Kyla," she insisted. "You're here with me now. That's all that matters. How are you feeling?"

"I'm confused. That's how I feel."

"What about me? You ready to do this?"

"It's all too soon to say," I told her, unable to make a firm decision in either Angie's or Asia's favor. "I mean, I'm here, and thank you for letting me stay. I want to make the best of this time, but I'm not sure what that means yet. Right now I feel uncertain. That's the best I can do."

"Uncertain about what in particular?" She came off agitated.

"Uncertain about what I should do. Obviously, I brought all this on myself, and now I need to figure out how to handle it. There's a lot to consider."

"Such as?"

"Everything, Angie. I just don't want to hurt anybody any further."

"*Anybody* meaning me?"

"Me, you, and Asia. Hurt any of us further."

"Let me tell you this. I know what I'm dealing with. I've known you a long time, in case you forgot. I know what you need, and it's me. I can fulfill every desire you have, and now that you're here, I'm about to show you."

"You don't have me yet, Angie. I just said I don't know what's going to happen."

Angie shook her head from side to side. "I'm not going to accept that. I won't lose you now that you're here."

I sat back in my chair. It seemed there was no reasoning with her. I'd have to make a decision fast, despite Angie's insistence that I was already hers. And, as David had said, if I had any chance with Asia, it had to be sooner rather than later. She needed time to cool off first. The thought of Asia saddened me. It suddenly hit me that for the first time since we moved in together, we'd spend the night apart for reasons other than business. Owing to my selfishness, we were apart. I missed her, even though I sat across from Angie and desired her just the same. No matter what I did, I would lose one of them from my life forever.

"Show me a little patience, will you?" I pleaded.

"Of course," she agreed unwillingly. "So how do you think you'll handle the house situation?"

"Angie. Really?"

"I'm sorry, okay? It's just something to consider, you know. I'm here for whatever you need. Moving. Bills. Anything."

"Thank you, but a sponsor I don't need."

Angie smirked and nodded. "You want me to back off? Give you some quiet?"

Which I had asked for earlier.

"Right now I need to close my eyes for a minute. I'm going to lie down, all right? I'll come find you when I wake up." I stood up and prayed she would relax, would believe I wasn't going anywhere, and would not come hound me again until I'd rested.

"I'll take that for you," Angie said and confiscated my plate before I could pick it up myself.

"You'll be here after my nap?" I asked.

"I sure will. I'm not leaving you."

Angie wrapped her arms around me. She was strong but soft. Her embrace instantly soothed the agitation and worry I felt. I relaxed for a moment and inhaled her fresh scent. She stroked my hair and squeezed tighter. Instinctively, regardless of my ambiguity about her and Asia, I lifted my head for a kiss, which she granted me. It was sweet, gentle, and assured me that I wasn't ready to disregard her yet.

"There's more where that came from. It's all yours if you want it," she told me. Before I could respond, she turned me around and walked me into the spare bedroom. "Now, go on and rest. I'll see you when you open your eyes."

She closed the door, and within seconds my eyes shut, with the taste of Angie's lips still on mine.

I couldn't rest. Ten minutes later my eyes reopened, and for no reason but a misguided impromptu impulse, I picked up the phone to call Asia and let her know I was gone. As the phone rang, I wondered how she would respond. Would her voice convey regret for kicking me out, or would she be relieved? I didn't get an answer to my question, because it was another woman that answered my call.

Fourteen

Asia

What I was doing would benefit no one, and I knew
it. But I wanted to. There was no way I would allow
Kyla to lie with Angie without showing her I could do
the same. It was out of my character; I had always been
loyal in my relationships. Kyla, however, needed to
know I could play the same cards she dealt. Years of
stringing women along was about to come back on her.
I wanted to call it karma, but it was pure vengeance.

Sam walked into the restaurant in all her delightful
youthfulness. Sam was thirteen years younger than me
and exactly the ego boost I needed after Kyla's disap-
pointing actions. Sam was one of those women with an
unbelievably angelic look: she had a full, round face
with pinchable cheeks, deep dimples, and large bash-
ful eyes. Her patients adored her calm disposition and
the delicate manner in which she interacted with them.
Admittedly, if I had been younger and single, I would
have considered dating her.

When I hired her a year ago, she had openly invited
me to seek her company should my and Kyla's relationship ever disintegrate. Aside from that early invitation,
we had always maintained a professional relationship.
No one, not even an appealing woman like Sam, could
have swayed me from Kyla. My faithfulness was all the
more reason why I wanted retribution for her infidelity.

"Hey, Asia." Sam took the chair opposite me at the small table.

"Sam. Glad you could make it." I picked up the menu. "Hungry?"

"Not really. I don't really eat lunch most days."

"No? What is it that you usually do over lunch?"

"Um . . . depends. Sometimes I sit in my car and listen to music. I go for a walk when it's nice out. Or I go home and take Nelly out."

"Yes. Nelly, your poodle . . . I remember."

Sam smiled nervously. "Is everything all right? Did I do something? Not always a good thing when the boss schedules an unplanned meeting."

"Of course there's nothing wrong, and trust me, this is all good. I just wanted to connect with you. See how things are going on your end."

Sam blushed. "Oh, okay. Good. I was worried. Everything is well. I'm glad you asked. What about you?"

"Going through some changes right now, but I think I'll be all right."

"Oh, I see. Anything I can help you with?"

"I'm hoping so." I leaned forward and took in her face: tender eyes, smooth skin, wet lips. "Do you recall the, um, the proposal you presented to me once upon a time?"

Sam leaned forward and met my gaze. "Of course I do."

"Is it still on the table?"

"It's always been there. Are you considering?"

"I'm ready. Shall we sign on the dotted line?"

"Do you have a pen?" she asked.

"In my back pocket." I laughed. "Sam, I appreciate you coming, but I think we should go. Is that all right with you?"

"Absolutely."

"Did you have plans for lunch today?"

"I was going to go home since I had a two-hour break." She tilted her head sideways. "Looks like that's working in my favor. Would you like to come with me? I mean, if that's okay."

"Yes, it's perfectly okay." We stood.

"Excuse me," I called to our server. "We won't be staying. Thank you."

The petite server rushed to our side. "Is something wrong?" she asked, concerned.

Sam and I glanced at one another.

"Everything is perfect," I answered without taking my eyes off Sam.

Twenty minutes later we were at her apartment in Dunwoody. It was a small place, with just enough room for a single woman and her dog.

"I'll be only a second." Sam excused herself to take a five-minute walk outside with Nelly.

I waited on the couch and tried to ignore my nervous energy. Kyla and I had been two different people in our single days. I hadn't slept around with women for sport the way Kyla had in her leisure time. After my initial experimental years, I had reserved my body only for women who showed promise in terms of a relationship. I had felt that way about Kyla, which was why I slept with her after just a couple of dates. She had been the only once since then. Sam was the first woman in twenty years who I wanted nothing more from than sex.

Sam returned while I checked my e-mail on my phone. She gave Nelly a treat and took a seat at my side.

"So . . . um . . . are you still hungry?" she asked me.

"Very," I answered and attempted to resurrect the suave demeanor I had exhibited at the restaurant.

"I don't have much." She looked toward the mini kitchen. "I'm sorry. I guess I should have told you that before I invited you over."

"Surely, you must have something I can nibble on," I said slyly.

"I might." She smiled coyly. "You know, now that I think about it, I have a feeling I might be a bit hungrier than you are." She licked her lips.

"You think?"

"I've been eyeing something on somebody else's menu for a while now. But"—she moved closer—"if the menu is being passed to me, I'll take it. Even if I get to sample only one item for now."

Always the innocent-looking ones, I thought.

I smiled. "No worries. Somebody else put the menu down. You're free to choose whatever you like. I think we have time for at least an appetizer right now."

"That's perfect." Sam came even closer, and I got nervous again. I hadn't touched another woman in nine years. It was strange and scary, primarily because two weeks prior I wouldn't have placed myself in that position, ready to give another woman specifically what I thought I saved for Kyla—forever.

"Do you mind? I need to use the restroom."

"Sure. Right outside the bedroom." She pointed and described the bathroom's location in greater detail, as if it were so far away that I needed directions.

Once inside I rested my head against the sink. I had to convince myself to do what I'd come to do. Spite was a quality I despised, yet it was the one emotion I craved. I had to fuck Sam and deal with the aftermath later.

When I opened the bathroom door, Sam smiled at me, her lips turned up in a sly smirk. Quickly, she steered me into her bedroom and closed the door, leaving Nelly whimpering outside.

Sam took the lead. I preferred it that way as a part of me simultaneously mourned and anticipated the moment. I shuffled fearful thoughts underneath the desire to complete my task. With the first kiss Sam placed on my skin, I shuddered uncontrollably. The fullness of her lips differed from the smaller ones I was used to. Her tongue, warm and thick, was unfamiliar, though pleasing, as she explored. Within minutes my clothes were at my ankles.

"Will you lie down for me?" she asked.

Her mattress was firm, unlike the soft cushioning of my bed at home. It smelled . . . different. It was the scent of another woman's perfume, her lotion, and her hair. It was everything other than Kyla. I tried not to yearn for Kyla and reminded myself that she was the reason I was in another woman's bed. Sam placed her head between my legs and kissed me.

"Mmm. Delicious," she told me.

I closed my eyes. "Bon appétit."

Fifteen

Kyla

The woman's voice was a light whisper, smooth, aroused, and familiar. I removed the phone from my ear and then placed it back again.

"I'm looking for Asia," I stated, confused.

"She's busy right now," the woman told me.

"Is she with a patient?" Asia rarely accompanied nurses on visits and vice versa, and even when she did, there was no need for any of them to answer her phone.

"No, she's with me," the woman replied confidently.

"Who is this?"

"This is Sam. Asia's in the bathroom right now, Kyla. Do you need her?"

My stomach turned. I knew Sam as the cute, sexy young nurse Asia had hired some time back. Although she had been cordial to me at the small holiday party Asia had for her staff at Christmastime, there was something about the way Sam had watched my and Asia's interactions that night that led me to believe she desired Asia as more than a boss. A woman picked up on those things. I mentioned it to Asia on our ride home that night. She admitted that Sam had clearly made herself available should anything ever happen with us. She had reached for my hand and had held it.

"We don't have to worry about that, do we?"

"Never," I had told her. At the time I hadn't known it was a lie.

Since then, to my knowledge, Sam had been nothing but an employee. Why were they together?

"Are you two on a job?"

Sam snickered. "No. We're at my place"—she snickered again—"having lunch. Would you like me to tell her you called?"

"No, I'll try her later."

"Good, because it's time for me to eat." She hung up quickly, before I could reply.

My mouth fell open. I had no doubt Asia was the meal to which Sam had referred. Maybe my suspicions were right. Had Asia been bored as well, and had she sought relief with Sam? I didn't believe this was their first lunchtime rendezvous. Maybe Asia wanted me to explore options with Angie so she could freely be with Sam. I was hurt, angry, and I felt deceived: I had been made the guilty party, Asia's scapegoat, when she was the one who desired to end our relationship.

My eyes singed with hot tears. I didn't know if I cried most from embarrassment or shame about what I wanted to do next. I felt embarrassment for having allowed Asia to play me as the bad girl while she cleverly hid her skeletons. I instantly wanted retribution. Without another thought, I stood and left the room. Angie was surprised to see me. She looked up from the book she was reading. I didn't say anything, only walked into her bedroom, removing my shirt and pants along the way. She was behind me in seconds. On her bed I lay on my stomach. She undressed, and we were skin against skin. The weight of her body was greater than Asia's, the pressure pleasing, though it reminded me of the heaviness of the situation. I readjusted myself until her thighs were wrapped around me. Angie kissed my back tenderly. Too gently. It was too much like Asia.

"No. Give it to me like you used to," I instructed her. Without hesitation, she grabbed my ass cheeks in the palms of her hands. She squeezed and then slapped them. The sting hurt, and my eyes watered. I put my face in the pillow. The satin case warmed from my tears. Angie slapped me three more times.

"This is what you want?" she asked.

"Yes. Yes . . . ," I cried.

"Turn over," she commanded.

I did.

Her expression was conflicted when she saw my tears. I wiped my face dry.

"Fuck me," I told her.

Angie regained her composure and buried her lips, her tongue, and her teeth in my neck. Her hand tightened at my throat, and she whispered in my ear.

"I'm about to fuck you like you've never been fucked before."

Sixteen

Asia

It was impossible not to compare Sam to Kyla. Kyla knew exactly what to do, how to stroke, caress, and please me. Sam was a novice with my body. She surveyed and examined with her fingers, and her tongue explored, trying to find the places I found delightful. She learned about the tickling sensations I felt when her tongue darted across my inner thighs. She took notice of the moans I murmured when she cupped my breasts with her hands and rubbed her palms against my nipples. She figured out that her two-finger stroke fit my body perfectly. She moved fast and slow depending on the movement of my hips.

She talked to me more than Kyla did. She asked if I liked it. She asked where I liked it. I didn't want to respond, but I told her "Yes" and "My pussy." I wanted her to make me cum; that was all I needed. She told me my pussy was beautiful. That it was wet, and she wanted to taste it. She did and told me it was good. That it was exactly what she had waited for.

Kyla

Angie pinched my nipples and bit my breasts. She stroked between my legs softly and then penetrated my wetness forcefully.

"Give it to me," I told her.

Angie slowed, then stopped. From her nightstand drawer she retrieved a healthy-size strap-on. It was long, thick, and matched the color of her warm beige skin. I helped her into it and adjusted the harness around her waist. The ridged penis bobbed, erect. I was ready for it. Angie positioned me on my hands and knees and took me from the back. The dildo slid into my wetness effortlessly. My pussy tightened around it as she began to pound me.

"Is this what you wanted?" Angie asked, her hands at my waist, my ass slapping against her sweaty skin.

"Yes," I breathed. "Go deep."

"You got it, baby."

She thrust deeper.

Asia

Sam rested her body in a sitting position, her weight on her heels, and lifted my waist into the air. Her fingers synchronized together harmoniously, thrusting deep, one plunging into my pussy, the other in my ass. The bliss was immeasurable.

"Your ass is so tight," she told me, her breath heavy. "Cum for me, Asia," she requested.

Her words excited me. I screamed and had one of the best orgasms I had had in a long time. With those innocent eyes and sweet mannerisms, Sam proved that her offer had been worthy of acceptance.

My mission had been accomplished beyond my satisfaction. And though my body relished the ecstasy, a sadness formed within me when I realized that the years I had shared my life with Kyla were over.

***

Kyla

Angie didn't lie. She gave me all the energy my body craved. She was relentless in her desire to take me to a level of pleasure to which I had never been. I came over and over, again and again. And even with this pleasure, still I couldn't shield my mind from thoughts and visions of Asia with Sam, and how the two of them must be laughing at me while they rolled together between Sam's sheets.

My pussy throbbed when Angie released the dildo. She wasn't done, though. Angie lowered herself again to my middle and began to suck. She sucked, licked, and penetrated me again, this time with her fingers. I tried to focus on the tip of Angie's tongue against my clit, and the pressure of her index finger and middle finger against my G-spot.

How long had Asia been cheating on me?

The pressure of Angie's sucking intensified.

What were they doing now? Was Sam pleasing Asia the way Angie was pleasing me?

My body twitched in anticipation.

Was Sam better than me?

Another orgasm formed and teased my senses.

Could Sam make Asia cum . . . like . . . this . . . ?

The most intense orgasm of the afternoon shook my body, thanks to Angie's tongue. I cried out Angie's name, though my heart longed for Asia. I knew it was over.

The Exchange
Seventeen

Kyla

Asia stood in the doorway while I packed every item I could in the rest of my luggage. I had been in the house only a few minutes, and the only words spoken had been mine. "I'm here to get the rest of my stuff."

It was Saturday morning, a week and a half after the morning I left. After Sam answered Asia's phone and I realized Asia had been having an affair with her all along, I never called back, and she didn't call me, either. I arrived at our house unannounced, half expecting Asia to be gone, and partly prepared to walk in and find Sam sleeping on my side of the bed. Instead, the house was quiet, and I found Asia upstairs in bed, still wrapped in the comforter. She didn't appear to be sleeping, but was just lying there. My heart hurt at the sight of her, her jet-black hair covering the side of her face, partially concealing an expression I could not decipher. Wherever she was at that moment, her thoughts were not in the present. She hadn't heard me come in and walk upstairs. She was startled when I spoke to her.

"I'm here to get the rest of my stuff," I told her and headed straight to the walk-in closet and retrieved luggage that I hadn't already taken to Angie's. When I walked back into the bedroom, Asia had gotten up and stood in a pink nightie at the door. Her long, smooth legs caught my attention, though only a second later I pictured them wrapped around Sam's head and I became repulsed. The line between love and hate had become increasingly invisible, and I crossed repeatedly from one side to the next, like the needle on a polygraph machine. Selfish as it might have been, I hated her for being with Sam. For making it seem like I was the only partner in our relationship who had a problem. At the same time, I loved her for every good memory I still had of her. Although I might have found solace in another woman's arms, it hadn't erased the nine years I had devoted to Asia. A minute later I remembered it was she who hadn't been committed to me all nine years. And I hated her again.

I emptied my drawers containing T-shirts and lounging clothes first and my undergarment drawer next, while Asia watched. Intentionally, for her viewing, I held up the lacy, silky, sexy negligees I had purchased over the years. Finally, she spoke.

"It's like that?" Her voice was raspy and angry.

"Yep." I continued to fill the bag.

"I haven't talked to you since you left, and then you come up in here, pulling out nighties and shit, flaunting whatever in the hell it is you and Angie have going on like that shit is cool."

"You're the one who asked me to leave."

"You didn't hesitate, either, did you?"

I rolled my eyes at her. "Like you wanted me to stay, anyway." I resumed packing.

Asia didn't respond immediately, then asked, "What's that supposed to mean?"

I ignored her and went into the closet. I returned with an armful of business shirts. I shoved them into a suitcase. I'd worry about the wrinkles later.

"What are you talking about?" Asia asked again.

I stopped packing. "Check this out, Asia. I'm giving you what you want, okay? You wanted me out, so now I'm gone. What you should have done is told me you wanted out, instead of waiting so I could take the blame for this."

"You *are* the reason for all this!" she yelled.

I couldn't believe she was still acting as if she hadn't done anything. "You keep wanting to make this all my fault."

"Who else's fault is it? Sure as hell isn't mine."

I went back into the closet and grabbed everything I could in one motion. I looked like an enraged, maniacal spouse who had just learned her husband had cheated on her. You'd think I was about to throw my own clothes out of the window into a blazing fire pit below.

I hurriedly stuffed the rest of my things into the last suitcase, scooped up my remaining toiletries in the bathroom, and prepared to leave. Asia blocked the door with her body, which was spread-eagle, like the Vitruvian Man.

"What, Asia?"

"I'm not about to let you walk up out of here with the audacity to think I made this shit happen," she snapped.

"Whatever. Get out of my way." I pressed a bag against her hip.

Asia started to sweat. Little droplets began to form at her hairline and around her nose. That happened only when her anger was borderline explosive.

"*You* fucked your two-timing friend, and you're saying that it's *my* fault?"

I took a small step back and looked her directly in the eyes. "You're the one fucking Sam, and now you're trying to stand here and play innocent, so, really, stop putting all this shit on me."

Asia's expression contained both surprise and guilt. Her breathing temporarily halted. She looked away and then stepped aside to let me out. Inside I cried at her silent confession. I had only assumed she had been intimate with Sam; by not denying my claim, she had proved that my assumption was correct.

I took the first two bags to my car, and when I returned for the last two, Asia's back was to me while she stood in front of the window. Through the reflection I saw that her expression was calm but powerful.

"You know," she said softly, "you had to know that someday all your indiscretions were going to come back to haunt you."

"Excuse me?"

She turned around slowly. "How does it feel?"

"How does what feel?"

"To know you're not the only one who can play your own game?"

She took a few steps toward me, then stood on the opposite side of the bed, her arms across her chest.

"What are you talking about?"

"You have to know I'm not the kind of woman to sit back and get played. Not again. Especially not by you. So I did what I had to do."

My eyes began to water. I picked up the remaining bags, ready to leave.

"So this was to teach me a lesson? That's what you're saying?"

She nodded. "Of course."

"For what?"

"Let's just say I was in a position to do what no one else could. I got you back. Now you know that what you can do, someone else can do better. In more ways than one, by the way." She smirked.

She stood firm and confident in her words. Her voice had softened, but her condescending tone hadn't faltered a bit. She had played me and deceived me for what? For teetering between her and Angie? Had she sought vengeance for all the women I had dated in the past? Had she maintained a facade for years, in hopes that I would eventually mess up and she could come out about her own indiscretions? Had this been her mission all along? My heart told me no, that what we had was real. Her nonchalant words seemed to indicate otherwise.

"Well, I hope you're glad your mission was accomplished."

"I am." She smiled. "It was worth it."

"Fuck you, Asia."

"No, boo. This is a fuck you. Haven't you been listening?"

"I heard every word you said, and like I said, fuck you. I can't believe this shit." I turned around to leave.

"Remember you brought this on yourself."

"I need to get out of here."

"Nothing stopping you now. Bye."

I walked out, and she slammed the door behind me. For emphasis, I supposed.

Outside I hurriedly tossed the luggage into my open trunk and closed it. I didn't really want to, but I felt compelled to look up at the bedroom window before I drove off. She stood there, the pink silk of her nightgown illuminated by the morning sun. Although her arms were crossed against her chest and she loomed high above me, her posture was less intimidating than her words had been just minutes before. Her shoulders were hunched slightly, and her head was tilted in a slight solemn bow. I didn't know what she had to be sad about. She had got what she'd asked for. I was gone.

Eighteen

Asia

I had to think fast when Kyla mentioned Sam's name. I didn't know how she found out about my afternoon with Sam or who would have told her. To my knowledge, Sam steered clear of the lesbian scene and knew few people in the lifestyle. She didn't have a group of gay friends, wasn't the partying type, and opted out of Pride events. In fact, I was happy to learn she hadn't already known Kyla when they met at the Christmas party last year. That Kyla knew about Sam startled me, and quickly, I had to regain control before she could use Sam against me. I needed her to know she couldn't toy with and disregard our relationship without repercussions. I wasn't going to be one of her ex-women who tapped to her every beat. So what if I had been spiteful and childish, maybe even silly? Even though my spirit dimmed as I watched Kyla drive away, I had successfully shown her I could give my body to another as easily as she had. What I needed to figure out now was how she found out about it. It hadn't come from me, and that left only one other person.

My interactions with Sam I had kept to a minimum since our lunchtime tryst. Ironically, I had behaved as Kyla had in the past, and had used a woman for sexual gratification, with no intention to pursue anything further. Sam had sent a couple of text messages with the suggestion that we connect again.

Later the same day, after I left her apartment, she wrote, I'm still full. So satisfying.

I didn't respond.

The next day, after work, she texted, Lunch again? I'd love to try another course.

We'll talk, was my reply.

I understood then I was not and never could be like Kyla. I didn't desire only a physical relationship with a woman. I didn't want to send explicit text messages to random women. I didn't want to fuck people just for the hell of it. It wasn't my style.

I probably would have ignored Sam's requests until she grew tired and got the hint that I had no intention of entertaining her any further. But with the knowledge Kyla had about her, I couldn't do that. I had to call.

"Hello, Sam."

"Asia. Good morning to you." Her voice was soft and flattering.

"How are you?"

"Better, now that you called. Glad to finally hear from you."

"Sorry. Just been a little busy."

Truthfully, I had spent too many days sitting in my office chair, contemplating the next stage of my life and how I would respond when I finally talked to Kyla again. I had, in fact, been lying in bed thinking of her, remembering the first time we made love. I remembered the evening clearly. It was just after Tiffany, one of the women she had been seeing along with Angie, had interrupted our first dinner at her apartment. The scene turned chaotic, with Tiffany issuing a final threat that karma would find its way back to Kyla. I trusted Kyla when she told me she had left Tiffany alone after that. I believed her when she said she wanted no one other than me. We gave ourselves to one another quickly and passionately.

I should have paid attention to the signs given to me that night. The fact that a crazed, clingy ex popped up showed Kyla clearly had unfinished business. Instead, I moved forward and did not hear the warning bells going off in my mind, the same way I didn't hear Kyla enter the bedroom to collect the rest of her things. I found it odd that it was another ex that caused the demise of our relationship. As it began, so it ended.

"So what's up?" Sam sounded disappointed by my response.

"About last week. Kyla knows about it. I'd like to know who you told."

"I haven't told anyone about us."

"There is no us," I said, correcting her. "Who did you tell about what happened?" I asked again.

"I haven't talked to anyone about our lunch date," she told me again, though it had to be a lie. I became agitated.

"How else would Kyla know?"

"I don't know, Asia," she answered innocently. "She didn't tell you?"

"No. I'm asking you."

Sam exhaled. "I wish I could tell you, but I have no idea."

"I'm going to ask you one more time. You didn't tell anybody about what happened?"

"I did not," she said clearly, articulating each word so I wouldn't ask again. "And maybe you shouldn't worry about it. She knows. Does it matter how? She's the one who left you, right?"

I avoided her last question. "I'd like to be sure this stays between us."

"I think it's too late for that. You might want to tell that to Kyla."

"I'll address Kyla when I need to."

"I suggest you let it go. Who cares? You're not together anymore, anyway." Sam adopted the sweet tone
I was accustomed to hearing. "So will we have another
lunch? Maybe even dinner?"

I wanted to tell her, "Absolutely no," but I couldn't
completely disregard her until I knew if she had lied to
me. "Let me sort some things out here."

"Don't worry that pretty head of yours too much.
What's done is done. Maybe Kyla needed to know she
shouldn't have let such a good woman go free. It's her
loss, you know—"

I cut her off. "I'll talk to you later, Sam."

I didn't trust her. I trusted her with my patients, but
not on a personal level. She already seemed too confident that she and I had become more than a one-night
stand. I prayed she hadn't turned into my version of
Tiffany.

There was no way she was being honest with me. She
had to have told someone, and that person told Kyla.
Or, maybe someone saw me at Sam's apartment, but
Kyla and I knew no one on that side of town. There
was only one person who could answer the question
for me, I thought, and then I wondered if Sam was
right. Did it matter how Kyla had found out? To me it
mattered. I didn't need my business spread around,
and if someone talked, I had to know who. Eventually, I would have to talk to Kyla and find out how
she learned what I had wanted her to know, anyway.

Nineteen

Kyla

With a car packed full of items, I drove the streets of Atlanta with no particular destination in mind. Finally, I stopped at a small park and sat on a bench to watch ducks swim about a small pond. Although I owned a beautiful home in the suburbs and also had a key to an East Point apartment, I felt homeless. But unlike a bag lady, I felt neither pity nor sorrow for myself or my circumstances. I didn't ask passersby for assistance, and no one stopped to offer me change or hand me a card with the name and location of a shelter I might consider. No, there was no need to worry about me. I sat and stared ahead because I felt lost. Asia's callous casualness had rattled me. For almost nine years I had remained monogamous and committed to a woman who wanted only to seek revenge for a past that didn't involve her. Never would I have thought that was Asia's true character. During our time together, she had been the antithesis of that.

The ducks fluttered about the water, squawking at one another and darting about in circles. The sun spread its light across the pond, and its mirror image was visible in shining twinkles across the surface. The weather had warmed to a welcoming sixty-five degrees in mid-March, and I appreciated the quiet time to think. I hadn't had any time alone since I had been at Angie's. Angie was up almost every morning before I woke, and I'd hear her in the kitchen, preparing breakfast for us. Twice she had omelets ready, which she served to me in bed at six thirty. One morning she had whipped together a sausage burrito, which sat ready on the table once I was dressed and about to leave for work. Another day she prepared a generous helping of hash browns and scrambled eggs. She seemed eager to prove she could be the woman she had promised she could be.

Throughout the workday Angie would send text messages to check on me. At least once an hour and between her appointments, I received reminder messages of how much I meant to her and how happy she was that I was at her place. She delighted in knowing that a few hours later I'd return to her. Oddly, the evenings we'd spent together thus far were similar to my nights at home with Asia. We sat next to one another on her living-room sofa, where we chatted about the day or watched whatever I chose on television while Angie pretended to watch next to me. Our interactions were smooth, calm, and easy. No conversation or exchange was overly exciting or stimulating, and I had begun to wonder if I truly had been missing anything besides breakfast in bed.

We avoided Asia, the topic that had me weighed down. I hadn't told Angie what I learned about Asia and Sam, and Angie hadn't pressed further on the issue of when Asia and I would sever the ties that bound us together. Angie seemed happy enough with my presence, more and more confident that it would be her and me in the end.

At night I didn't sleep on the futon in the spare room, as I had originally intended. I was in Angie's bed every night, and almost every night we made love. I wanted to open not only my body, but my heart as well. That was why I was at her place, right? Before the revelation about Asia, I felt like my desire for Angie had been more sincere. Now I felt I used her as a rebound and sought her touch, her warmth, and her affection every time I became frustrated or annoyed about what Asia had done to me.

You would think that finding out Asia had cheated would fling me right into Angie's arms. It didn't. I lay in Angie's arms for comfort, but I was distracted by thoughts of Asia, my mind busy inspecting details of our past as I tried to figure out how I had missed her cheating. A part of me wanted to confront her and ask her questions. I wanted to know how in the hell she had deceived me all that time. Had she faked appointments with patients? Did anyone, especially the business owner, really have to work weekends as often as she had? She had her staff for that.

I had begun to drive myself crazy, analyzing every time I now suspected Asia had told me a lie. I was curious if she and Sam had already been sneaking around by the time I met Sam at the Christmas party. I tried not to fabricate stories in my mind and create fictitious events. Yet I couldn't stop myself.

I recalled a two-minute interlude at the restaurant where the Christmas party was held when neither Asia nor Sam was in sight. An easy enough explanation would be that they both had to use the restroom at the same time. Now I wondered if there had been more to it. Maybe they had escaped for a quick kiss. Maybe Asia had taken Sam aside and had apologized about the fact that it was taking longer than expected for our relationship to end. The assurances Asia had given me about Sam on our ride home that night had been false. Maybe she had hoped I would create a fuss about Sam, start a big fight, and she would find a reason to plant enough

doubt in my mind that I'd sabotage what we had. She
must have felt relief when Angie successfully injected
herself between us. Asia deserved an Academy Award
for her performances the past couple of weeks. On the
inside she must have been tickled.

I checked the time. It was ten o'clock, and I needed
to get back to the apartment soon. Angie had planned
for us to have lunch at one of my favorite restaurants,
and from there we would visit an art exhibit I hadn't
yet seen. In addition to treating me to an afternoon of
two things I love most, food and art, Angie had begun
making plans for the following week and had even
asked where I wanted to vacation in the summer. I told
her I wasn't sure and to surprise me. Honestly, inside
I wasn't certain Angie and I would be an official couple
in the summer, so the surprise might be on her.

On the way to the apartment, I wanted to talk to
someone about the swirl of emotions that ran through
my mind, but I didn't know who to call. Nakia had
listened as I told her part of the story when I returned
to work last Wednesday. She had offered condolences
and had said she'd pray for the situation. Since Nakia
became a mother to Aidyn, she had become much
calmer and peaceful in her demeanor. Her advice had
entailed delicate whispers of assurances and prayers
that "all would be well." As soon as I'd accepted her
kind words, she'd dashed right into a new story about
Aidyn.

I could call David, but his response would be the
same as it had been earlier in the week: take my ass
home or go to his house, anywhere but Angie's. But between him, Marlon, and Marlon's son MJ, I would have
less breathing room at his house than at Angie's. David
was in disbelief when I told him Asia had been cheating on me with Sam. He'd insisted I talk to her about it,

but I had refused to call her. He would be disappointed to learn that rather than having a calm sit-down chit-chat with her about both our indiscretions, instead, I stormed into the house and packed up the rest of my things. He might have a heart attack if I told him about the episode.

Yvonne and I weren't close enough that I'd share such a sensitive matter with her, at least not until there was some sort of resolution. Andrea might be able to provide her clairvoyant insight, though she and Asia had become chummy, and I hated for her to look into her crystal ball and see all the damage we had done to one another. Actually, I wished she had seen all this coming and had forewarned me.

My mother might listen, and my father most certainly would, though I knew that they too would fret about the breakup. The more I thought about it, the more I realized that our breakup would affect everyone close to us. Those who loved Asia right along with me would have to readjust their feelings toward someone new, perhaps Angie, and relinquish the hopes they had for me and Asia. That wasn't going to be easy, as I knew how crazy everyone was about Asia. "What happened?" they would all ask. I would have to reveal that she cheated on me and I found out only after I cheated on her. How ridiculous that would sound to their ears.

There was really only one person I wanted to talk to, so rather than call anyone on my ride home, I decided to save the conversation for the only person who could answer the questions I had. When I would call her remained undetermined.

Twenty

Asia

For two hours after Kyla left, I walked through the house, from room to room, with a pad of paper and a pen. I jotted down all the items Kyla and I had purchased and accumulated over the years and determined how we would split them between one another. I wanted to present her with the list the next time we spoke or when she decided to show up again, whichever came first.

As I walked around, I wondered if one of us would want to stay in the house. But given that it held so many memories, why would we? Would I be able to bring someone new into the space? Would she be able to hear whispers and echoes of what once was? The days and nights Kyla and I would laugh until we cried while we would play wrestle on our bedroom floor. What if the secrets we had shared were etched between the crevices in the corners of each room? What if the walls really could talk? What would they say? What had they observed? I shook my head. Fuck the philosophical bullshit. I picked up the phone and placed a call to the real estate agent that sold us the house. I left a voice mail message, saying that we would soon need her services again, only this time to sell the beautiful home she had sold to us. I added "sell the house" to my Kyla to-do list.

I had just begun to prepare a turkey peppercorn sandwich when the doorbell rang. I didn't know who it could be other than Kyla. I almost hoped it was so we could proceed with the review of the separation list sooner than I'd thought. Cautiously, I walked toward the foyer, but first I peeked out the dining room window. A taxicab sat waiting in the drive. Finally, I walked in the foyer and opened the door.

"Surprise!"

I screamed from excitement. Before me stood Melanie and Jovanna with a suitcase at their side.

"Oh my God, what are you doing here?"

"So glad you're home," Melanie said, then waved to the taxi driver.

"Come in, come in. I can't believe you're here."

Melanie and Jovanna stepped inside the foyer, and I closed the door behind them. Melanie hugged me.

"I had to come check on my friend," she said.

I hugged her back. "So good to see you both." I released Melanie and hugged Jovanna. She was so petite next to Melanie and me.

Last time Kyla and I saw them in Chicago, Jovanna had gained about twenty pounds since the first time we met them in Atlanta. Today she was slim, but curvy, and her mane of curls was gone. She sported a short hairstyle, the back and sides tapered and only a few luscious curls on top. She wore skinny jeans, a weathered T-shirt, and a leather jacket with crisscrossed and angled zippers, which gave her a rockish appearance. She looked good.

Melanie was polished in dark straight-leg jeans, a white fitted, button-down oxford, and a deep navy blazer. Her brown skin was still smooth and vibrant, and her bright eyes were alert with excitement.

"Yeah, we haven't been here in a few years, and we had a free weekend and figured why not," Melanie said. "I wish we had come under different circumstances."

I lowered my head and then looked at Melanie. "It's all right. It is what it is. Come on. I was making lunch."

I wasn't dressed or prepared for company, but I was happy to have them with me.

"What's this?" Melanie asked when she reached the kitchen counter. She tapped the yellow pad of paper.

"Divorce proceedings."

Melanie perused the paper, while Jovanna stood close to her side.

"So you're going to present this to Kyla and see if she's in agreement?" Melanie asked.

"I sure am. We bought almost everything in this house together, aside from a few things we brought from our old places. She has her favorite things in here, and so do I."

"I see you're giving her the bed." Melanie laughed.

"She can have that shit. She'll have someone new in it in no time."

Melanie eyed me sideways.

"Okay, sorry. I won't sour the mood. Want a sandwich?"

They looked at one another to make a decision.

"No, that's okay. We were hoping we could take you out. I had a feeling you'd be crammed up inside today," Melanie stated accurately.

I smiled at my uneaten food. "I appreciate that, absolutely. Let me shower and change. You two need to freshen up? I'll take you to your room."

"Oh, we reserved a spot at the Hilton for a couple nights. We didn't want to impose on you much further. We already showed up without your knowledge," Jovanna told me.

"What? You didn't come all this way to stay at a hotel." I frowned.

"Well, you know, we didn't know exactly what would be going on here, especially surprising you and all. We crossed our fingers that we wouldn't interrupt anything," Melanie explained.

"Go on and cancel those reservations right now. You hear me? You're staying here."

Melanie gently cleared her throat. "So Kyla isn't returning?" She almost sounded hopeful that I would tell her Kyla was about to walk through the door any minute.

I shrugged. "She was here this morning. Not sure if or when she'll be back."

"What happened this morning?" Jovanna wanted to know.

"She came in to pack up the rest of her stuff," I told them.

"Damn. For real?" Melanie was disappointed again.

"Yep."

"I still can't believe this," Melanie said.

"Believe it." I sighed. "Come on. Follow me."

I gave Melanie and Jovanna a quick tour of the first floor, taking them through the family room, the dining room, and the living room. Upstairs I showed them the master bedroom, the bathrooms, and the guest bedrooms, giving them the room at the end of the hallway.

"Give me twenty minutes, okay? Make yourselves comfortable," I told them.

Melanie nodded. "Thanks. And take your time. Just glad we're here to keep you company." They both smiled in my direction. Melanie then led Jovanna into the guest bedroom.

Behind the closed master bedroom door I smiled too. I was grateful for their thoughtfulness and for their willingness to take the time and spend their money to come visit me. In the midst of this gloomy situation, it was refreshing to have some positive energy around. As Melanie had said, I wished their visit had been during happier times. I hoped that by the time they visited again, I'd be in a different place, literally, under a new roof and with or without someone new at my side.

Twenty-one

Kyla

After two glasses of wine in the early afternoon, I relaxed comfortably in the corner booth of the small Italian restaurant Angie brought me to. The encounter I had had with Asia no longer pressed as harshly against my brain and heart, and for the first time since I had been at Angie's, I began once again to see Angie as the woman I had become more and more fond about. So what if it was through Riesling-induced glassy eyes. Didn't that count?

Angie talked about what it had been like to have the "hard to settle down" reputation she had in Atlanta prior to Deidra. Many women had sought her, and only a handful had been able to claim her as their official woman. Before Angie settled with Deidra, she had courted me and a few other women simultaneously. As she told her story, she pointed out that it was me she would have chosen had I accepted her offer back then. Before she and I met almost ten years ago, and while she was in her twenties, she had a few serious relationships, none of which lasted more than two years. In between women, Angie took full advantage of being single, just as I had prior to Asia.

The conversation became light as Angie and I began to compare lists of women we had entertained. Embarrassed, we realized we had slept with two of the same women. On the third glass of wine, we compared our sexual experiences with them. I ranked Vicki a five based on her inability to kiss, and not just my mouth. Angie ranked her a three. "She wasn't freaky enough," she explained. She ranked Trish an eight. "She was down for almost anything, but not everything." I gave her an eight for the same reason.

"And what's my score on your scale?" Angie smirked.

"Why do you ask?"

"Because I want to know where I rate with you," she explained. "I want to know where I fall in comparison to the women you've been with. So, one to ten, where am I?"

I had never told Angie she had provided the best sexual experiences of all the women I had been with. Before Angie, I didn't think anyone would ever top my first experiences with Stephanie, the one who introduced me to the world of female pleasure. On top of the physical ecstasy Stephanie gave me, I was also in love with her. I was sure nothing could top the love and lust combination I had for her. And no one had until Angie. The difference with Angie was the blank space where there had been no love. I hadn't been in love with any other women I had sex with, either, but Angie brought something else out in me that none of them had. In Angie's bed everything was one hundred–one hundred. What she gave, I gave. What I demanded, she delivered, and vice versa. There were no insecurities, no hindrances, no concerns about the other's intent. We focused solely on freedom and pleasure, and she succeeded in bringing to life every experience I desired. I let her know.

"You're not even on the scale," I told her. "I can't rate you from one to ten. You're more like a twenty."

She leaned forward confidently. "Is that right?"

"Yes, that's right."

"Well, what are you waiting for, then? Let's do this," she suggested, referring to a relationship.

"You know why. Because there's more to it than sex."

"True, true. I can love you at a twenty too."

I stared into my wineglass. "Yes, you've told me that."

"Am I not showing you too?"

"You are." That was all I said.

"Okay, you're tired of me saying that. I got you." She toyed with her napkin for a second. "Don't you want to know where you rank?"

I laughed. "I do, but I'm scared to ask."

"No need to be afraid. I think you already know."

"No, I don't know. Tell me."

"You're kind of all right," she teased, making a "so-so" hand gesture.

"I'll take that." I laughed.

"For real, you're my number one. Others came close, but you set the bar pretty high. The ones before you didn't compare. After you, none quite got there, either. Even after all that time with Deidra, we never had the same kind of intimacy that you and I have. You know what happened once?"

"What?"

"I called her by your name."

"No, you didn't!"

"Yep, I sure did. She was pissed the fuck off too."

"You said my name *when*?"

"During sex. It was a night after we hung with you and Asia, and she had gone down on me. I was still thinking about you, and I called your name. She never let me forget that shit."

"Oh my God, Angie. I wouldn't have let you forget it, either. I bet Deidra can't stand me."

Angie laughed. "She, um, she might feel some kind of way about you, but I let her know she better not ever say anything to you about it. She always took it out on me."

"When did this happen?"

"Couple years ago."

"I don't know how she still came around after that."

"It didn't matter. She knew how I felt about you before that night, anyway. She chose to stay, anyway." Angie paused a moment. "I have to ask. If we're each other's number one, it seems that you and Asia, like me and Deidra, never had the same kind of intimacy you and I do, right?"

I looked away. It was one thing to let Angie know she was my best, but I didn't want to elaborate. I didn't want to divulge how she compared to Asia, even though I had regretfully told Asia that Angie was the best sex I had ever had. I was pretty sure it was something she hadn't forgotten. I told Angie more, though.

"You're right. Asia's good. She's phenomenal," I said, correcting myself. "It's just . . . routine, you know? There's no lack of pleasure, but it's just the same every time."

"Yeah, you kind of let that slip the other night." She chuckled. "You were on a schedule, huh?"

"Seemed that way." I sighed.

"Had you tried to spice it up? Liven it up a bit?"

"Not lately, no. We got stuck in the flow, and we stayed there."

Angie was thoughtful. "It probably wasn't too late."

"Too late for what?"

"To make it right with you and Asia."

I snorted. "Well, it's too late now."

"Why? Because you're head over heels about me now?"

I grinned, buzzed. "Because she's fucking somebody else," I finally told her.

"Say what? Stop playing."

I sipped more wine. "I'm serious. I found out the other day, when I called her."

"You called, and she said, 'I'm fucking somebody else'?"

"No. Someone else answered the phone. Sam. One of her nurses."

"Shut the hell up."

"Yep. Asia was at her place, having lunch."

Angie leaned back in her chair. "Don't jump to conclusions, Kyla. That doesn't mean anything."

"Lunch. Eating. And not eating food."

Angie's lips formed a silent "Oh."

"Asia finally admitted it this morning, when I went to get my stuff. I told her I knew about Sam. She said she did it to get back at me for all the women who never could."

"What? That doesn't even make sense. How long have they been sleeping together?"

"I don't know. I assume for a while now."

"Why?"

"Because Asia doesn't sleep around. That couldn't have been their first time together."

"I don't know, Kyla. She seemed real pissed the other night, when I brought you home. A cheating woman wouldn't be that mad."

"You said she didn't say anything or act mad," I reminded her.

Angie shifted in her seat and looked out the restaurant window. "Well, no, but I could see it on her face, you know," she told me.

"She put on a good performance, pretended like I was the one who did her wrong." I finished my wine, considered another, and remembered it was only two in the afternoon.

"Damn, Kyla, I have a hard time believing she cheated on you. She's not the cheating type."

"What's the cheating type? Me?"

"Stop. That's not what I was saying. She doesn't come off as the kind of woman to cheat, especially with an employee. She's smarter than that."

"She's smarter than I thought to get away with it."

Angie exhaled. "That's some crazy shit."

"It is, and I want to know how she did it."

Angie nodded in agreement. "If that matters to you, find out."

"It does matter. Here I was, feeling all bad and guilty, and she was with somebody else, anyway."

She silently agreed again with a nod of her head. No matter how she thought it happened, I could tell she felt it worked in her favor.

"Don't feel bad or guilty. You followed your feelings. No one can be mad at that."

"That's bullshit, Angie. Asia followed her feelings and fucked Sam. I shouldn't be mad? You followed your feelings and fucked me. Deidra shouldn't be mad?"

Angie shook her head. "My point is, we aren't fucking just to be fucking. Not anymore, right? There's more to it now. You're mine. You followed your heart. That's different than cheating just for a good cum."

"I don't agree with that, and I doubt Asia would, either. Doesn't matter, anyway." I sighed, ready for that glass of wine. My buzz had diminished.

"Come on. This is supposed to be a good day." Angie removed the napkin from her lap and set it on her empty plate. "Let's get going. We have someplace else to be."

I sighed again. "Okay."

Angie paid the bill. When we got to the car, my phone rang.

"It's Asia," I told Angie, surprised.

"Really?" Her lips pursed, and she frowned angrily. "Are you going to answer?"

"You think I should?" What did she want already?

"Up to you."

I stared at Asia's name on my screen, undecided about what to do. Finally, just before the last ring before voice mail picked up, I answered.

"Hello?"

There was no response, just a shuffling sound in the background and muffled voices. I heard car doors open and then close, more shuffling, and then Asia's voice.

"I know exactly where I want to take you," she said.

My heart pounded.

"Lead the way," a female voice happily responded. It wasn't Sam. How many women did Asia have?

Twenty-two

Asia

After I changed into fresh clothes, Melanie, Jovanna, and I hopped in my truck.

"I know exactly where I want to take you," I told them, with Houston's restaurant in mind.

"Lead the way," Melanie said.

"This area is gorgeous," Jovanna said, admiring the large homes lining the blocks.

"Thank you." Wistfully, I browsed the homes as we drove out of the subdivision. "I'm going to miss this area."

"You really plan to sell the house?" Melanie asked from the backseat.

"Kyla will probably agree to selling it."

"You all right staying in that big house by yourself right now?" Jovanna was curious.

"I don't like it, but what can I do?"

"Kyla can stay while you two work out the details," Melanie replied.

Jovanna turned in her seat to face Melanie. "Yeah, you would say that. All women don't want to live with their ex during a breakup."

Melanie rubbed Jovanna's cheek. "It all worked out, didn't it, Jo?"

Jovanna smiled, kissed Melanie's palm, and faced forward again. "What if Asia wants to date?" Jovanna asked, then touched my hand quickly. "Not saying you are already, but you shouldn't do that with someone in the house. I don't think so."

"Asia doesn't have a lady-in-waiting, do you, Asia?"

I bit my bottom lip and didn't respond. Sam did qualify as a woman I could have if I wanted her.

Melanie leaned forward in her seat. Her hands grasped the back of Jovanna's headrest. "You didn't."

"Didn't what?" I played innocent.

"Find someone to pass the time with."

"Well . . ."

Melanie shook her head. "Oh, damn, you've been holding back. Details, please."

I smiled as I pulled into a gas station. "Soon as I get back." I grabbed my wallet out of my purse, filled up my truck with gas, and then tossed my purse with the wallet inside into the backseat, next to Melanie, before I took off again.

"All right, here's what happened." I prepared to tell them the story and began to worry what impression it might leave on Jovanna if I told her that both Kyla and I had slept with other people, Kyla first, with her ex, and then me, with an employee, out of revenge. "Don't judge me, okay?"

"Never," Melanie answered. Jovanna didn't say anything.

"Well, there's a nurse that works for me, Sam. She's fine in every kind of way, and after I hired her, she made herself available to me, and not just for work. She was very open about wanting to sleep with me. I don't get down like that, and I don't sleep around, definitely not while I'm in a relationship. The same day I asked Kyla to leave, I called Sam. She was still willing, and so we met for lunch and I took advantage of her open invitation."

"Damn, Asia!" Melanie responded. "What happened to not rushing things?"

"This is out of character for me, for real," I explained as I took the ramp onto the expressway. "I had to get back at her. I felt like she had played me all the nine years we've been together. Check this out." I glanced at them both. "Kyla knows. I don't know how she knows, but she threw it in my face this morning. I hadn't even decided how and when I was going to tell her before she confronted me about it."

"Oh, shit. How'd she find out?" Melanie squirmed in her seat.

"Only Sam could have said something, and she swears she hasn't said a word."

"This doesn't sound good," Jovanna said.

"You didn't tell anybody?" Melanie asked.

"Nope. You two are the first."

"Sam was the only other person there?" Melanie questioned.

I laughed. "Of course. No threesomes, girl, no threesomes."

"Just asking." She laughed back. "And Sam is denying telling anybody?"

"Claims she hasn't told anyone."

"Anyone see you arrive at or leave her place? Any way the other nurses may have found out?" Melanie questioned.

"I thought about somebody seeing me too, but I can't think of anyone who lives out that way. And I sure as hell hope my nurses don't know."

"She's got to be lying to you. Sam, not Kyla," Melanie concluded.

"Be careful," Jovanna advised. "There are crazy people out there. Isn't that right, Mel? I hope Sam isn't one of them."

"She's one of my best nurses. Patients love her, and from the outside she looks sweet as pie."

"Humph." Jovanna snickered. "Exactly the ones to look out for."

"If I have to go back to Sam, I will. Right now only Kyla can tell me how she found out, and I'm going to ask her. Eventually."

"Yeah, if you really want to know, you're going to have to ask," Melanie remarked. "Look, I know it's going to sound crazy, but I'm going to ask, anyway. Are you sure it's over? They say two wrongs don't make a right. In this case, maybe they did. Maybe she'll appreciate you now."

"Melanie, if you don't quit with that shit."

"I'm serious. Some relationships can survive infidelity. Takes hard work, but it's possible if you want it to work."

"I don't think you'd be saying that if you saw the way Kyla was parading around with her panties while packing up this morning. It doesn't look like she wants to work it out."

"She's pissed about Sam," Melanie asserted, analyzing the situation.

"Well, I'm pissed about Angie."

"Exactly. You both messed up. Now clean up that mess," Melanie said.

Melanie was ridiculously optimistic. I wanted to turn the tables and ask if she'd be amenable to patching things up with Jovanna if she were in my shoes and Jovanna had fucked one of her exes. I couldn't do it with Jovanna there. I'd have to wait until later.

"Right now I can't imagine forgiving Kyla for what she's done. And after the shit I said to her this morning, she may never forgive me. Who's to say she wants to come back, anyway?"

Melanie shrugged. "Like I said, you gave her free rein. I don't think she was right, but I'm just saying."

"I thought you two came here to make me feel better." I glanced at Melanie through the rearview mirror and poked my bottom lip out.

"We did," Melanie insisted. "We're here to help."

"Good. Then help me find out how in the hell Kyla learned about Sam, and help me kick Sam's ass if she's the one talking."

We all laughed, even though I was partially serious. Between Kyla, Angie, and Sam, I didn't know if my fight-free days had come to an end.

I parked in the restaurant lot, and we got out. I observed the attentiveness Melanie and Jovanna gave each other. I noticed the way Melanie reached in the truck to grab Jovanna's purse, which she had left on the floor. Jovanna then smoothed the rumpled collar of Melanie's button-down shirt. They held hands as we walked toward the door. I felt alone in that moment, and I missed Kyla. I didn't want to, but I couldn't help it. I missed her touch, I missed her companionship, and I missed having someone next to me. Was that reason enough to forgive her? Then I spotted the yellow piece of paper peeking out of my purse. No. I'd get over it.

Twenty-three

Kyla

"Soon as I get back," I heard Asia say with my volume level maxed and my ear pressed to the phone. The next sounds were muffled, and a few seconds later the call disconnected. She must have both called and hung up accidentally. She had no idea I heard the conversation she just had. I put the phone down.

"So what's up?" Angie stared at me while we sat at a stoplight.

"She called by accident. I heard her talking to two women. I can't place who," I said, wondering aloud.

I considered who Asia's closest friends were, those to whom she would divulge such private information, and the first person that came to mind was her best friend, Tracy, who lived in their hometown, Dallas. They spoke on the phone several times a week but saw one another only on our trips to Dallas. The other people in Asia's life were loyal and consistent. However, they were merely associates with whom we would connect when we went out. The only other person I knew Asia talked to regularly was Melanie, one half of a couple we met during a Pride weekend. We had connected with them online, and Asia and Melanie had meshed instantly. Just as she did with her best friend, Tracy, Asia spoke with Melanie throughout the week. We visited with them during our last trip to the Midwest and partied in Chicago together. Were they close enough that Melanie and her girlfriend, Jovanna, would travel to Atlanta to see Asia?

"What did she say?"

"She was talking about selling the house, and then she was about to tell them about the lady she has in waiting. See? What did I tell you? She hooked up with Sam before you and me."

"She said that?"

"I didn't get to hear everything, but that's what it sounds like."

As cautious as I tended to be when it came to conversations with Asia, I had to approach her about her cheating. "I'll get to the bottom of it."

"I hope so. Then we can move on."

"Right." I reached for Angie's hand and squeezed it. Frustrated with Asia again, I absorbed all the comfort Angie gave.

A saxophonist played through the speakers, and she turned up the volume. I turned it back down.

"What do you think about exes being friends?" I asked her. "Was this bound to happen? Me and you? Is it not possible for exes to be just friends?"

She smiled. "Better not ask Asia or Deidra that question."

"I know that's right," I agreed.

"Deidra never liked it. I mean, she got along with Asia just fine, and there was no stress about them being exes. I know if she never saw Asia again, she'd be cool with it. I didn't care about them, either. Did you?"

"Honestly, no." I had rarely thought twice about Deidra and Asia. "They could have showered together and washed each other's back, and still I wouldn't have worried about any attraction or longing between the two of them."

"That's the way I felt too. But you . . . Deidra couldn't stand me and you being friends. I told her there was nothing she could do about it."

"She wanted us to stop hanging out? Why didn't you stop if you knew it bothered her? Wasn't it your responsibility to make her happy, even if it meant sacrificing something you wanted?"

Angie looked at me. "Like I told you before, I didn't think Deidra was my forever, even with the love I had for her in the beginning. Being your friend was worth the arguments it caused."

"I don't even want to think about the conversations you two must have had. I'm sorry."

Angie rubbed my leg. "It's not your fault. I did what I wanted to. I did what I had to do to keep you in my life."

"Asia never said anything about us," I told Angie. "I don't know if us being friends bothered her or not."

"Maybe it didn't. Not if she was confident that you had no feelings for me. When you think about it, the shit was crazy, all four of us hanging out. It never bothered me that Deidra and Asia had been intimate. Most of my lesbian friends have dated each other at some point. It can work if there are no feelings. How often is that? Somebody usually has some lingering feelings. Don't you agree?"

"The kind of feelings you claim you had for me all this time?"

"Exactly. And the memories of us that I shared with Deidra made it harder. It's not the easiest for a woman to be cool with a woman that used to fuck her women. That her woman used to be in love with. Trust me, I know."

"When did you fall out of love with Deidra?" I asked.

"I still love her."

"Bullshit, and half the time you don't sound like it. And that's not what I asked you, anyway."

"Damn. Um, this is going to sound like I'm an asshole, but I fell out of love with Deidra a long time ago. It was cool the first couple of years. Then she fell into the ATL trap, trying to floss and create an image. Always had to have top-of-the-line gear and always wanting to be seen, like she was the shit. Look around the apartment at that expensive-ass furniture she had me buying. That futon in the extra room, six hundred dollars. Shouldn't nobody's futon cost six hundred dollars. It turned me off."

Several years ago, Asia had commented about Deidra's style and taste, and had suggested it had become extravagant, which I had noticed too. She was like an undiscovered talent, molded into a pretentious star under Angie's care.

"You don't admit you had something to do with that? You treated her to all the fanciness," I said.

"True. It didn't have to transform her. Look at you. Living up on the hill, dressed right, looking right. You're still grounded. Kind of," she replied. "She changed into the kind of woman I tried to avoid. Snobby. You see how boojie her salon is, acting like every woman that sits in her chair has to be famous. That shit isn't cute."

"So why'd you stay? Why'd you continue to support her every move, trying to be up in everything?"

"Because I still wanted her to have whatever she wanted. I still wanted to see her succeed. Doesn't matter. She didn't want any of what I had to offer in the end."

"Right. She said you were too much," I stated, recalling Angie's explanation for their breakup. "You keep saying you still loved her, even though you weren't in love with her. Is that natural, you think? To fall out of love with the person you're with and just love them?"

I wondered if that had happened with Asia and me. Did the love we shared slip out of the "in love" category, and instead did we only love one another? I believed that there was a difference between the two and that a relationship had to be more than just love for it to work. Didn't it?

"I've heard people use that as an excuse, yeah. I think it depends on the person you're with. I wouldn't fall out of love with you." She smiled gently.

"How do you know that?"

"Because in all these years I never have." Her words were soft and smooth. "I've always been in love with you."

Angie had expressed her desire to love me and share her life with me. She hadn't told me before that she was in love with me, even with the implications. She tilted her head to the side.

"Don't worry. You don't have to tell me you love me back. I know you can't."

"What happens if I don't accept your invitation? What if I can't love you back?"

She gripped the steering wheel tightly. "I'd say you're one crazy-ass woman."

We laughed; then she shrugged one shoulder.

"If you decided I'm not for you, then I'd have to walk away knowing I gave it my all."

"Walk away? So we wouldn't be friends anymore?"

"I don't think so."

"Wait a minute." I twisted in my seat. "We've been friends all these years, and now, because you might not get your way, you wouldn't want to be friends? That's selfish, Angie."

"No, it's realistic."

"How is it different than nine years ago, when we stopped sleeping together?"

"It's different now because even though I wanted you, we were just sex partners. You walking away from that, it hurt, but not half as much as it would now. If you leave me now, then I know you don't want me, Angie, the person I've shown you I can be to you. I can't do that. Kick it with you after that? Hell, naw."

"You're so confusing. We just said some exes can be friends."

"Not in this case. Not now. Don't try to tell me you want to be friends, either, Kyla. If you don't want me as your woman, you still want me as your friend, even now?" She shook her head no. "Fuck that shit."

I understood her perspective and had to agree. If I decided we shouldn't pursue a relationship again, and thus passed up a sincere opportunity to be together, there would be no reason to remain in each other's lives.

"That's not going to happen, though, right? You don't want Asia back after she fucked somebody else, do you?"

I flinched. "I don't want to talk about Asia anymore."

"Good. About time. It's a new day, and we're supposed to be having fun." She ran her hand over my head.

By the time we reached the museum, I had pushed thoughts of Asia, Sam, and the conversation I overheard to the back of my mind. I had enjoyed lunch with Angie and wanted the afternoon to continue without stress. I trusted Angie's words and agreed that it was a new day, so I permitted Angie to open the car door for me. She was elated.

"Thank you for allowing me to treat you like the lady that you are."

"Anytime," I replied, suddenly appreciative of her gesture. It would take something major to reject the affection I believed Angie wanted to shower on me.

I smiled at her, and she at me, and hand in hand we walked toward the entrance.

Twenty-four

Asia

"Hey."

"Oh, hey." I sat upright. I had been lying in bed, reading a magazine article about how to react when in a disagreement with another. "Come in."

Melanie entered the bedroom and closed the door quietly behind her. She spotted the chaise across the room, next to the fireplace. It was so far away.

"You mind?" She pointed to the edge of the bed.

"No, go ahead." She sat opposite me at the end.

"Jo was tired. She fell right to sleep."

"You two had a long day of traveling."

"Yeah." Melanie fingered the pattern of the comforter. "I was hoping I'd have a chance to talk to you privately, anyway." Her brown eyes remained lowered and followed the slow trace of her finger.

"Me too."

"Really?" She looked up. "What's up?"

"You first." I put the magazine aside.

"I have a confession," she whispered. Melanie sat straight, her arms in her lap, like a trained woman on the stand who was about to detail events that would incriminate her. "There's a little something I never mentioned before."

"What's that?" She had my attention.

"I almost cheated on Jo before. I've been able to forget about it like it never happened, but it's been on my mind again since you told me about you and Kyla."

"What? With who? Sunday?"

"Hell no, not her crazy ass." Melanie shook her head. "She was fine, though. What a waste."

"Well, with who, then?"

"It was about a year before the whole Sunday incident. The worst part is that it was with one of our friends."

"Oh, shit."

"Jo doesn't know." Melanie looked nervous. "It's one of those really silly, caught-in-the-moment situations that I wish I could erase." She took a deep breath. "One night I went out with the guys at work. Many times we celebrate when one of us wins a case. John had won a case, and that night we went to our usual bar. Ali was there."

"Ali? Jovanna's Ali?" I asked, though I knew the answer.

"Yes."

"Oh, my God."

"Ali was there with Noni. Remember her? She's the one Ali used to pine for. They had gotten into a little dispute about the usual, Noni not wanting to commit to a relationship. It got heated, and Noni left. I didn't even know Ali was there till me and the guys were ready to go. She was at the bar by herself, and Ali doesn't drink. Ever. But that night she had a couple. She needed a ride home, and I offered because I didn't want her to get in any trouble driving drunk. The whole way to her place, she cried about Noni and then went into how much she envied me and Jo and what we have. I felt bad for her.

"When we got to her place, I asked if she was all right. She said she was, but she kept crying, so I went inside with her for a while. We talked some more, and I tried to console her. We actually started to fall asleep. When I got up to leave, she thanked me, hugged me. She told me Jo was lucky and kissed my cheek. I told her Noni was really missing out on someone special. I guess she was real sensitive, because then she kissed me. I don't know what I was thinking, but I kissed her back, and before I knew it, we were back on her couch, taking off each other's clothes." Melanie winced at the memory.

"After a few minutes, just when I was about to take her panties off, it was like something hit both of us at the same time, because we both stopped, looked at each other, and got up. I straightened myself up and got ready to go. There wasn't some kind of 'Don't tell anybody' conversation. We just knew it was a mistake, and went on as if it had never even happened. Next time I saw her, there was no awkward moment or anything."

"Jo has no idea?" I asked, shocked.

Melanie lowered her head. "She doesn't. It would kill her. They're best friends."

"She would kick your ass, Melanie."

"She sure as hell would. Let me tell you the craziest part."

"Hmm?"

"That was the night Jo's grandmother died. She called me just after I left Ali's with the news."

I gasped, put my hand over my mouth.

"I'm not into ghosts and shit, but I think her grandmother put a stop to it. Intervened and slapped me and Ali out of it. My point in telling this story is this. I could have told Jo what happened and dealt with the consequences. The timing was bad, but I still could have told her, even if it was well after the funeral. Inside I know that even if I hadn't had her grandmother's death as an excuse, if me and Ali actually had sex, I wouldn't have told her then, either. I wouldn't have had the courage. I'm all about honesty and coming clean, but shit, I'm a criminal lawyer. I know what not to say and how to sweep shit under the rug." She exhaled. "It took a lot for Kyla to tell you about what happened with Angie. Her actions were wrong, but she still had the balls to tell you."

"You're suggesting what? Forgive her because she confessed?" I agreed that honesty was the best policy, but telling the truth didn't automatically grant forgiveness.

"It's your decision. Had I come clean to Jo, it wouldn't have been to pursue something with Ali. It would have been out of respect. Despite her actions, Kyla respected you enough to tell you the truth."

"The difference, Melanie, is you and Ali didn't have a history of fucking in the past. You didn't even have feelings for her. It was one incident, which is really more forgivable than fucking somebody you have feelings for." As soon as the words came out and I heard them, I disagreed with myself. "No, never mind. It's just as low to almost fuck your girlfriend's best friend."

Melanie closed her eyes. "It is. That's the only reason I'm telling you this. Not to upset you. Just to let you know people, all people, make mistakes."

"You're right. I know plenty of people who have cheated in their relationships. I don't play that kind of nonsense. It happened to me once before, and I swore I wouldn't be stupid like that again."

"So that's it? You're mad because you feel like you got played again?"

"Yes."

"Do you still love her?"

"Of course I do," I admitted. "I don't like her, though."

"That's cool," she said, understanding. "You don't have to like her right now, so long as you still love her. Just think about it."

"Sure," I half lied.

"Now, what did you want to talk to me about?" Melanie wanted to know.

"It almost seems irrelevant, but now I understand. Earlier you were saying relationships can survive infidelity. I was going to ask if you'd be as forgiving of Jovanna if she told you she had feelings for someone else. Somebody she used to date."

Melanie leaned back and repositioned herself across the foot of the bed, her head resting in her hand.

"I want to say yes. It would be difficult, but I love her enough to try. Because of what happened with Ali, I'd almost think it was karma. That I deserved it. Oddly, that's something Ali would say. She's all about karma."

I nodded. "I don't know if Kyla accepts what goes around, comes around. She didn't seem real receptive to my sleeping with Sam. How many people would really sit back, like, 'Okay, it's all right. I deserved it'?"

"Tell her why you did it."

"I did. I told her I did it to get back at her. Told her she couldn't fuck me over like I was one of the silly women from her past."

Melanie was confused. "What do you mean?"

I remembered Melanie had no idea about Kyla's illicit past. "Let's just say Kyla had her taste of women before she settled down with me."

"Ah, okay. That bad?"

"Bad. And I was the idiot who trusted her to be faithful when she wasn't to anybody else."

Melanie investigated the facts. "She cheated on a bunch of women?"

"No, she slept around. A lot," I said.

"So?"

"So? She's been with half of Atlanta."

"What's that got to do with it if she didn't cheat? You can't crucify her for her past, not now, not nine years later. She was faithful to you for nine years and came clean about it right away. She probably learned her lesson."

"You think that's why she's at Angie's now? Because she learned her lesson?" I asked sarcastically.

"It's not cool that she's over there. All I'm saying is talk. Hear what she has to say, and this time listen," she advised.

"I don't know, Melanie. I appreciate you throwing your pom-poms in the air, cheering for us. I don't know if this is mendable."

"Maybe it's not. Maybe it is. That's why I wanted to see you in person, see if I could help. Part of that was to tell my story. Did it help at all?"

"It helped me realize people don't really know what they'll do in a situation until they're faced with it. I doubt you ever thought in a million years that you would be making out with Ali, and I never thought I would sleep with one of my nurses. The shit we do . . ."

"Speaking of nurses, that's next on our agenda. We have to find out what Sam did. I don't believe she's innocent," Melanie stated.

"Me either," I agreed.

"We'll figure it out."

"Okay."

Melanie eyed me slowly. "Are you good with what I shared? Please don't think I love Jo any less. There's nothing I wouldn't do for her. For us."

"I'm fine with it, and I believe you. I feel a little embarrassed for her not knowing, with that being her best friend and all. That's the kind of shit that makes people snap when they find out."

"She never will. If she does, I know where it came from." Melanie winked at me.

"Go on. Get out of here before I go tell her."

Melanie laughed and got up. She stretched her lean frame, her back cracked, and then she bent to hug me.

"That hugging thing is not going to work on me. Sorry," I kidded.

She laughed again. "Stop it, Asia." She released me and headed for the door. "See you in the morning."

"Good night."

Soon as she left, I turned off the lamp and closed my eyes. I wondered what would have happened had Melanie confessed to Jo. I had no doubt that the incident between Melanie and Ali would have been unforgivable in Jovanna's eyes. I guessed ignorance really could be bliss.

Twenty-five

Kyla

Angie's phone rang at seven in the morning. She loosened her hold on my waist and picked it up, irritated. The sudden sound had awakened us both.

"Too early for this shit," she murmured after she checked the screen for the caller. "Hello?"

I could hear Deidra's loud voice on the other end, though I couldn't understand her words.

"What for?" Pause. "It's too early. Come back." Angie groaned. "Well, I'll drop them at the salon, then." Her voice grew louder. "You're the one who said you didn't want the damn boxes. Bye, Deidra." She pressed the END CALL button angrily.

"She's here," Angie told me.

I turned over. "What do you mean, she's here?"

"All of a sudden it's urgent that she get her boxes."

"Right now? At seven in the morning?" I sat up. "I can go. Tell her to come back in a little bit." I didn't want to be in the middle of their exchange.

"She said she's not coming back. Wants them right now." Angie got up and covered her body with boxers and a tank top. "I'll handle her. You stay in here." She walked out of the room, leaving the door ajar.

Deidra's boxes had been moved from the hallway to a corner in the living room. Every time I looked at them, I wondered how long Angie would have two women's belongings in her place. I bunched the pillow under my head and said a prayer. *Lord, please don't let me get in a fight this morning.*

A minute later the front door opened, and Deidra came in.

"Damn, good morning to you too," she said bitterly. I didn't know what kind of look Angie had given her, but it must have been fierce.

"Good morning, Deidra," Angie said, annoyed.

The hardwood floors creaked as Deidra walked across the room. "Can I get a little help or what?" Her tone was bitter.

"Why didn't you bring your own help?"

"Because I thought you were still ladylike enough to help a girl move."

Silence.

"What's the problem?" Deidra continued. "Think I'm going to run back there and attack your girlfriend? Shit, go get her. She can help too."

"Just get your shit, Deidra."

"It's not shit," Deidra countered.

"It was shit last week, acting like you didn't need it anymore. What's so urgent now?"

"Nothing, really. I only wanted to see if I was right. I am."

"About what?" Angie asked, aggravated.

"About Kyla moving in already. I saw her car outside, which means you and her are some snaky-ass bitches. Or better yet, Asia came to her senses and kicked her out. Either way, you're happy, I see."

There were sudden noises, scuffles, and thuds.

"Stop, Angie!" Deidra yelled.

Were they fighting? Didn't Jesus hear my prayer?

"Shut the fuck up," Angie growled, her voice low and aggressive. I heard more quick movements.

"You bitch," Deidra growled back.

That was when I heard the slap. It was one of those "I've been waiting years to slap the shit out of you" smacks. It was loud and forceful. I didn't know who delivered it, and I jumped up, with only my panties on, and ran into the living room, my breasts bouncing and exposed.

Angie had Deidra pinned against the wall, her face red where Deidra had hit her. Obviously, Angie had caught Deidra's arm too late, but after the slap she had held on to it, and now she had it in a tight grip. Deidra tried to free herself with hard punches to Angie's body with her free arm. Their altercation stopped when they saw me.

"Ain't this about a bitch?" Deidra fought harder to get away.

"Get out of here, Kyla," Angie cautioned.

"Why? Can't she stay and see what kind of woman she's dealing with? This isn't the first time she put her hands on me!" Deidra screamed in my direction. I looked around the room and saw that Deidra's boxes were toppled over on their sides near the door. They had been thrown, likely not by Deidra. I took a step back.

"Go back to bed," Angie instructed again. She hadn't let go of Deidra's arm. Deidra's brown skin bulged under Angie's hold, her veins thickening. Both of them watched me, Angie furiously, Deidra spitefully.

"Stick around long enough, you'll be next," Deidra warned. "Soon as she's done wining and dining you, she'll try to own you."

Angie put her other hand over Deidra's mouth to shut her up. "Get out of here," Angie advised me again.

I turned away from them and went back to the bedroom and took cover in the bathroom.

"She'll find out sooner or later," Deidra yelled, loud enough for me to hear. "All that sweet shit is just a cover-up. You ain't shit, Angie. First time she makes you mad, she'll see you for who you are, you abusive bitch!"

"Shut up and get the fuck out of here." Angie spoke through her teeth.

They quieted down. I heard footsteps and then the sound of boxes being tossed into the hallway. The door slammed next, and then there was total silence. A few minutes later Angie knocked on the bathroom door. I was sitting on top of the toilet cover, with my head in my hands.

"Kyla." She slowly opened the door and peeked her head in.

The redness on her face had vanished, though a small welt remained where Deidra's ring had made an impact.

"You might want to put ice on that."

"Later. I want to make sure you're all right. I'm sorry about Deidra." Angie's anger had cooled, and her eyes were no longer filled with fury. She had returned to the gentle Angie I'd always known.

"Deidra? That wasn't just about Deidra, Angie. You two fight like that?"

Angie stepped inside and leaned against the sink. "We've had moments, times when we're both pissed off and acting irrational. It happens."

"Pushing, shoving, hitting. Really?"

Angie hesitated. "I admit we've had some real intense arguments, and it's gotten out of hand, yes. She was on some bullshit today. I got mad and threw her boxes. She hit me because I wouldn't stop."

"Stop tiptoeing around the complete truth. You've hit her before, like she said?" I prayed the answer was no.

"It's happened before, Kyla," she confessed. "But you have to know me better than that. It's not my normal character." Angie shook her head. "Deidra is just one of those people. No matter how boojie she tries to be, she's got some hood in her. She brings out the worst in me."

As tender as Angie had always been to me, and from what I had witnessed of her and Deidra over the years, I couldn't imagine her putting her hands on Deidra. How could you hit someone you claimed to love? *Maybe the same way you could cheat on them,* my subconscious replied.

"I bet her wrist is bruised," I said.

Angie waved my comment off with a flip of her hand. "Maybe. I didn't want her fighting me, or you, for that matter. I don't hit women. I'm not an abuser. But I do protect myself and those I love."

Angie's words came across as sincere, as they always did. Indirectly, she had again professed her love for me. It felt different, and I was suddenly uncomfortable. I was inclined to consider a relationship with someone whose sexual past was as extensive as mine. But could I be with someone with a violent history, no matter how infrequently the incidents occurred?

"Please don't let this mess us up," she pleaded.

"Those moments are in the past."

"The past? It was ten minutes ago," I challenged.

"You know what I'm saying. You're not her. I'd never hurt you. Just let this go. Deidra is officially history. There's no reason for her to come around anymore. Nothing else connecting us."

Angie reached for my hand and lifted me up to her. I rested my breasts against the ribbed texture of her tank top. She lowered her mouth to my neck and kissed it.

"Now you separate your things with Asia, and we can be together," she told me. "It's time for us to be together."

I closed my eyes and tried to allow her lips and tongue to cloud the visions in my mind of her and Deidra's altercation.

"Soon," I responded. "This will be figured out soon."

It had to be. As soon as I talked to Asia I would know what to do.

Twenty-six

Asia

"You should call her."

"Call who?"

"Kyla."

"Why?"

Melanie and I sat at the kitchen table, while Jovanna prepared a breakfast of fried ham and eggs. We sipped on freshly squeezed orange juice and waited.

"Because you two need to talk this out before too much time passes. Find out how she knew about Sam. Address that. Then, depending on how the conversation goes, you'll know if you need to pull the divorce list out for her. Me and Jo are here for your support."

"Why don't I invite her, Angie, and Sam over and we make it a party?"

"We can do that," Jovanna said as she flipped two eggs. "I don't have a problem confronting women." She shot a small smirk at Melanie.

Melanie returned it and then looked at me. "See why she can never find out?" her expression said.

I nodded. "Sure. I'll call," I announced. I wanted to get it over with, whatever would happen, because to continue just thinking about it would get me nowhere. I didn't think I needed their help, although I was happy to have Melanie's and Jovanna's backup. I didn't think Kyla and I would ever become overly aggressive with one another. You never knew, though. She could say something to piss me off, or I could do the same to her.

"After breakfast. Let me let her and Angie get their morning screw in."

"You are so crazy," Melanie said.

"I'm just saying that's what they do." I turned to Jovanna. "Sure you don't need any help?"

"No thanks. Got it." She slid two sizzling fried eggs onto a plate. "On a serious note, Asia, say you talk to Kyla and she begs your forgiveness. You will not forgive her?"

"I'm not one to forgive cheating. It happened to me a long time ago, and I hated the feeling." I stared at my hands. "But honestly, now I'm not sure anymore. You two have almost convinced me to be open-minded."

Jovanna set a plate before Melanie and another in front of me. "I don't believe anyone should be a doormat and allow a person to get away with just anything," she said. "However, mistakes happen, you know? Sometimes a person gets caught up in a moment. It happens."

Melanie eyed Jovanna curiously. Jovanna met her gaze directly. "At least it's out in the open. You two can talk this through, not hold anything back. No secrets. Can you imagine what it would be like if Kyla hadn't told you and had come home and acted as if nothing ever happened? Can you imagine how that would make you feel once you actually found out? Because the truth always comes to light, you know." She continued to stare at Melanie. "More juice, Melanie?" Melanie didn't answer, so Jovanna picked up the pitcher of juice, along with Melanie's glass, and poured.

"I understand how you feel, Asia," Jovanna continued. "I used to be a hard-ass too, with rules about what I would and would not accept. *Pero* sometimes we can be so set about what we will not allow that we forget that love can survive anything. That everyone deserves a second chance. More for you?"

I raised my glass silently, afraid to take my eyes off of Jovanna to sneak a look at Melanie.

Jovanna went on. "If you love her enough and believe it'll never happen again, then she may be worth forgiving. Especially if she didn't really intend to hurt you. Thing is, you have to know in your heart that if you decide to forgive, you truly have to forgive. No holding on to it, no throwing it in her face later. Trust me, she knows it was wrong. It may not be fair what she did to you, but it wouldn't be fair to remind her of it, either. Making her feel guilty won't help. I bet she feels badly already. I'm about to make my own plate. Do you two need anything else?"

"No," I answered quietly.

Melanie shook her head from side to side, and Jovanna went back to the stove.

"As I said, once you forgive, if you decide to forgive, you also have to trust that she'll be true to you," Jovanna said. "That can be hard sometimes, especially if you think you see opportunities for her to be unfaithful again. It might make you act a little crazy, because you want to believe she wouldn't have stayed with you if she were going to mess up again, you know? Trust your instincts in those moments, as hard as it may be."

Jovanna returned to the table with her food. "Moving forward, make sure you surround yourself with a few good people. People you can rely on. People you know will always tell you the truth, even if it hurts. If they know something, they will tell you. They trust you with the truth because they know you deserve it." She stared at Melanie and spoke to both of us. "They will be honest with you, even if Kyla can't. The truth may hurt, but releasing it is the best feeling in the world."

Jovanna took a bite of her food. "Mmm, this is so good, if I say so myself." She closed her eyes and relished the smoky flavor of the ham. "Anyway, it sounds to me like Kyla is pretty honest, though. That's a good start in my book. I agree with Melanie. I recommend talking it through, and if you two can work it out, wonderful. Now, if she happens to mess up again, well, then you have the right to cut her loose." Jovanna laughed heartily. "You're not eating, Melanie." She pointed to Melanie's untouched food. "So that's my two cents," she continued before Melanie could respond. "I'm glad I could share that with you. I don't think Melanie knew I had anything I could share on this trip. Well, surprise. I do know a little something, after all." She winked at me.

I cleared my throat and finally glanced at Melanie, whose gaze was locked on Jovanna. She was no longer on the witness stand. She had already been convicted and had been given a once-in-a-lifetime get-out-of-jail-free pass.

"Thanks, Jovanna. We, um, I needed to hear that," I said.

"*No problema.* Love is a powerful emotion, and every relationship has its moments. The true test of strength and love is whether you stay in those moments or you flee." She sipped her juice. "Now that I got that out, let us know how we can help."

The situations were different, yet the principle was the same, I thought. Someone in each relationship messed up, Melanie and Kyla, and the other person, Jovanna, and I, had the choice to forgive or not to forgive. Jovanna had chosen to forgive. What would I do? I was suddenly convinced I wanted to talk to Kyla.

I wanted to take advantage of their presence and call Kyla with them around. I grabbed the cordless landline phone from the counter and dialed Kyla's number. She didn't answer. I was upset, mad that my joke about her and Angie having sex might be true. That was probably why she didn't answer. A few seconds after I hung up, the phone rang. She'd called back. Jovanna and Melanie smiled.

"Hi," I said.

"Hey," Kyla said back. "You called?"

"I did. I was hoping we could talk. Today."

"Yes. I wanted to talk to you too." Her voice was subdued, softer than I'd expected.

"Great. Where would you like to meet?"

"Um . . ." She was quiet for about a minute. I waited. "It's another nice day out, so what about Piedmont Park, the entrance on Eleventh? Meet me in a couple hours?"

I checked the clock. It was 9:05.

"I'll see you at eleven."

"Okay. See you then."

I put the phone back on the charger.

"Two hours," I announced to Jovanna and Melanie, even though they'd heard.

"How did she sound?" Melanie asked.

I thought for a moment. "You know, if I had to choose one word, I'd say she sounded grateful."

"That's a good sign," Melanie said. "You'll call us if you need us?"

"I will. We'll be at the park, so if anything goes down, someone should be able to call nine-one-one." We laughed.

"We'll clean the kitchen," Jovanna said. "You can go up and start getting ready."

"Thank you both. I'm so glad you came."

"I am too," Melanie agreed, directing her words to Jovanna. "Thank you for breakfast, Jo. Thank you . . . for everything."

Jovanna walked over to Melanie. They kissed.

"I appreciate you more than you'll ever know," Melanie whispered.

"Te amo," I heard Jovanna say as I walked away.

Twenty-seven

Kyla

My heart jumped when my phone rang. I hoped it wasn't Deidra calling to harass me next. Angie and I had gotten back into bed. I had lain on the edge of one side, with the hope that she would keep a little distance between us. She hadn't. She had scooted behind me and had wrapped her arm around my stiff body, locking me underneath her strong hold. When I picked up the phone from the nightstand and saw Asia's name on the screen, I left Angie in bed and headed to the bathroom. I looked back at Angie, who had a concerned look on her face. I waited too long to answer and missed the call. I cleared my throat, exhaled to calm my nerves, and called right back. I didn't want the stress I felt to be apparent in my tone.

She wanted to see me. That wasn't what I had expected her to say. I thought maybe she had called to curse me out further, to dig her verbal fingernails deeper into my thin emotional skin. Or maybe she had called to tell me she and her lady friends had packed up half the house and had put it on a moving truck, which was on its way to Angie's place. She had to make room because Sam was about to move in. She did neither, and I was both happy and nervous that she wanted to get together. Her voice comforted me.

"We're meeting at eleven."

Angie was uneasy. That morning's incident and her admission to hitting Deidra in the past had eroded the confidence about us that had been building. She walked over to me and put her arms around me.

"Good," she said. She squeezed. "Now you two can figure out the next step to finalize this."

Silently I told myself I didn't know what was next anymore. I said another silent prayer and asked that the whirlwind events and emotions of the past few weeks come to end after I talked with Asia.

I wasn't going to rehearse a script, as I had before. I wasn't going to plan what I would say or anticipate Asia's responses before they were spoken. I would talk to her openly and honestly and would find out what had happened that caused her to cheat. Had she really only wanted to get back at me for the hearts I had carelessly disregarded in my past? Or maybe, instead, we both had felt the same weariness in our relationship, and she found an outlet with Sam. Whatever her explanation, however the discussion progressed, I dedicated myself to accepting her words and prayed she would accept mine.

"I will be back later and will let you know how it went," I told Angie.

"I'll be ready for you."

Angie ran her hand down my arm and rested her fingers around my wrist. I tensed and tried to pull my arm away. She held on.

"Don't do that, Kyla." She stroked my wrist with her thumb.

"I'm sorry. It's just, you know, I don't know what to think right now."

She sighed. "Think about the way I've treated you. That's all you have to focus on. You're not Deidra. You . . . you bring out the very best in me, not the worst. I'd never lay a hand on you."

I didn't say anything.

"I don't know how all this will turn out, but you have to trust me. The same way we don't judge each other by our pasts with women intimately, don't judge me about Deidra. All that shit happened with Deidra. It wouldn't happen with you."

I tried to respect Angie's words and understand her point. In my heart I believed she would never bring physical harm to me, but my knowledge about Deidra had punctured the protective armor I tended to feel in her embrace.

"I understand what you're saying. I'd be lying if I said it didn't bother me some. I'll try not to let it interfere," I lied. It was too late. I could shake off the high number of women Angie had slept with. I couldn't pretend she hadn't been abusive to one of them.

"That's fair. Do you need anything before you go? I can make us some breakfast."

"I think I'm okay. Thank you. I'm going to shower."

"Sure, okay. I'll let you get ready." Angie kissed my neck again and got back in bed.

In the shower I first washed the spot where she had kissed me. The damage was done. Even if Asia didn't want me back, I didn't think I could stay with Angie. After I dried off with a lavender towel Deidra must have left behind, I searched for relaxed jeans and a fitted sweater in my suitcase. I added a colorful scarf that Asia loved on me. I didn't want to be overzealous in my preparation, but I still wanted to look nice. I was reminded of our first date, in the middle of the night. and the effort I had exerted to find the appropriate outfit. I had wanted to make a good impression on her then, and now I wanted an appropriate look for the meeting that might formally renew or terminate our relationship.

Once dressed, and with my make-up applied, I packed a small purse and went to Angie. She was still in bed and had fallen back asleep. Her eyes opened when I grabbed my keys from the dresser.

"You look really nice," she told me.

"Thanks. I'll, um, I'll be back."

"When?"

"I don't know how long this will take. We have a lot to sort out."

"Right. I'll be here whenever you get back."

"Okay." I started to walk out of the room.

"Hey. Come here." She sat up against the headboard.

I returned and sat next to her on the edge of the bed. Angie ran a hand over her tousled, loose curls. In her I saw Stephanie years ago, when she was troubled by our relationship, unsure where it was headed. I also saw Asia's face nine years prior, willing to love me, but only if I was certain I could love her back. In Angie's expression I saw something else, something I couldn't pinpoint. She seemed an agitated combination of the two as she struggled with how to handle our status.

"I feel responsible for what's happened. I know Asia cheated and everything already, but I know this didn't make it any better. For that, I'm sorry. But think about this. You might not have found out about Sam if me and you hadn't rekindled what we've had all along. Did you think about that?"

"Angie, I told you, we didn't have anything all along. What are you talking about?"

"I don't believe you would have come back to me so easily if you hadn't felt something too. Look, I know what you said and all, but that's what I believe. And right now I want more than anything for you to come back to me tonight." Angie looked toward the window. "If that doesn't happen, I don't know what I'll do."

"That's a lot of pressure, Angie. I don't know what to say."

"Nothing. Just come home later. I'll see you when you get back."

I tried to stand again, but she pulled me close. "I love you, Kyla." She kissed me hard. Her lips covered my mouth, eating away the lipstick I had just applied. "Say you love me too," she whispered heavily.

What had gotten into her? I didn't answer, and she kissed me more forcefully, sucking my lips into her warm mouth. Finally, she released me. She was breathless.

"See you later," she said, then abruptly crawled underneath the covers again.

I left before she could stop me again and called David on my ride to the park.

"You know, I was about to call the cops on you and Angie. Girl, don't ignore me like that again," David screamed at me when he answered the call.

It was wrong of me to have left David hanging and not to have kept him updated about Asia after his many years of supporting me through all my battles and rooting for me during success stories.

"I'm sorry. It's been crazy."

"That's your middle name lately. Everything all right?"

"I'll let you know later today. I'm on my way to see Asia now."

David shouted like a woman stricken by the Holy Ghost. "Hallelujah, praise Jesus."

I laughed through my nerves. "What a difference twenty-four hours makes. Yesterday I went home and took the rest of my clothes—"

"Shame on you, girl," he interrupted.

"Whatever. She said some horrible things to me. Things I never thought I'd hear from her. It hurt."

"Baby, what did you expect? For her to give you a handshake and a pat on the back? These kinds of things go down like a Black Panther riot."

I shook my head. "This morning she called, real calm, and asked if we could meet."

"Hmm." David thought for a second. "Either she got nervous after you wanted to take the rest of your stuff, and she wants you to come home, or the meeting is to finalize the breakup officially. Lord Jesus. No hootin' and hollerin', fussin' and cussin', you hear me? Too early in the morning for that."

No, it's not. I thought of Angie and Deidra.

"I'm trying not to anticipate how the conversation will play out. I'll see what she has to say first. I still really want to know when she started cheating on me."

"Mmm, baby girl, I understand. If you're right about Sam, I think you have a right to know what's been going on with them."

"Me too. I'll let you know how it goes."

"Will you be back at Angie's tonight?"

"Right now I don't have anywhere else to be, but she's being real strange right now, acting like we're a couple already."

"Are you surprised? You kept choosing her over Asia, so what did you expect? You go handle your business the right way, and don't make me come banging on Angie's door tonight. I expect to hear from you."

"I'll call. Promise."

"Let me go so I can go update Marlon on the latest in the Kyla saga. Girl, you never fail to keep us entertained."

"Glad to be your comic relief." I laughed, but I really didn't find him funny.

"I'm teasing, baby. Talk to you later."

I heard him call Marlon's name before the call disconnected.

I drove the rest of the ride with my music blasting. It was loud and annoying, but the booming bass provided me with the distraction I needed. A couple blocks from the park entrance I found a place to park and started my walk. The area was already busy, even though it was a Sunday morning, owing to the many nearby restaurants and the park itself.

I passed Asia's truck on the first block I walked down. It was empty, which meant she was already waiting for me. My pace quickened. I was suddenly eager to be in her presence again. Toward the end of the second block, as I prepared to cross the street, I saw her standing on the opposite side, near the large open gate. My phone vibrated.

You look nice today, she said to me via text.

When I looked up again, she smiled at me.

So do you, I responded quickly. She wore leggings, boots, and an oversize top that hung off her left shoulder. Her straightened hair was silky and soft, and it brushed across her skin.

We met less than a minute later. The moment was both comforting and awkward. It was strange because we didn't know how to greet each other. Her posture seemed to indicate that she welcomed my presence, and it was nothing like the last visual I had of her, which was of her standing in the bedroom window, with her arms crossed. She stepped forward in response to my approach, then stopped. I stopped too, automatically, and then stepped closer. We were face-to-face, and the current of energy decreased. I wondered if we would still be face-to-face an hour from the moment. Would we have reconciled, or would we have said good-bye forever?

Twenty-eight

Asia

On the ride to meet Kyla, I thought of Jovanna. I had come across many women who had stayed silent after learning of their girlfriend's skeletons, out of fear they could do no better. Those were women who clung to their woman's arm, their self-esteem so diminished, they remained passive in response to their partner's affairs. Jovanna was not that kind of woman. She was the opposite. She was secure enough in herself and the relationship to understand there would be mistakes. She was wise to know there would be moments of action and regret. There might be times when a partner lost focus. In her case, Melanie had erred, and Jovanna had had the strength to forgive silently.

I hadn't done that. When Kyla had come to me about her feelings toward Angie, I could have taken the opportunity to talk to her. Instead, I had given her the thumbs-up to date someone else. I was still mad at Kyla and in no way agreed with her actions, but I had come to understand that we both could have handled the situation differently. After I witnessed the smooth way in which Jovanna revealed what she had known all along, her commitment became an example to me. She had gotten past Melanie's mistake, and she trusted both Melanie and Ali enough to remain loyal companions to both of them. I tried to remember this as Kyla approached me.

"Hi." Kyla said softly when we met.

"Hey."

We were quiet for a few seconds.

"Let's find somewhere to sit down." I tilted my head toward the interior of the park. We didn't say anything while I led her to a bench. I stayed near the path, far enough away that our conversation would remain private, but close enough for passersby to break up a fight.

"This is all so crazy," I began. "I don't know where to start."

Kyla picked at her nails, as she tended to do while she thought of what to say. "I have questions for you. But you go first."

"How's Angie?" I asked. If she told me Angie was great and they were madly in love, then I would have a different kind of conversation with her. Would she have agreed to meet me if they were? She could have told me on the phone there was no reason to meet, because she and Angie had officially reunited.

She stared ahead and searched through the trees for answers. "Angie's fine."

"She's fine? That's it?"

"Yeah, I mean, she's Angie, you know. She's ready for a relationship."

"Of course she is. She made that clear to me the other night."

"She did? She said you two didn't say anything to each other."

"What? Get the fuck out of here. Angie made it clear she's a backstabbing bitch who wanted you all along, kissing you and shit in my face."

Kyla was dumbfounded. "I can't believe she lied to me," she said softly.

"Trust me, she did if she pretended like I was cool with her bringing you home drunk. I was ready to kick her ass."

Kyla lowered her head. "Speaking of, she had a little encounter with Deidra this morning at the apartment." She turned her head to me. "Did you know they've had physical fights?"

"Hell no, I didn't know that. They had a fight while you were there?"

"Deidra popped up, and they started arguing about Deidra moving the rest of her boxes out. I didn't see it happen, but Deidra slapped Angie hard as hell. Then Angie told me it's happened before. And that she's hit Deidra too. Deidra was yelling all kinds of shit, like Angie is really abusive."

That knowledge about Angie had affected her feelings toward her. I could tell by the weary twist of her lips that Angie had disappointed her. Was that the only reason she was there?

"You've never seen that side of her before?"

Kyla shook her head from side to side. "No, never. She has always been nothing but gentle and kind with me."

I ignored that. "Well, Deidra never said anything to me about them fighting, but it happens. Plenty of women I know have been in fights with their girlfriends." That was one green check mark on the positive side for Kyla and me. Even though I joked about it, and had somewhat prepared myself for it, I truly could not imagine either of us laying a hand on the other.

Kyla looked directly into my eyes. "I can see getting into a fight with the woman your girlfriend is cheating on you with," she stated firmly.

"Why her? Isn't it the girlfriend you should be mad at?"

"Of course. But knowing the woman has been around you, smiling in your face, while cheating with your girlfriend behind your back is enough to make any woman want to fight her."

"Exactly," I agreed.

We stared hard at one another. She seemed like she wanted me to say something else.

"Look, I asked you to meet me because I wanted to know where you are with Angie. This all happened way too fast. One day you told me you had feelings for Angie, and the next you were fucking her on your lunch break." I stopped and took a breather. "What do you want to do? Is being with Angie where you want to be?"

Kyla snorted and then inhaled and exhaled just like I had. "Shouldn't I be asking you that question? Is Sam where you want to be?"

"Sam," I repeated. "That was nothing."

"You made it a whole lot more than nothing yesterday."

"Yesterday I was mad. You came home and packed up the rest of your shit. I had to say something."

"What does me packing up have to do with you fucking Sam? Nothing."

"It has everything to do with you and Angie."

"Is that right? Why do you keep trying to put Sam on me, when you were the one screwing her before I even told you about Angie?" she asked loudly.

"What? What the hell are you talking about?"

"I'm talking about you cheating on me with Sam. You fucking Sam the same day I moved out? That must have been real convenient for you, Asia." Her body shook with anger.

"I did have sex with Sam. I won't deny that. What's this about me cheating on you? I never cheated on you."

"Bullshit."

"Bullshit my ass. What are you talking about? And how in the hell did you know about Sam, anyway?"

"Ask her."

"I did. Funnily enough, she told me to ask you. What kind of game is this?"

"No games over here. That's you talking about getting me back for all the women who couldn't. That's a game if I ever heard one."

Two joggers slowed their pace to witness our heated exchange. I waited until they picked up their pace again before responding to Kyla.

"Getting you back for all the women who couldn't? What the hell does that mean?" I asked.

"You said it, so you tell me. Talking about doing what every woman couldn't."

"Right. Getting you back for your inability to stay committed. What was I supposed to do? Let you fuck around with Angie while I sat back and did nothing?"

Kyla shook her head back and forth and threw her hands in the air. "You were fucking Sam, anyway!"

"No, I wasn't," I said. "Where did you get that from?"

"I don't believe last week was the first time you were together. Don't try to play me stupid like that."

"Well, it was, believe it or not. I never cheated on you."

Kyla lowered her head again, her eyes pinched tightly closed. "Look," she said, without opening her eyes, "how long were you cheating on me?"

Why was she so confident I had cheated on her? "Listen to me carefully. I've never cheated on you. I slept with Sam to get you back for sleeping with Angie."

She opened her eyes, frustrated. "You're trying to tell me that the same day you kicked me out, you happened to go to your nurse's house and fuck her? Really?"

"That's what I'm saying, and that's what happened." I squinted my eyes. "How did you know I was at her place?"

Kyla ran her fingers through her streaked strands. "I called you while you were there."

"I didn't get a call from you."

"Sam answered," she told me. "She made it very clear why you were there."

I jumped up and started to pace. That lying bitch. I knew she had lied. I recalled her smug expression when I returned from the bathroom that day. She must have just hung up the phone with Kyla.

I stood in front of Kyla. "What did she say to suggest we had been sleeping together?"

"Nothing." Kyla looked up to me, squinting her eyes at the sun. She bit her bottom lip. "She didn't say anything about you two having an affair. Nothing more than that day. I assumed you had been with her before." Her confident tone faltered, her words uncertain.

I sat back down. "Why?"

"Because you don't fuck around. At least I didn't think you did. I assumed you had been having an affair for a while. Yesterday you made it sound like it had been your plan all along. To cheat on me. Get me back for all the women I didn't treat right."

I didn't know whether to laugh at her, cry for her, or hit her upside the head for being so stupid. "Kyla, who does shit like that? You really think I waited nine years to cheat on you to get you back for what? For women you hurt in the past? If that's not the stupidest shit I've ever heard. I slept with Sam because I was hurt. I was angry. I thought it would make me feel vindicated. You must know, Kyla, that I would never do anything to intentionally hurt you."

Kyla was quiet for a long time. What she was thinking about, I couldn't decipher from the blank stare she directed at the ground. She didn't blink, only focused on a pebble in the dirt next to her foot. Finally she spoke.

"I want to come home."

Twenty-nine

Kyla

For several minutes I processed Asia's words. I compared them to what Sam had said to me, to what I knew and believed about Asia, to what I had assumed about their situation. Asia had told me that the day she went to Sam's apartment was the first time they slept together. When I spoke with Sam, she hadn't insinuated there was anything more to their interaction beyond that lunch date. From what I knew about Asia, she didn't give up her sweetness just because. After I listened to her explanation, I believed she had been hurt enough to seek revenge by sleeping with Sam. It was I who had assumed it wasn't their first time. My decision to return home might have seemed swift and hasty, but it felt right.

Asia inhaled deeply when I told her I wanted to come back home. I couldn't read her expression as she held her breath, her cheeks puffed while she thought about her response. Finally, until she could hold her breath no longer, she exhaled. "You can come home," she said, her voice steady, her tone uncertain. "What about Angie?" she asked.

My final verdict—that I didn't want to pursue a relationship with Angie—probably seemed rushed and impulsive, since I made it the day after I moved the remainder of my clothes out of the house and only hours after I left Angie's bed. In my heart I had no doubt Angie would love me to her fullest ability. I believed she would try to grant me every wish I ever had, would love me through every hurt, and would protect me from any harm that came my way. It was unfair, but I didn't believe I would be able to forget 100 percent that she had hit Deidra in the past. I would always be on edge, unsure if a disagreement with her would result in a black eye or a busted lip. I agreed with Angie that different people could bring out different sides of us, positive and negative. Asia had done that for me. Most women hadn't been able to bring out the emotional love I had to give. I had allowed unexpected feelings for Angie to overshadow the deeper connection Asia and I had established. I didn't believe I could love Angie the way that I loved Asia.

"I hope Angie will be all right." I lowered my head and recalled the intense kiss she had forced on me before I left her place. How Angie would actually respond when I told her I planned to moved back home had yet to be determined.

"What about you? How can you be so sure this is what you want? Isn't your ass still warm from Angie's bed? How do I know this isn't only because you found out Angie has violent tendencies?" Asia asked, testing me.

"This is what I wanted when I came to you that day after the conference. I wanted to be honest about how I felt. I didn't expect those feelings about Angie to arise, and I wanted to talk about it. You . . . it was you that told me to explore."

Asia got defensive. "You didn't have to." Her tone was sharp and edgy.

"I didn't. You're right. You wanted me to grovel, beg for your forgiveness? If there's one thing I have always expected from you, it's honesty. You taught me that. If you didn't really want me to explore more with Angie, I wish you hadn't told me to."

"Say I came to you and said I had feelings for somebody else. You would have said what?"

"I don't know. I would have been mad too. But I hope I wouldn't say anything I didn't really mean."

"I can get with that," Asia admitted. "These past couple of weeks may have been different had we talked it out. But . . ."

"But what?"

"We might never have even gotten here if you had been up front from the start."

"About?"

"About not feeling excited about us anymore, Kyla." She stared into the slow-moving clouds. "About your feelings of boredom. You didn't say you were bored, but that's what you meant. We could have tried to work it out, make it better. Every day isn't going to be a trip to the amusement park, but we can do our best."

"I realize that now. I know there are things I could have suggested we do or experiment with so it wouldn't have felt like we did the same thing all the time. It gets hard, you know. Easy to fall into the same day-to-day rut."

"True," she agreed.

We were quiet as we observed a family set up an afternoon picnic nearby. The kids, a boy and a girl, chased one another in circles across the grass while their parents laid out a blanket.

"This won't be easy," Asia stated.

"No, it won't. What will you do about Sam?"

She got upset again. "I don't know yet. She lied to me, never mentioned you called or anything. I shouldn't have messed with her in the first place. That was *my* mistake."

"Why Sam? Why did you choose her?" I wanted to know.

"Because I knew I could."

"She laid it there like that for you, huh?"

Asia smiled smugly, inappropriately. She didn't answer.

"Was it good?" I asked.

Her head snapped to the side. "Kyla . . ."

"I want to know," I declared.

She hesitated. "No," she said.

Inside I smiled.

"You don't want to know," she added.

Once again, my double standards surfaced the second I processed her words. I was sick to know sex with Sam had pleased her, even though Angie had continued to exceed my expectations in bed.

"If we want to make this work, we can't talk about this. About them. If I forgive you, if you forgive me, we have to let it go," Asia said.

I couldn't help it. I wanted to know what Sam had done that pleased Asia. My pride fought hard against humility, and won.

"Was she better than me?"

Asia rolled her eyes. "I can't believe you just asked me that. If she was, what difference does it make? If she wasn't, what difference does it make? We're talking about reconciling, and you're busy wondering how good sex was with somebody else. I know all about Angie rocking your world, but you don't see me over here sweating about it. You know why? Because love wins. It should. If loving me is more important to you than how many times Angie can make you cum, then put this shit to rest and let's move on."

I was quiet again. I wanted to go home with Asia. I wanted to rekindle our relationship, to restore the connection of our earlier days. To do so, I would have to forget about Sam and Angie. How could I forget about Sam if she continued to work for Asia?

"Will she still work for you?"

"I'm thinking about that. I don't have a valid reason to let her go, Kyla. Fire her for telling my girlfriend we fucked each other?"

I cringed.

"That's a lawsuit waiting to happen," she continued.

"How can she still work for you after what's happened? You slept together."

"Same way you and Angie stayed friends after fucking."

My persistent repetitious questions were pissing her off.

"That makes you uneasy?" Asia asked. "I don't know what to tell you, because I doubt I can let her go without good grounds."

"It's fine. It's fine," I said, yielding to the truth she spoke.

"I'll handle her lie. Otherwise, it is what it is. I chose her, and now I'll have to deal with the consequences."

I didn't like the idea of Asia working with Sam after they slept together, especially if Asia enjoyed it. I hated that they would see each other regularly, and it bothered me that I would have to face Sam again eventually. I had brought it upon myself; there was nothing I could do but swallow my own pill.

"What now?" I asked.

Asia stared up at the sky again. "Come with me." She stood up and reached for my hand.

I had touched her hand innumerable times over the course of nine years. In that moment, her skin around mine felt like it had the first time. I shoved aside the curious question of how her touch had felt to Sam. I had to find the strength to think it irrelevant in terms of our future.

She led me back toward the park entrance and then toward our cars. "Follow me home," she instructed when we reached her truck.

"Right now?"

"Yes, right now. Is that a problem? You need to see Angie first?"

"No, I'll get with her later. I'm ready," I told her. "I'm ready to come home."

"Let me say this before we go." She took a step closer to me. "I didn't know what to expect when I called you this morning. Even if the conversation hadn't ended this way, I wanted to apologize for the some of the shit I said to you. I wanted to hurt you way you hurt me. I did that with words and actions. I didn't mean most of it."

"Most of it?"

She grinned. "Right. Most of it." She added nothing further. "See you in the driveway." She got into her truck before I could respond.

I walked the additional block to my car. Once inside it, I pulled my phone from my purse; I had felt vibrations twice while I sat with Asia, signals that I had missed two calls. They were both from Angie. She had left one message, which I listened to as I pulled up behind Asia's waiting truck.

"Kyla, I decided to step out for a while. I hope to see your face when I get back." She paused. "I'll be gone from about six to nine, okay? Remember everything I said. All right. Bye."

So much had been said, so I didn't know what she wanted me to remember in particular. That she loved me and had always loved me? Did she want to remind me that she had claimed she would never hit me, though she had hit Deidra? What was the point of her message? No matter what she wanted, I knew I had a three-hour window in which to retrieve my things from her place. I didn't want to go through a drawn-out good-bye with her and decided I would leave a note and her key, which I would no longer need. I prayed she would understand.

Thirty

Asia

We pulled into the garage, my truck first, Kyla after me. The garage felt complete with both of our cars there. Each day I had entered the garage without her car there, I had felt as empty as the open, bare space. The presence of her car comforted me.

"I have a surprise for you," I told her before we opened the door to the kitchen. She smiled.

The kitchen had been spotlessly cleaned. It was empty, and the house was still. I walked to the family room and found no one, no Melanie, no Jovanna. Maybe they were napping. I headed upstairs, and Kyla followed. When we reached the second floor, we started to walk down the hallway, but then we both stopped and covered our mouths, I from a desire to squelch my laughter, Kyla from shock. She appeared scared and confused, while I was tickled. From the guest bedroom, we heard moans of pleasure and words of delight. Exactly what position they were in, we couldn't see, but whatever it was, Melanie was euphoric. I took quiet steps backward and led Kyla back downstairs.

"Who is that?" She tried to whisper and failed.

"Melanie and Jovanna."

"They're here?"

"Yep. They came yesterday. I had no idea they were coming. They just showed up."

"I wondered who that was," she said.

"When? What do you mean?"

"Yesterday. Yesterday you called me," Kyla explained. "Had to be by accident. I heard them talking. I tried to figure out who it was, and thought maybe it was Melanie. I can't believe she came all the way to see you." Kyla tilted her head sideways. "So they know, then?"

"Yes, they know. They came to see how I was doing."

"That was really sweet. That makes this kind of awkward, Asia." She sounded sad. "Me showing back up after all this. We must look all kind of unstable to them."

I shook my head. "As a matter of fact, the opposite is true. They're actually very supportive of us. They encouraged me to call you so we could talk things out."

"Even with *all* that's happened?" she asked.

"Yes, with all that's happened. They know everything. They believe in love. They believe in us. It helped. You should thank them." I smiled at her.

"They must not have expected you back so soon." Kyla laughed.

"I guess not. Certainly sounds like fun. Shall we? What better way to show them our gratitude."

She gave me a puzzled look. "Shall we what?"

"Join them." My stomach shook as I tried to contain my laughter with a convincing expression.

"You mean in their room? In their bed? A foursome?"

"Sure. Why not? You wanted to spice things up with us, right? This is the perfect opportunity. I think they'll be down."

"I've always thought Jovanna was kind of fine." Kyla licked her lips sensually. "You're right too. This will liven things up for us right away. Come on." She put her purse down and walked toward the staircase again.

After what we had been through the past couple of weeks, I wanted Kyla to get angry with me and show disgust at my suggestion. I knew I shouldn't have played with her, but I thought the joke would die as soon as it began. Instead, Kyla considered my suggestion. I was furious instantly.

"You've got to be fucking kidding me!" I screamed. "We're trying to make things right, and you go and agree to some shit like that? Get the fuck out, and don't come back."

Kyla blinked at me, like she didn't understand my words.

"What? You suggested it. What's the problem?" she asked.

"*You* are the fucking problem," I told her.

She frowned at me. Then a moment later she fell to the second step and burst out laughing. "Shh . . . ," she told herself and covered her lips with one finger, but she couldn't stop her laughter. She pointed at me and gasped for breath.

Damn, she got me. "I should kick your ass," I said as I went to her and wrapped my fingers around her neck in a playful choke.

She was crying. "I got you good." She wiped her eyes. "You should have seen the look on your face." She continued to laugh. "That's what you get for playing with me."

"I can't believe you." I loosened my light grip around her neck and put my arms around her shoulders.

"That was funny as hell." Her wet eyes looked into mine. "It's just me and you now. Got it?"

"Got it." I lowered my head and kissed her salty lips. More warm tears began to fall. She no longer laughed.

"I'm so sorry," she whispered softly between kisses. "I wish I could make all of this go away." Her body began to shake.

I held her tightly. "It's okay, baby. It's okay."

"I wish none of this had ever happened. I know I made mistakes before, but this is by far the worst ever."

"We're going to work this out," I whispered, trying to assure her. "Together."

She responded with a squeeze. Behind her, at the top of the stairs, stood Melanie and Jovanna, covered in robes. Jovanna's head lay against Melanie's chest. She smiled down at me, and Melanie gave me a thumbs-up. They walked back to their bedroom.

"I love you," Kyla told me.

"I love you back. I'm so happy you're home."

Thirty-one

Kyla

"You want to go back by yourself?" Asia asked after I told her I wanted to go back to Angie's to pick up my things. We had gone into the bedroom and were lying face-to-face on the bed. "You don't think she'll try to stop you, do you?"

"I don't think so. She said she won't be there from six to nine."

"What about Deidra? Think she'll show up again?"

I hadn't thought about that. "I hope not."

"We can ride with you. There's enough room in my truck for all of us and your things."

"Yeah, okay. Just in case somebody shows up. I don't want any trouble."

Asia's phone rang in her purse, which was next to me. "Hand it to me, will you?"

I reached in her purse, got her phone, and handed it to her. A piece of paper with our names on it caught my eye. I pulled it out when she answered the phone. Her name was at the top, to the left, and mine was at the top, to the right. Beneath our names was a list of different items from the house. She had listed the chaise in our bedroom under her name and the bed under my name, along with the chest of drawers. She had listed two small paintings we purchased in the Dominican Republic under her name and a hand-carved sculpture from Jamaica that I loved under mine. Items from every room in the house were on that sheet of paper.

"That was Melanie, checking to see if it was okay for them to come to our bedroom," she told me.

"What's this?" I asked.

"Oh." Asia snatched the paper from my hands. I tried to take it back. "I told you I didn't know how the conversation would end. If it had ended badly, I would have shown you this list. I had already taken it upon myself to divide things up. Why? You disagree with the list? I didn't get it right? I tried to give you everything you like."

I straddled her and was able to retrieve the paper from her slim fingers. "Let's see." I scanned it. "You gave yourself all the kitchen appliances. Really?"

"I cook more than you do."

"Oh, right. You have to make your spaghetti."

"I know what you're hinting at, and that's not funny, Kyla," she said.

"I'm just saying. How many times a month do we have spaghetti?"

"So that's what bored you? My cooking?"

"Lord, I was just teasing."

"No, you weren't. There's humor in all teasing, or so they say."

I kissed her. "I love your spaghetti. Especially the sauce."

"Mmm. Whatever." She grabbed my waist and tackled me, turning me over. "When you start cooking more, you do the menu, okay?"

"I'll start cooking more, then. Bet that'll spark things up."

"Just don't burn the house down."

I was offended. "Quit playing. You know I can cook."

"You're all right. I cook better," she stated matter-of-factly.

"This sounds like a cook-off challenge to me," I told her.

"Fine, but you know I'm going to win." She kissed my nose.

There was a light tap on the door before it opened. Melanie and Jovanna popped their heads inside. I rolled off Asia and stood. They both rushed to me.

"We're so happy to see you," Jovanna said with a hug.

"Yes, not the same without you," Melanie told me after Jovanna released me, and then she embraced me herself.

"Glad to see you both." I touched Jovanna's short hair. "You look really good. Love your hair." I glanced back at Asia discreetly, and was so swift that neither Melanie nor Jovanna noticed the move. Asia stuck her tongue out at me.

"Thanks." Jovanna smiled.

"Asia's been a great sport, letting us stay," Melanie said.

"She wouldn't have it any other way," I told her.

"I'm happy you came. Seems like you're enjoying yourselves." Asia winked at them and giggled.

Jovanna elbowed Melanie. "See, I told you they were home."

Melanie laughed and shrugged her shoulders. "Hey, we're all grown women. What was that yelling about? That's what, uh, startled us."

"Nothing," I said quickly.

Asia chuckled again. "Inside joke. Sorry, guys."

"What do you have planned for tonight? We saw on Facebook that there's a party tonight," Melanie hinted.

Asia looked at me. "Well, first we have to take care of some unfinished business. Want to roll with us by Angie's?"

Melanie and Jovanna exchanged concerned glances. "What's up at Angie's?" Melanie asked.

Suddenly I felt ashamed again and was too embarrassed to answer the question.

Asia answered for me. "Going to scoop up Kyla's things."

"Oh, yeah, yeah, sure," Melanie said happily. "We'll go along. We got your back."

"Good. Thanks. So what's up in Chicago these days? How's everybody?" I asked. From what I remembered of their circle of friends, they were all some of the sexiest lesbians I had ever met.

"Everyone is really well," Melanie answered.

"Please tell them I said hello, especially Ali. I loved her. She was so sweet."

The room was still for a second too long. The quiet tension sent prickles up my neck.

"I will," Jovanna responded. "She really enjoyed you too."

"Are she and her lady friend still together? I forgot her name."

"Mika? No, it didn't work out. She's still looking for her Miss Right."

"That's too bad," I replied.

Everyone remained silent. The atmosphere became tenser still, and I felt the kind of uneasiness I experienced when I talked about someone without knowing they were standing behind me and then suddenly they made their presence known. I didn't know what I had said to alter the climate.

"Let's go downstairs and catch up more now that Kyla's here," Asia suggested. She got up from the bed. "Meet you in the family room?"

"Sure," said Melanie.

Melanie and Jovanna left, and Asia grabbed my hand and escorted me into the bathroom. She closed the door.

"I didn't get to tell you," she whispered.

"Tell me what? What was that all about?"

"Last night Melanie told me about an incident with her and Ali."

"With Ali? What kind of *incident?*" I leaned against the counter.

"She told me that one night she and Ali had been drinking. One thing led to another, and they almost had sex."

"Jovanna's friend Ali? You're talking about her, right?"

"My reaction too." She got excited, then quieted down again. "Well, Melanie thought Jovanna didn't know about it, because Melanie never confessed about what happened. This morning we were talking, and surprise, surprise, Jovanna has known all along."

"What? She told Melanie at breakfast? In front of you?"

"Not really. She said it indirectly while talking about you and me. She was really letting Melanie know that Ali had told her what happened after it happened. All this time Melanie's been carrying the secret around, thinking Jovanna didn't know."

"Wow, that's a big-ass secret. Now I know why everybody got so quiet. Damn, this has been a crazy weekend for everybody," I acknowledged. "Emotional all around."

"I'm glad they came," Asia said. "Where do you think we'd be if they hadn't?"

I didn't even want to admit that had Asia not called, I would probably still be in Angie's bed, confused and wondering what I had gotten myself into with her.

"You know, they helped me realize that it took courage for you to tell me about Angie. I couldn't see beyond my own feelings to listen to what you had to say and how you were feeling."

"I tried to be honest with you, with the hope that we could talk it through." I shook my head. "Like I said, I just wish none of it happened." I didn't know what else to say.

"Let's try to put all this behind us. They got their closure, and so do we."

We kissed.

"Yes, we do," I said.

Asia, Melanie, and Jovanna sat anxiously in the truck while I entered Angie's apartment building. On the ride over we had discussed various "if, then" scenarios. If Angie wasn't home, as she had promised, then I'd send Asia a text that said Clear. If Angie came home while I was inside, then I would text Asia, Subject has returned. If Angie attempted to talk me out of leaving, then I would text, Harassment. Asia would ask, Assistance needed? I would respond, Okay or Be on the lookout. Finally, if Angie tried to stop me physically from leaving, then I would text, Disturbance or Assault. My word choice was dependent on the severity of Angie's demands. Asia would respond, Nine-one-one? If I could respond and didn't need 911, I would text, Situation under control. If I responded Help, or didn't respond at all, Asia would place the call to 911. The three of them would get out of the truck and await the officers' arrival..

Inside Angie's apartment it was dark, aside from the dim light in the kitchen. I checked the kitchen to make sure Angie wasn't at the table. Next, I entered her bedroom. She wasn't in bed. I checked the bathroom and the closet next, then looked in the second bedroom, where my luggage sat. Angie wasn't there. Clear, I said to Asia via text.

Most of my clothes were still shoved in the suitcases and bags I had hurriedly taken from the house the day before. In the still of Angie's apartment, I again acknowledged how swiftly the reconciliation with Asia had occurred. Had I again moved too fast, but in reverse? I wondered if I would have been as receptive to Asia if I hadn't learned of Angie's violent tendencies. Did I think of Angie as an abusive woman? Not really. But that was the problem with women. We tended to excuse the behavior someone exhibited toward someone else in the past, thinking it wouldn't happen to us. Then it did.

I understood Angie's attempt to equate her abuse with a cheating past. Maybe she was right. Maybe she would never hit me, just like she claimed she would never cheat on me. I wasn't comfortable taking any chances.

I picked up my small travel case and gathered a few items I had left in the bathroom. Once I had zipped the case, I threw a duffel bag over my shoulder and grabbed a suitcase in each hand. It would take two trips to remove all my luggage. Asia popped open the trunk when I got outside, wobbling from the weight of the bags. She met me at the rear of the truck.

"I'll arrange this," she said and took one bag from me. "Go get the rest of your stuff."

When I returned to the apartment, it was still quiet. I halted at the dining room table and used a pad of paper and a pen to write a note. What was I supposed to write? *I decided I love Asia most.* True, but it was too blunt. *Can't be with you. I think you might hit me.*

Again, true, but I didn't want to say that, either. Finally, I put the pen to the paper.

Thank you for being so kind and opening your home to me. I appreciate all you have to offer in a relationship, but I decided to return to Asia. I hope someday you find the woman who completes you. Love always, Kyla. I tore the paper from the notepad and decided to leave it on the futon.

I rounded the corner and went into the second bedroom for my remaining bags, and there, atop one of the suitcases, sat Angie. She stared solemnly at the floor. Where did she come from? With my hand to my chest, I screamed.

"You scared me!" I yelled at her.

She stared blankly. "So this is it, huh?"

Her demeanor was sad. And odd.

"I thought you weren't going to be here," I stated.

"I had a feeling you were leaving. I decided I wanted to see you one more time." She stood. My suitcase rocked.

I reached for my phone. *Subject has returned!!!!!*

"What are you doing?" she asked.

"I had to send a message."

"Right now? In the middle of our good-bye?" She was agitated and annoyed. Angie had never been angry with me. She looked at the paper in my hand. "What is that? A note? You were about to creep out of here and leave me a note? Don't you think I deserve more respect than that?"

My phone beeped. It was Asia's reply, and I needed to respond. I tried to read my phone, but Angie came close, pressed my arm to my side, and held it to my hip with one hand. She took the paper from me with her other hand, read it, then balled it up and threw it over her shoulder.

"Are you sure you want to leave me?" Her face was only a couple of inches from mine, her breath warm against my cheek. The warmth and her closeness no longer excited me the way they had weeks earlier. My phone beeped again.

"It's best. I love Asia. She's where I want to be."

Her fingers gripped my arm tighter.

"Deidra left me because of you, and now you want to go and leave me?"

"What? What are you talking about? You said Deidra left because you were too controlling." I recalled Angie's explanation of their relationship collapse.

"I lied. She left because she knew I was still in love with you."

What? "You shouldn't have lied to me about that, Angie. You shouldn't have been over at my house, in front of me and Asia, acting like your world was crumbling down because she left you."

"I already told you I wasn't in love with her anymore. I told you I have always loved you."

"But you never said she left because of me. That's wrong."

"It is what it is," she replied nonchalantly. "I knew you would have responded differently if you knew the real reason. I handled it the way I needed to in order to get you. And now you're leaving, anyway. Ain't that about a bitch?"

Another beep. I tried to free myself from Angie's hold.

"I . . . really . . . have to get that." I struggled some more, but she wouldn't let go.

"Whoever that is can wait." Angie frowned at me.

"No," I protested. "It can't."

"Yes. It can," she said firmly.

I became frightened. How had she been so gentle with me all these years and suddenly so aggressive?

"I don't know what you want me to say. I already told you I didn't know how you felt all this time, and I also told you I didn't know how this would turn out between us. Now I do. You can't be mad at me for choosing Asia."

"Well, damn it, I am." She let go of my body and put a fist to her chest and pounded against her heart. "How can you do this to me?" That same fist then aimed at my face. I ducked, and the punch landed on the mirror behind me. The glass cracked, then shattered, sending pointed, sharp pieces to our feet.

No one—not my mother, my father, my sister, David, any friend or foe—had ever hit me. I was shocked and angered. "Did you just try to hit me?"

Angie grabbed her bleeding knuckles with her left hand. I pushed her away, and she stumbled backward, slipped on glass, and fell to the floor. *So this is how it starts. . . .*

"Kyla, no," she yelled. "I wasn't trying to hit you."

"That swing was pretty fucking close to my face," I yelled, standing over her.

She denied my accusation. "I told you I'd never hit you. I hit the mirror because I'm mad. I'm hurt."

"You hit the mirror on purpose? Who does shit like that?"

Angie stood quickly and cornered me.

"Get away from me," I ordered. "Now I know I made the right decision. Move so I can leave."

Her bloody hand reached for me. I dodged her touch, and her bloody fingers swiped my sweater, leaving a red smear on the cable-knit pattern.

"Wait, wait." Angie winced and tried to talk through her pain. "This wasn't supposed to happen like this." Her tone softened.

"Too late. It has. Glad I got to see it now."

"This isn't me, Kyla. You've got to know that. You've never been so upset, you kicked, hit, or threw something? Something to get your anger out?" She tried to plead her case softly.

"Maybe. But never another person. And I never would, especially not somebody I claim to love."

"I do love you, Kyla. I've been trying to show you that."

"I might consider responding to that if I hadn't seen your fight this morning. And now this? You've shown me who you really are."

"You're going to let today overshadow all these years? Let it ruin all the good times we've had?" She was mad again.

"Yes. None of that matters now," I told her.

"Kyla." She said my name, nothing more.

I grabbed my bags and studied her bleeding hand. "Humph. What would your father say?" I scoffed.

"You better leave my father out of this," she snapped and grabbed a tight hold of my arm, the same way she had held on to Deidra that morning.

I freed myself somehow, turned around, and ran through the apartment, into the hallway, and toward the elevator. A man had just stepped inside it, and he held the door for me. Angie followed me out of the apartment, but she slowed down when she saw the man. She reached the elevator just as the door closed in her face.

Thirty-two

Asia

Kyla ran out of Angie's building, distraught and angry, just as the squad car arrived. She rushed toward me, Melanie, and Jovanna, and her eyes bulged when she noticed the officers who had gotten out of their vehicle, each with a hand at their waist.

"What happened?" I asked anxiously when I noticed the bloodstain on her sweater. I studied her face for bruising.

"What's going on here?" asked one of the officers, a gentleman with red hair sprouting from under his tight cap. His partner, a black woman, walked at his side.

Melanie spoke. "Melanie Benson. This is Kyla Thomas." She gestured toward Kyla. "She came to retrieve her belongings from a friend's apartment. We became concerned by the length of time it was taking her and called nine-one-one."

"Where's the disturbance?" he asked, irritated.

Angie burst through the front door with a washcloth wrapped around her busted, bloody hand. She stopped when she saw the officers.

"The friend?" The male officer nodded toward Angie.

"Yes," Melanie answered for me.

"Ma'am, this way," the officer instructed, his voice increasingly aggravated. He waved his fingers for Angie to approach us. She did so slowly.

Angie's expression dimmed, becoming innocent, relaxed, and her hesitant walk was the only sign that she was concerned.

"Shit," the female officer muttered, but we all heard. She and Angie exchanged glances. The officer shook her head from side to side, as if to say, "Don't say anything."

"These ladies indicate that there was a disturbance in your place involving this woman here," said the male officer. He pointed to Kyla and then spied Angie's hand. "Care to explain?"

Everyone stared at Angie. She held her hand up and inspected it, as if she was noticing the wound for the first time. Her eyes went to Kyla. She pleaded through mildly angry eyes. Just as Angie was about to speak, Kyla offered her side of the story.

"I was staying with my friend Angie for a few days, and I came to get my things. Angie was trying to help me with my luggage, and it was so heavy that she hurt herself with it," she lied.

Mr. Officer sighed. Melanie groaned. I held my breath to stifle the curse words ready to fly out. Why would she defend Angie?

"The luggage was so heavy that she's bleeding, huh? That's what you're saying?" The male officer asked, trying to call Kyla's bluff.

"Yes. She, uh, she picked it up and fell forward. Hit her hand," Kyla replied.

No one said anything.

"I had a lot of things in the suitcase," Kyla added softly, unconvincingly, and unbelievably.

Mr. Officer tapped his partner's shoulder, and they turned around for a private conversation.

"What was that about?" I mouthed to Kyla.

Melanie held up a hand to me to hold off conversing until the officers left. I tried to catch Angie's attention, but her eyes were focused on the female officer. Finally, they turned back around.

"Ma'am," he said, addressing Angie, "what your friend says here is correct?"

Angie met the female officer's eyes. She gave a gentle nod. "Yes. That's correct."

Mr. Officer studied Angie's hand one more time. Then the blood on Kyla's sweater. Then he glanced at my face, Jovanna's, and Melanie's. Everyone was silent and tense.

"You three." He pointed to me, Melanie, and Jovanna. "We appreciate your concern for your friend, but next time, make sure there's a disturbance before you call nine-one-one, got it?"

"Yes, sir, we understand. Thank you for your time," Melanie answered on our behalf.

Mr. Officer tipped his hat to us and headed back to the squad car. The female officer stayed in her place. She peeked over her shoulder once her partner got into the driver's seat and then turned back to Angie.

"What the hell happened, Angie?" she asked. "I was hoping this wasn't a call for you that we were answering."

"Yes, Angie, what the fuck did you do to Kyla?" I demanded.

"Hold on, miss," the officer said. She held up a hand to me. "Angie? What's up? 'Cause we know that's a bullshit story she just told for you."

"It's nothing. Kyla's moving out, and we . . . you know . . . I'm not happy about it. I didn't hurt her, if that's what you're thinking. If that's what anybody is thinking." She looked around, glancing at me last. "I wouldn't hurt her."

"It's your lucky day. Good thing my partner trusts me, and good thing Kyla lied for you. You know better than to be getting your ass arrested. We've had this conversation before," the officer warned.

"Who are you?" I quizzed, irritated. I couldn't hold it in any longer.

"I'm somebody who's been knowing Angie for years," she answered, her eyes cold and unwelcoming. "Long enough to know exactly who you are and who she is." She eyed Kyla from head to toe and nodded appreciatively. "I understand. But leave it be, Angie. Kyla, get your things in the car," she instructed.

Melanie and Jovanna helped Kyla with the luggage, and they got inside the car. Mrs. Officer stood between me and Angie.

"I bet you two have some things you'd like to say to each other, but it's not going to happen. Not now. Not at all," she said in Angie's direction. "Miss, get Kyla home. Angie, I'll follow up with you after my shift."

We remained standing in a triangle. I wanted to make it clear to Angie that she was to avoid Kyla and to leave her alone.

"Don't contact her again," I told Angie, ignoring the officer's instructions.

"Miss," the officer interrupted.

"What? Shouldn't we get this out with you right here?"

"If you don't want my partner to come back and arrest somebody, *anybody,* this better get wrapped up right now, hear me?"

"Treat her right," Angie advised me.

I snorted. "Kiss the crack of my fuckin' ass."

"Miss!"

Melanie got out of the truck again.

"Get your friend," the officer told Melanie.

"I'm done. This is done. Thanks for your help, *miss*."
I squinted at the officer.

She dismissed me with a shake of her head and led
Angie toward the front door. We waited until Angie
was inside the building and the officer was in the squad
car with her partner. They followed us and made a turn
in the opposite direction once I was heading to the
expressway ramp. Kyla was replaying the events in the
apartment.

"I can't believe she tried to hit you," Jovanna said.

"Claims she wasn't aiming at me," Kyla told us.

"You don't believe that, do you?" I looked over at
Kyla. "You wouldn't have had to duck if she wasn't aiming at you. That's bullshit. Why did you lie for her?"

"Because nothing really happened. Our whole evening would have been caught up in that, had I told the
truth. Not worth the time."

"That was a quick lie, Kyla, but a bad one," Melanie
joshed. "That was the best you could come up with?"

Kyla laughed. "They didn't buy it, anyway. I'm just
glad it's over." She reached for my free hand. "It's really over."

Her eyes softened. It was over, I agreed to myself.
The first trial of our relationship had been more sig-
nificant and severe than I could have imagined. But
part two of our relationship was just about to begin. I
squeezed her hand. Through the rearview mirror Melanie and Jovanna smiled at me. I smiled back and drove
us home.

The Return
Thirty-three

Kyla

From the bed I stared at my luggage as it rested outside the closet door. I wondered if the suitcases and bags were as tired as I was from the shuffling from here to there and back again. I sat as still as the luggage, upright and stiff, suddenly unsure how to relax in my own home. Maybe I needed to unpack right away—place my belongings in the drawers and on hangers, tuck the luggage in the closet—and then, perhaps, we all could comfortably readjust to our appropriate places.

The four of us had lost our partying spirit after we left Angie's house, and had chosen to spend the evening inside. We had made a stop at the grocery store, and then Melanie, Asia, and I had sat at the kitchen table while Jovanna cooked Melanie's favorite chicken dish. We ate until we were full, talked, and laughed until our stomachs hurt. Melanie and Jovanna were the first to yawn and turn in, since they had an early morning flight. Asia and I quietly cleaned the kitchen together, as we had in the past. In our bedroom I didn't know what to do. Snuggle in her arms when I had freed myself from another woman's arms less than twenty-four hours earlier? Were we ready for that?

"How do we do this?" I asked while she undressed.

"Do what?"

I struggled to find the right explanation. "How do we erase the past few weeks and start over?"

Asia pulled a large T-shirt over her head, one she had slept in a thousand times before. "I don't know," she admitted. "I've never been here before. Day by day, I suppose."

I stood and began to undress. I didn't bother with a change of clothes, as all my belongings were packed and I didn't feel like going through them. I decided to wait until Asia was at work to settle back in, unpack, and sort through everything. Back in bed, the warm sheets were satiny against my skin and smelled of Asia. I inhaled the enchanting floral scent.

"Music tonight?" Asia asked from across the room, where she stood next to the Bose stereo system.

"Yes, please." That would help ease my nerves.

Asia put on a jazz CD. The speakers released an all too seductive melody, one Angie had played just a few nights before, while I lay in her bed, our bodies hot and intertwined. I squirmed and shuddered.

"Something else please," I requested.

"Sure." She switched to Anthony Hamilton.

Asia dimmed the light and scooted in bed beside me. We faced one another without words. Her eyes probed mine, curious and cautious. The reflection in my eyes mirrored hers. Anthony started the conversation. "No matter what the people say, I'm gonna love you, any-way. . . .You are my life. I can't let go."

"Like I said earlier, this will take some time," Asia said, apparently feeling the same uncertainty I felt.

"Even if we fuss or fight, try till we get it right. You are my life. I can't let go."

"I'm willing to do whatever it takes," I told her.

"Even if we disagree, you can put it all on me. You are my life. I can't let go."

"No talking about the past," she said.

"I'll try." I couldn't be certain I would never mention Sam's name again. What if Asia worked extra hours? Would I forever be plagued with fear that she might be with Sam?

"Don't, Kyla," she warned sternly. "As much as I might want to know about the past couple of weeks, I don't need to know. Understand?"

"Yes," I answered.

I understood exactly what she meant. A part of me still wanted to know about her experience with Sam, even though my heart would be crushed by the details. Did I need to hear who seduced whom that day? I didn't need to know if Asia had screamed words of pleasure or cried tears of regret. I would never know if she had murmured Sam's name in the low, lingering way she whispered mine. I wouldn't know if they had lain in each other's arms in an afterglow, or if Asia had dressed quickly, thanked Sam for her time, and offered her a raise for a job well done.

"All that I know now is to give you all of me. And no matter how long I take. And every part of me belongs to your love. Help me, help me."

"Let me say this, and then I'm going to sleep." Asia sat up, rested on one elbow, and stared down to me. "This was big, Kyla. A big-ass interruption in our relationship. This is the first, last, and only time I will forgive you for some shit like this. If you even think you have feelings for somebody else ever again, I'm out. No talking about it, no waiting for it to pass, no exploring your feelings. It's done, period."

"It won't happen again," I assured her.

"No, don't say that to me. You told me nine years ago I was the only one, and look what happened. Don't make statements you can't live up to."

"Why are you getting angry?"

"I'm not angry. I'm making a point. I can say confidently that I'll never cheat on you. You, Kyla, you can't."

"Then tell me why you'd want to be with me if you can't trust me."

"I didn't say I couldn't trust you. I said you can't tell me you'll never cheat on me."

"Same thing, isn't it?"

"Of course it's not. I trust you, or you wouldn't be here in the bed next to me right now. What I don't want you to do is tell me another lie that you'll never cheat."

"So somewhere in the back of your mind, you're always going to think I'll cheat on you?" I asked, knowing I had silently considered the same about her and Sam.

Asia lay back down. "Not what I said, either. I'm not about to walk around biting my nails in fear that you'll cheat on me. If it were to happen, though, I wouldn't be surprised."

I became defensive. "Wait, let's not forget how quickly and easily you hopped in somebody else's bed."

"Yep, I sure did, and that's a memory I'll always have. How about that? How does it feel to know you're the reason I fucked somebody else?"

"Damn, Asia, why do you have to say it like that?"

"Because that's what it was, Kyla, nothing more, unlike you thinking you're falling in love and shit with an ex."

How did we transition from such gentle moments in the afternoon to arguing already?

"Asia, that's not what happened, and this entire conversation isn't fair. What the hell happened between this afternoon and now?"

"Nothing happened. I just have to let you know this before you get too cozy on your side of the bed. And you don't have to think it's fair or agree with how I feel, but that's how it is."

Asia put her back to me and turned off the lamp on her nightstand.

"No matter what the people say . . . I can't let go. . . ."

I wanted her to turn that song off too. The only thing I agreed on with Asia was that no, this wasn't going to be easy.

Thirty-four

Asia

"Good morning, Sam."

Sam entered my office, fresh and exuberant, as if she had just returned from a weekend island getaway. Early that morning Kyla and I had seen Melanie and Jovanna off for their flight home to Chicago. Afterward, Kyla had told me she was taking another day off and would be home unpacking and getting settled back in. She was back in bed after I showered, apparently still irritated by our conversation the night before. I didn't know why she was so angry. I had only spoken truth.

"I'm meeting Sam this morning," I had told her backside while I sat on the edge of the bed.

"Okay."

"Once I handle this, we can move on."

"Seems like there's no moving on to you regardless," she commented.

I wanted to tell her that if she couldn't handle my truth, then she should rethink whether or not she wanted to be back home. I still had the divorce list in my purse and all. However, that would have been another hasty comment I didn't mean, so I kept those words to myself. I chose another route.

"I hope you replay what I said and understand I meant no harm. You must know that if I didn't believe in you, I wouldn't be here. I do trust you, and that's all that matters." *Don't make a fool of me twice. . . .* I held that in too.

She accepted my words with a shift under the covers and a soft "Mmm-hmm." She turned back over.

I had finished getting ready, so I kissed her good-bye on her cheek and left. I sent Sam a text before I left the garage. I asked that she meet me at the office at 9:30.

"Good morning to you too." Sam smiled sweetly and innocently.

"How was your weekend?" I asked and pretended I cared.

"Very nice, thank you. Yours?" She was polite, as always. She no longer appeared irritated by our Saturday morning telephone call.

"It was quite busy. Some things came up for me."

She lowered her head and then lifted it. A layer of hair covered one eye. I think she did this move on purpose. Two weeks ago I thought it was kind of cute. It did nothing more than irritate me as she sat before me.

"Really? What kept you busy?" she inquired.

"I had some friends in town," I told her. "I also talked with Kyla."

"I see." She blinked underneath her black hair. "Does that have anything to do with this meeting?"

"Everything to do with this meeting."

"What would you like to know?" she asked calmly.

"I'd like to know why you felt you could answer my phone. Why you didn't tell me Kyla had called. Why you told her I was with you and, most of all, why you lied about it. You had no right to do any of that."

Sam readjusted herself in her seat. She crossed her right leg over her left and placed her hands around her right knee. "Well, Asia, I answered your phone because it rang," she answered smoothly. "I didn't tell you Kyla had called, because you had just informed me that it was over between you two. I didn't see why it mattered that she'd called you, especially if it was going to interrupt our meeting. I told her you were with me because I wanted her to know. I lied about it because I didn't think you'd find out. You did say you two broke up, remember?" She paused. "Is this honest enough for you now?"

"Sam—"

"Wait. Before you even try to tell me I crossed lines by my actions, please remember you're the boss who slept with your employee. You made this bed. Now lie in it. I am. It's nice and comfy." She grinned.

All the words I wanted to say, I couldn't, as they might have landed me in a lawsuit. Melanie had warned me. Instead, I swallowed every "Bitch," "Heifer," and "Ho" comment I wanted to make, and for the second time in two hours, I chose new words.

"I'd very much appreciate it if you'd keep what happened just between us. As your boss, I made a mistake and crossed a line I shouldn't have. Please do not share this with any of the other nurses, your friends, nobody. I'd like to put this behind us."

"You and Kyla are back together I take it?"

"Not that it's any of your business, but yes, we are."

"Wow. She does move around quickly, doesn't she?"

"Watch your words about Kyla," I cautioned.

She smiled. "Well, it's wonderful you two are back together."

"I agree, it is." I didn't know how to take her comment.

"Do you know why it's wonderful?" She licked her lips anxiously.

"Not for you, no. Do share."

"Because now I get the satisfaction of seeing Kyla's face again with her knowing I fucked her woman. That's all I ever wanted. Thank you, Asia."

"Excuse me?"

"Kyla. Your dear, sweet Kyla. The woman you love so much . . ."

"What about her?" I became more annoyed.

"Years ago my cousin was head over heels for Kyla. Made a fool of herself for Kyla, actually. I was quite young back then, but I heard all about the night she met you at the dinner party that Kyla had failed to invite her to. Does that evening ring a bell?"

Of course it did. "Tiffany?" I was confused. What did Sam and Tiffany together have to do with Kyla? The incident when Tiffany snuck into Kyla's apartment and crashed the dinner party was years ago, just after Kyla and I began dating.

She laughed. "You seem bewildered. Let me break this down for you." She wiggled excitedly in her seat. "I've known about you and Kyla all along, before you and I even met. When you hired me, I put it together and saw an opportunity I couldn't resist. And, well, I knew eventually you wouldn't resist this, either. When Kyla called while you were at my place, it was like a gift from heaven. I couldn't have planned it any more perfectly if I had tried. Like Tiffany said, what goes around, comes around. Now every time Kyla sees me, she'll know I had you. I know what your pussy tastes like. Smells like. The sounds you make when you cum. You're a good fuck, Asia. I see why Kyla wants you back."

"So this was a setup?" I asked, thrown off my game.

"Not at all, Asia. You hired me on your own, remember? I just took advantage of the situation."

The twisted irony of the whole situation was that Sam had done to me and Kyla what Kyla had accused me of doing to her: Sam had got back at Kyla for Kyla's past indiscretions. Indeed, the entire situation was karma in its worst way. Kyla's past continued to haunt and stalk us; it was inescapable. I had to regain control.

"Do you want to remain employed here?" I asked her.

"Of course I do. This is the most fulfilling and satisfying job I've ever had." She grinned.

"If you do, then none of this ever happened, hear me? Keep Kyla's name out of your mouth, keep my name out of your mouth, and move on. I don't give a shit about Tiffany, and frankly, I think you're just as crazy as her, trying to get back at somebody so many years after the fact. That's childish. My mistake, though, was not remembering you're only twenty-six. Grow the hell up."

"I think you should watch your tone with me," she warned. "We wouldn't want this to get out, would we?"

"It won't. You're messing with a grown-ass women over here. Don't forget that."

Sam shrugged nonchalantly. She sucked the inside of her cheek, and her dimple caved deeply. "That's cool. I got what I wanted."

"So did I." I shuffled a few papers on my desk. "I'm done. You're dismissed."

Sam clucked her tongue and stood up. "Best of luck with Kyla. Hope it works out for the two of you."

"Why are you lingering? Don't you have an appointment to get to?"

"Sure do." Sam headed to the door. "Have a wonderful day, Asia."

I ignored her. What I couldn't ignore was the nagging question of whether I had made a mistake when I allowed Kyla to come back home. No doubt I loved her, no doubt I wanted to be with her, but at what cost?

Thirty-five

Kyla

"Thanks for coming by."

David and I had just finished putting my clothes away. We tucked the luggage in the closet, where it would stay until my and Asia's next trip. Finally, the suitcases could rest again.

"No way would I miss this chance. First good move you've made in a while, boo."

"I hope so, because now I don't know what to do. I don't know how to ease back into how we used to be."

"From what I hear, you don't want to be how you used to be. You want to be better. Start there. Everything that had you all confused in the head, change it. You bored? Figure out something exciting to do that doesn't involve an ex. Tired of the same meal? Cook something new. Bored in the bedroom? Whip out some new tricks, 'cause I know you got some. What you don't want to do is fall back into the same ole, same ole, or you'll be calling me because you went and messed up again."

"I don't plan to mess up again," I vowed.

"Good. I hope you learned your lesson, baby girl. Asia ain't one to be played a fool. She got your ass back good."

"I know. That's what I'm talking about. I can't shake knowing she's been with somebody else."

"You best shake it off like a loose wig, girl. Asia is a one-in-a-million kind of woman, so appreciate what you have."

"I will," I assured him.

"So what are you going to do to knock her socks off? 'Cause that's what you have to do now."

"I don't know. I'm mad at her," I told him, contradicting my declarations to forgive and forget.

David rested his face in his hands. "Lord Jesus," he prayed into them. "Help this child."

"She told me last night she wouldn't be surprised if I cheated again."

"Kyla, baby, sit down right here." He patted the bed. I went over and sat down. "You can't be mad at her for saying that. You got hot in the pants and up and moved in with some other woman all in a couple weeks. If she had done that to you, how would you feel? You'd be a hundred percent certain she'd never do it to you again? Probably not. Now what you have to do is make sure it doesn't happen."

"It won't."

"I believe you mean that. I also believed you a long time ago, when you said she was the one, and a few weeks ago you went crazy and thought Angie was the one. Don't let your head fall off like that again."

"It's on straight. I'm not going to lose her again."

"Cool. Time to reassure her with all these affirmations."

"For real, David, you and Marlon have been together longer than me and Asia. You two have had a totally monogamous relationship this whole time? Neither one of you has ever stepped out?"

His lips pursed. "Well, you know, baby girl, it's different for men."

"What do you mean? Cheating isn't gender biased. It's the same regardless. Who messed up? You or Marlon?"

"Nobody messed up, Kyla. It's just . . . we're made different. We have, you know, testosterone. We have needs that need to be satisfied."

"Everybody does. What are you dancing around? Who cheated?"

David rubbed his scalp. "I wouldn't call it cheating. I call it accepting."

"Stop talking in code to me!" I yelled.

David sighed. "On occasion we've allowed other men in our bed with us," he confessed. "Only together. Never separate. It would be cheating if one of us did it alone."

My eyes bucked. "What? I can't believe you never told me this!"

"Pop them eyeballs back in your head, girl. I ain't got to tell you everything," he said, defending himself.

"But threesomes, David? How does that help your relationship?"

"It keeps our relationship healthy."

I became angry. "So you've been on me about how I was feeling about Angie, and now you want to tell me you and Marlon have been sleeping with other men in your relationship? How is that right? How is that any better?"

"Because it's not cheating. We agree on it. What's also different is you had feelings for Angie, or so you said. We don't have any emotional connection to the men. It's just sex. That's all. Purely physical. Don't forget about the threesome trysts in your past. You were the side woman. Did you feel like the woman you were with was cheating on her man with him right there?

No. I don't claim that what we do is right for everybody. It's not. Every now and then it works for us. It's open, honest, and we keep it safe. Best way to do it if you're going to do it."

"So if I had told you instead that me and Asia and Angie had all been sleeping together, you would have supported it? Or better yet, all four of us, Deidra included?"

"I didn't say that, and you're taking it too far."

"No I'm not. You just have double standards. I can't believe you. I'm disappointed."

"Don't be disappointed. I love Marlon, and he loves me. The occasional men we let in our bed are there for nothing but ass."

I covered my ears.

"Honey boo, stop acting shy after you just came from sucking on somebody else's kitty cat. Remember, my relationship is sharp and intact, honey. It's yours that we're repairing. Now, if you plan to have a long monogamous relationship with Asia, let's make that happen."

"You have just blown my mind. I can't even think straight right now." I shook off visuals of David and Marlon having sex with other men, but together.

"You're a big girl, Kyla. Don't go getting elementary on me about this."

"I'm not. I'm just saying. I never would have thought. You never know what people are doing behind closed doors."

"That's true, because it's nobody else's business. Unless someone is hurting somebody, which you were. Now, forget about Marlon and me, and let's figure you out. What are you going to do to wet her appetite again?"

I raised my eyes to the ceiling in thought. "I could buy her flowers."

"Humph," David scoffed. "Go deeper."

"Spa, mani and pedi day? Romantic dinner?"

"Typical, but you're getting there. What else?"

I thought more and tried to recall all the moments that had made Asia smile. "One of her favorite singers is on tour and coming to Atlanta soon. I can get us concert tickets."

"Now you're getting hot."

"These are all things, David. Anybody can buy her something. How can I prove I love her and won't hurt her again?"

"By doing just that. Stop thinking about it, put your Nike shoes on, and just do it. These gifts are all the extra perks to show how much you do care."

So I did. I placed an order of two dozen roses for delivery on Tuesday. I went online to purchase tickets for the soulful songstress's concert in a few weeks. While online, I came across an old CD of the artist's that Asia didn't have. I called a small, old-school independent record store, and they had it in stock. I'd pick it up and present it to her as a prelude to the show.

I called Nakia at work and asked her to retrieve a size six, slim-fitting, chocolate-colored crochet dress that had been placed on the racks a couple of weeks ago. It was perfect for the same colored heels Asia had purchased months prior but had nothing to wear with. I wanted her to wear the dress to dinner.

"You worked things out?" Nakia asked happily.

"Yes. I'm back home, where I belong."

"Good. So happy for you. Before I go, let me tell you what Aidyn did Sunday."

I spent the next three minutes listening to Nakia describe Aidyn's first soccer practice experience and how his little, swift feet outsmarted the young players on the other teams. "We have a David Beckham on our hands, I'm telling you. My little man is just as handsome too."

"Yes, he sure is. Don't forget the dress. Take it up to my office, please."

"You got it. We'll have you two over for dinner again soon. Aidyn would love to see his godmomma."

"It's a date."

Next, I made reservations at an upscale Italian restaurant Asia favored for Thursday evening. Finally, I scheduled after-work massages, manicures, and pedicures at an expensive hotel and spa. I booked us a whirlpool suite with a city view for Friday night.

"How's that?" I asked David after my calls.

"It's a great start. You'll have to keep this up. Keep her happy, keep her smiling, and keep up the momentum."

"I'll go broke if I keep this up."

"She's worth every penny, isn't she?"

I laughed. "She won't want me with an empty bank account, will she?"

"She seems dedicated to you for better or for worse." David snapped his fingers. He had an idea. "Maybe that's it. You two should get married."

"Married?"

"Honey, yes. Every lesbian is walking around these days flaunting a ring on her left finger. You can't just be in a relationship anymore. You have to be engaged or married. Don't you know that's the in thing?"

I had heard through friends of friends about a few lesbian couples that had gotten hitched. I hadn't considered it for me and Asia. It wasn't legal in Georgia and seemed like a waste of time, energy, and money.

"I don't think so, David. I love Asia, but what's the point?"

"To profess your love to one another."

"We've already done that. Privately, just me and her."

"I hear you, baby. You could at least get rings. Both of you are walking around with bare hands, looking unattached. Claim your woman, honey."

"Don't you think that seems desperate? Like I'm trying too hard to make myself seem like I can commit?"

"Maybe so. Think about it before you dismiss it, though. Janet said, 'Diamonds are a girl's best friend.'"

"You are really trying to break me, aren't you?"

"Trying to help you do anything to keep you and Asia together and happy."

"Thanks, but let us get past these first few weeks before I get on bended knee."

"Good. Now that you have the rest of the week planned out, what will you do tonight?"

I hadn't thought about the evening. It was Asia's reality show night, and I didn't know if she'd want to be distracted by other plans. I shared this with David.

"That's the problem, girl. You two are too set in your routine. That's why the DVR was invented. Record that shit, and come up with something else to do."

"Stop yelling at me. I got this."

"Handle it, then, baby. Do your thing."

"Run to the store with me?"

David checked his watch. "I have a little time before I need to get home."

"Thanks. First, I have to take care of something I should have done earlier."

From my drawers I removed every intimate item I had showcased for Asia the day I packed and left for Angie's. I had to get rid of everything that might bring back memories of Angie. I stuffed them in a garbage bag, and then I tossed the bag in the trash bin outside.

Once in the passenger seat of David's car, I grabbed my cell phone, scrolled through my contacts until I found Angie's name, and hit DELETE.

Are you sure you want to delete this contact? the phone asked.

I was sure. I hit OKAY.

Thirty-six

Asia

I had an attitude all day. What I had learned about Sam and Tiffany irritated me, and I couldn't let it go. Even my revenge on Kyla had backfired, and it would forever be associated with her prior indiscretions with Tiffany. I had worked hard to erase what I knew of Kyla's sexual promiscuity, and unfortunately, it would be in my face each time I saw Sam. Sam and I each had our own vendetta, both geared toward the same person.

When I thought about it some more, I gave Kyla an ounce of credit in the situation. She had been honest with Tiffany by telling her she no longer wanted to see her. It was Tiffany who couldn't handle the truth. And Kyla had been honest with me about her feelings for Angie. And it was I who couldn't handle her truth. Both Tiffany and I had responded from fearful, insecure places with our vengeful actions. I wasn't big on self-help psycho babble, but I had learned that from the magazine article I read while Melanie and Jovanna were in town.

Regardless of Sam's intentions, I had to follow Jovanna's advice and honor the demand I had made of Kyla: not to bring up the past. I wasn't going to tell her about Sam and Tiffany's relationship as cousins, mostly because I didn't want her to know my cheating had been in vain. Sam and I had gotten what we wanted, yet I still felt slighted.

Kyla had been quiet most of the day. She had sent me just one text, saying she hoped the conversation went well with Sam. That's over too, was my response. Her car was in the garage when I got home at seven. Before I opened the door, I could smell garlic in the air. My mouth responded, and I swallowed. Inside the kitchen Kyla stood next to the table, with a timid smile on her face, comfortable in black jeggings, a yellow T-shirt, and an apron I bought her years ago that said I ONLY LOOK LIKE I COOK.

"Hi. Let me get that for you," she said quickly, then reached for my bag and took it out of my hands. "Welcome home. I made dinner. Here. Sit. Relax." She took a chair out for me.

I sat.

"I'll get you something to drink. What would you like? Wine? Something stronger?"

She hadn't put my bag down before she was in the cabinets, searching. The straps rested in the crook of her arm.

"I can make you anything you want," she offered, breathless, her words streaming together.

I softened. She was trying to make up and was so nervous, she couldn't stop her rambling chatter.

"Hungry? Do you want this? Let me get you a plate. It's a garlic shrimp pasta. I hope you like it."

"Kyla."

"That's not what you want? I can make something else. Whatever you want." Kyla opened another cabinet and shuffled through boxes and cans. She frantically searched for ingredients to make an entirely new meal. "There's some rice in here. I can thaw some chicken too," she offered.

"Kyla." I stood and walked over to her. I took the bag from her and set it next to the refrigerator. I rubbed my hands down her arms. "Breathe, honey. Breathe."

"I just want everything to, you know, get better. Be better."

I hugged her, and she rested her head on my shoulder. "It will be," I told her. "Day by day, remember?"

She exhaled, her breath warm against my chest. "Okay. Let's eat. You ready? Sit back down."

I washed my hands and took a seat back at the table. We ate quietly initially. I think both of us were afraid to begin a routine conversation about our day. And on that particular day I didn't think either of us wanted a rundown of the day's events. The details of my conversation with Sam, I wasn't going to share. It wasn't necessary to rehearse the details of her moving back in, either.

"Guess what I found out today?" she asked suddenly.

"What?"

"David was here today, helping me. Anyway, he told me that he and Marlon have threesomes sometimes."

I quickly shoved a bite of food in my mouth. *So it runs in the family,* I thought. "That's surprising. They seem so solid."

"That's what I said."

"Personally, I don't understand the purpose of being together if you're going to openly fuck other people. What kind of relationship is that? That's just an excuse for people who don't know what real commitment is. Real commitment is faithful, monogamous, honest, and involves two people. I can't be the only person who still believes in that, could I?"

"No. No, you're not. So yeah, that's that," she said softly. Her eyebrows turned upward in desperation. She had realized that was the wrong topic to discuss. She started over. "I made plans for us for Thursday and Friday nights. I hope you're okay with that."

"If it's me and you, I'm okay with that." I smiled.

Visibly, she relaxed. Her shoulders unfurled, and she straightened, her confidence restored.

"Oh!" I wiped my mouth with the napkin from my lap. "It's almost time for my show."

Her lips curled into a delicate smile. "Not tonight. We're recording it. I have something else planned for us."

"But that's my show. You know that," I protested.

"Watch it later on DVR," she said, and I protested no further.

We finished dinner, and I was both surprised and pleased that Kyla didn't ask me questions about my conversation with Sam. Instead, she quickly piled the dirty plates, glasses, and utensils in the dishwasher.

"Ready?" she asked.

"Yes."

"Right this way."

She led me into the family room, where she had moved the large coffee table, clearing the space in the middle of the room. Covering the carpet was a portable dance floor, and at its edge were two pairs of four-and-a-half-inch heels, a pair for each us, it appeared.

"Instead of dancing with the stars on TV tonight, let's dance with each other. I bought a learn-at-home instructional DVD with all kinds of dances on it. Salsa, waltz, all that stuff. Let's teach ourselves."

I really wanted to see one of my favorite celebrities perform as he was close to winning the entire competition. He could wait, though. Kyla's spontaneous gesture was a sweet and refreshing surprise.

"This is too sweet, Kyla. Thank you."

"You're welcome. Come. Put your shoes on."

I removed my Adidas and put on the ankle-strapped heels. Kyla did the same and inserted the DVD. A vibrant Hispanic woman welcomed us to dance with her and her attractive male partner. We selected a fun cha-cha for our first attempt. We learned the basic count, though we stumbled over each other's feet. We watched the professionals perform each new step, and after each one the woman would turn to the camera and point enthusiastically and say, "Your turn!" It didn't take long for us to pick up the routine, which was only a few minutes long. We held hands, twisted our bodies in unfamiliar directions, and wound our hips, making gyrating motions. Warm and sweaty, we slapped high five when we mastered the dance, or so we thought.

"No wonder all those people on the show lose so much weight. That's a lot of work," I said as I sank onto the couch, tired. "That was fun."

Kyla plopped down next to me. "Next week, new dance?"

"Absolutely." I kissed her sweaty nose.

"It's only nine forty-five," Kyla observed. "Your show is still on. Want to catch the end?"

We took off our shoes and turned the channel to the show. We tuned in just as the spotlight shone on the famous actor, whose arms were wrapped tightly around his sexy dance instructor. The host then announced that they had made it to the show's finale. He was on his way to winning. His partner jumped into his arms, and they hugged. I smiled to myself and kissed the top of Kyla's head. I was on my way to winning, too.

Thirty-seven

Kyla

Asia and I still hadn't made love. Even after the flowers, the concert tickets, and the romantic dinner, there was no sex. At night we held each other tenderly, though we hadn't connected intimately. One night I began a stroke up and down her spine slowly and softly. I felt the heat between her thighs as her body responded. She breathed deeply, but her body suddenly stiffened. I didn't know what to do, so I rested my hand at her waist and went to sleep. The following night Asia leaned in for a good-night kiss just after our heads rested on the pillows. The kiss deepened, our lips happily reunited. Until Asia abruptly backed off once again.

My body missed and craved her, especially as we lay next to one another for our couple's massages. I wanted my hands to caress Asia's body and bring about the soft moans that escaped her mouth when the masseuse rubbed her in the right spots. It was Asia's hands I desired against my skin, rubbing my calves and thighs. I had to have her. I had grown tired of knowing Sam was the last woman she had been intimate with.

An hour later, we were back in our suite, our bodies soft and scented with seductive jasmine flower oil. Asia was sprawled facedown on the bed in yoga pants and a T-shirt.

"I feel so good. That was just what I needed," she moaned.

I stood at the foot of the bed, hovering above her. "Is that all you need?"

"Hmm?" Her question was muffled by the sheets.

I crawled above her on the bed and kissed the bottom of her spine through her shirt. "I asked if that's all you need."

Asia rolled over to face me. The hesitancy she had previously exhibited had diminished. "I was hoping you'd ask that."

Her face was bare, and yet she was more beautiful than ever. Her dark eyes betrayed her yearning for me. Her breathing was already heavy.

"Well? What do you need?"

"You," she told me. "I need you. Come here," she requested.

I bent to her parted mouth and kissed her. Her tongue was as soft and warm as the touch of her skin. We kissed deeply, passionately, slowly, then aggressively. Asia ran her hands up and down my waist, caressing me through my tank top, until finally her fingertips found their way underneath and explored my skin. We still kissed. Her thumb circled my navel, and then her hands rose to my breasts, cupping, squeezing, pinching.

"Ahhh . . . ," I breathed into her ear, and then stuck my tongue inside. She squirmed and dug her fingers into my skin in delight. I sucked and licked her earlobe, down and across her neck. She accepted my kisses willingly, lifting her neck and pressing it to my face. Her hips circled beneath me, searching for mine. I lowered my body and ground with her. Asia's hands reached for my ass and found it. She held on with each thrust against her body.

"I missed you," she whispered.

"I missed you too," I told her.

She opened her legs farther, and I took advantage of the space, settling my middle against hers. We rubbed. I throbbed.

Asia lifted my shirt over my head and bit the skin at my collarbone. It hurt in the most pleasurable way. She nibbled against the bone, then made her way over to my shoulder and down my arm. She took my hand in hers and placed it inside her pants. My fingers drowned in her wetness. Her juices provided an easy glide into her warmth. She inhaled sharply at my insertion. I rested my fingers deep inside, with a slight stroke of my middle finger against her innermost pleasurable spot. Her muscles tightened, then loosened and tightened again. Finally, I did strokes in and out, exerting pressure against her G-spot, my thumb against her clit. I brought her to a near climax and then stopped to remove her pants completely. I turned her so she was facedown on the bed and brought her hips up in the air. I buried my face in her ass, jasmine oil and sweat dampened my cheeks, and still I dove farther, my tongue as deep as I could go. Asia screamed.

"Shit! Kyla, shit . . . Fuck me, baby."

My fingers found their home again inside her, and I fucked her with both my hand and my tongue. Asia's ass slapped hard against my face, coming down on my fingers, and I thrust faster and deeper until I felt her rush. Her back arched, her insides gripped my fingers tightly, and warmth ran down my hand and wrist. And still she wouldn't let me go.

"Make me cum again."

And so we kept fucking, our bodies slippery and greasy. The room became hot and smelled of flowers and sweat. I sucked her ass cheeks, then opened them wider, and ate her ass while my hand continued to rock her pussy.

"That's it, baby. That's it," she told me. She came almost immediately.

When her body calmed, I freed myself from her hold. She lay on her back and scooted up.

"I want to taste you," she said. "Give it to me."

I went to her, put a knee on each side of her face, grabbed the headboard, and lowered my hot pussy to her face. She devoured it. She licked and swallowed my wetness, her tongue dove inside, and then she opened my clit, its delicacy fully exposed, and flicked her tongue across it. The intensity was overwhelming, so much so that I almost couldn't handle it. Asia gripped my waist tightly and wouldn't let me budge as the tip of her tongue continued to stroke. The feeling was hot and unbearable and frighteningly delicious at the same time.

"Asia," I cried. My eyes began to water. I wanted to scream from the searing sensations building at my clit. The more I squirmed, the tighter she held me, her tongue creating an increasing burning sharpness between my legs. The hotter I became, the more my body trembled involuntarily, and the more I anticipated what was next. My lower back warmed, my stomach twitched, and my insides pulsated. Like lightening, I came, experiencing one of the strongest orgasms of my life. A gush of wetness exited my body like never before. I could barely hold on to the headboard; I was light-headed, dazed, between the heat flashes and the dizzying orgasm.

Asia calmed the burn with a soft suck, my entire clit in her mouth. She held it, her tongue soothing the pounding throbs. I wiped my tears. Eventually, I lifted myself and lay at her side. She stroked my hair.

"You all right?" she asked. Her voice was sultry, like the first time we made love.

"I'm fine," I answered. My body temperature cooled. "That was amazing. And painful."

"But was it good?" she asked, though she knew the answer.

"It was . . ." I waited and then looked to her. "The best."

Thirty-eight

Asia

It had been a month since Kyla had been back home, and each day had been wonderful. We were back in a honeymoon phase, adoring each other with appreciative eyes and fresh, optimistic outlooks. Every Monday we partook in our at-home private dance lessons, witnessed only by the encouraging instructors behind the TV screen. Every other day of the week we did whatever we wanted to. Spontaneity had become the theme of our relationship. We were reenergized and recharged, ready to explore our lives together again.

The only piece of the past that remained a constant in the present was Sam. I grimaced every time I needed to work on the nurses' schedules. I kept Sam busy, making her lunches short and assigning her patients who were a good distance from the office. I remained grateful that Kyla had not asked about Sam. If she was nervous about Sam and me continuing to work together, she never expressed it. She obeyed our rule not to bring up the past and to let it be.

Since the day Sam revealed her connection to Tiffany, I had seen her only once, at the agency's monthly meeting I held in the small conference room at the office. Sam had arrived and had taken a seat next to me. I wanted her to take a different seat, but I had no valid reason for asking her to move, and doing so would have provoked questions from the clueless nurses who were already there. So she sat next to me, doodling hearts on her notepad occasionally. Once her knee rested against mine, and I kicked her underneath the table. I didn't think anyone noticed, and she kept her body parts to herself for the rest of the meeting.

"Sam, can you please stay for a minute?" I requested after I dismissed everyone else. I waited until the other nurses had filed out of the room before speaking. They chattered among themselves in the outside sitting area.

"Yes, Asia?" She sat back down.

I turned in the swivel chair to face her. "From now on, sit across the table from me, not next to me. And don't ever pull any shit like this again."

"It's just a chair. You don't own it," she shot back.

"As a matter of fact, yes, I do."

She blushed like a schoolgirl. "Okay, no problem. No harm meant. I was only teasing you."

"Sure. That's all," I said, dismissing her.

"What? We can't talk anymore?"

"What's there to talk about? I just asked everyone if there were any questions about work. Aside from that, we have nothing to discuss."

"How's Kyla?"

"That's irrelevant to you."

Sam licked her lips slowly. "Yeah, maybe it is."

"Trust me, it is."

"I'm not thinking about you two anymore, anyway, I have a new girlfriend."

"Good," I said flatly.

"She's older. Respectful. Treats me right. Like a lady."

"I'm happy for you." I gathered my papers and put them into my folder and stood up.

"Maybe you can meet her at this year's Christmas party," Sam continued.

I didn't give a shit who she brought to the party. "Sure. Whatever. It's time to go."

Sam led the way out of the room, and from behind I cursed the heavens for blessing this woman with such beautiful looks and all that craziness. It was an oxymoron.

On a Monday afternoon I had another appointment with Mrs. Johnson. Every week she had asked me about Kyla, and at each meeting I had told her we were getting better with each passing day.

"That's what it's all about. I'm proud of you," she told me on this day. Then she coughed.

"It's like we've started all over again."

"You have, baby. That's how it was for Mr. Johnson and me. Second time around can be better than the first."

"I think you're right about that. Without everything we just went through, I don't know if we would have this level of appreciation for each other. I mean, I still wish none of it had happened. But there's nothing we can do but make the best of it. We are."

She placed her old, wrinkly, cold hand on mine. "Life and love are precious. Treasure each moment." Mrs. Johnson closed her eyes. "I'm tired, baby. Wheel me by the window so I can listen to the birds sing while I nap."

I positioned Mrs. Johnson in front of the doors to her balcony, opened one of them slightly, and allowed a warm spring breeze inside. I lifted the leg rest on the wheelchair so her frail legs could rest in a relaxed position. She inhaled deeply, and her body shook.

"Smells good out there."

"The lilac bushes have blossomed. Would you like me to bring some blossoms inside for you?"

"Yes. I would love that," she answered weakly.

I held her hand a moment before I left to retrieve scissors from the kitchen drawer. In a cabinet I found a small clear vase. I poured a little water into it and set it on the table across from her.

"I'll be right back."

Outside I went to the lilac bush and snipped several of the fragrant blossoms. This part of my job I dreaded. To each of my patients, I gave my best. To welcome them into my life brought me joy. To nurture them back to health was rewarding in a way like nothing else. Sometimes we won the battle; sometimes we lost. I was sad that Mrs. Johnson and I would lose, though I was happy to have had the opportunity to inherit some of her keen wisdom. The greatest lesson I learned from Mrs. Johnson about love and relationships was to appreciate the struggle, to have respect even through loss, and in the end to know that, no matter the outcome, I had given my all.

On my walk back inside I called her daughter, Patrice.

"It's time," Patrice whimpered. I consoled her.

Inside, I placed the lilacs in the vase and allowed the beautiful scent to fill the air.

"Thank you," Mrs. Johnson uttered and then closed her eyes again.

I was grateful for the brave life Mrs. Johnson had led, for the confidence she had to love unconditionally, and for the strength she had to understand others completely.

"No. Thank *you,* Mrs. Johnson," I whispered.

Thirty-nine

Kyla

Angie called and interrupted a smooth late Monday afternoon at work. I didn't recognize the number and picked up the call.

"Don't hang up," were the first words out of her mouth.

Her voice startled me. I hadn't expected to hear from her again. She wasn't supposed to contact me ever.

"Why are you calling me?" I questioned.

"I wanted to see how you're doing," she answered innocently.

"That's not necessary."

"Everything is good?"

"Angie, what do you want?" I asked, irked by her call and mad that I had answered the phone.

"To check on you, like I said."

"I'm fine," I answered.

"Good." She didn't say anything else.

"Is that all, then?"

"You and Asia are doing well?"

"We certainly are. What else? I have work to do."

"Nothing. I guess that's it. Just wanted to hear your voice. Make sure you were okay with your decision not to be with me."

"And why wouldn't I be?"

"Because despite what you saw that day, you know I know how to treat a woman like a lady. I always treated you with love and respect."

"Punching me is not loving. Nor is it respectful."

"I didn't hit you," she objected.

"You aimed, and you swung. That's good enough for me."

"You really won't let that shit go, will you?"

"Absolutely not. Look, no need to check on me. Don't make this a habit."

"I won't."

"Good."

"Maybe I'll see you around," she suggested.

"No, you won't."

"You never know. Atlanta isn't all that big."

"It's big enough. And unlike last time, if you run into me again, there's no need to speak."

"Um, we might need to."

"I doubt that."

"One last thing."

"And what's that?"

"Remember that no matter where you see me or who you see me with, you're still my number one."

"Do you need anything else?"

"Nah. I'm good now," she said smugly, satisfied. "See you."

"No, not if I can help it. Bye, Angie." I hung up the phone, but not before jotting down the number on a Post-it note, which I placed on my terminal. I needed to know it so I could ignore her, should she call again. *Stalker.*

I rapped my fingers against my hardwood desk and considered what to do next. The last month with Asia had been so fulfilling and we'd been so loving with each other that I didn't want to cause any unnecessary stress by telling her about Angie's call. I decided against it. We had agreed that the past would stay there, and for me, even if not for Angie, that was what she was: history.

In a moment of hindsight, I wondered why I had been tempted to risk what I had with Asia for a false fairy tale with Angie. I didn't know if she was the sweet little grandma who had my best interests at heart or the wolf in disguise, coy and sly as she lured me in. I was glad to have seen her true colors before I got comfortable with her and thus made the hugest mistake of my life. I was even more certain now that Asia was the only woman I'd have for the rest of my life.

In response to David's suggestion that Asia and I get married, I had asked Asia about it one night. She hadn't dismissed the idea, nor had she said it was something we should consider right now. Was there a need to put on a big show for family and friends when we had already survived as a couple and had made it this far? We didn't think so, but we told one another we'd revisit the topic at our ten-year anniversary.

I took a break from work and scoured a Web site devoted to Atlanta happenings with the hope of finding an event that would interest me or Asia. I came across a small announcement about an Atlanta-based author's book release event. The author had written a novel titled *Smooth Jazz Ridin'*, a true-to-life tale about the lesbian scene in Atlanta and what it had been like dating one of Atlanta's most well-known lesbians but always being "the other woman." The author, Styler Park, was quoted as saying: "I secretly worked on this book with a woman who has remained anonymous until now. She is a salon owner and has been the live-in girlfriend of one of Atlanta's top lesbians. While all the names have been changed for privacy purposes, trust me, you'll recognize yourself in this story. This is like the Video Vixen meets Atlanta. Everybody is about to be put on blast!"

I read the author's quote three times. She had to be talking about Deidra. No wonder Deidra had performed disappearing acts over the past year. She must have been planning and timing the breakup all along. If the book recounted the years of her relationship with Angie, that meant I was in it. Why else would she be referred to as the other woman? If I was in the book, that meant Asia was too. And likely every other woman Angie had ever dated, and every story Deidra had ever been told, whether the truth or a fabrication. That wasn't good. I knew that Asia and I had agreed to leave the past in the past, but if my suspicions were correct, my past was about to bite us in the ass. Again. I picked up the phone and dialed Asia's number.

"Hey, babe."

"Hi, honey." She sounded sad.

"What's wrong?"

"It's Mrs. Johnson. I don't think she'll make it through the day."

Asia had told me about Mrs. Johnson and how close they had become. I knew how fond they were of one another.

"I'm sorry."

"Thank you. Did you need something?"

I didn't want to dampen her day any further. I'd wait to share the news about Deidra.

"No. We can talk about it another time."

"Okay. I'll see you at home tonight."

"Okay."

"Wait. Slow waltz tonight?" she asked before hanging up.

"Sounds perfect."

I closed my eyes when I hung up the phone. I was worried. Our relationship had been reborn, and any exploitation by Deidra could send us spiraling back into a tense state. I sighed. Maybe I needed to keep Angie on my radar, after all. I picked up the Post-it note and entered her number into my cell phone again. Just in case. I worried for Deidra too. If Deidra had blasted Angie and their violent past, I had a feeling Angie would need the assistance of her lady cop friend again.

I added the author's Web site to my "Favorites" list for follow-up and logged off my computer. Rather than worry about Angie and Deidra and whatever the past might bring to the future, I was going home to put on my Monday night dancing shoes and dance the night away with my Asia. No matter what the people might say, I wouldn't let her go.

Discussion Questions

1. Kyla experienced boredom in her relationship for over a year. Should she have told Asia about her feelings earlier? Do you think it would have resolved her boredom or created friction in their relationship?

2. Do you believe it is possible to be a platonic friend to an ex? Are any of your exes friends, and if so, what are the boundaries of your friendship?

3. How do you think Kyla should have responded to her feelings about Angie when they first surfaced? Should she have ended her friendship with Angie?

4. When Kyla confessed her feelings for Angie to Asia, Asia suggested that Kyla explore her feelings further. Do you agree with Asia's response? How would you have responded?

5. Seeking vengeance, Asia had sex with Sam. Do you agree or disagree with Asia's response?

6. As one of Asia's close friends, Melanie suggested that Asia talk to Kyla, in hopes that the two would reconcile. If you were Melanie, what would you have suggested to Asia? Attempt to reconcile with Kyla, or end the relationship?

Discussion Questions

7. In the story, we learned that Melanie almost cheated with Jovanna's best friend, Ali. Ali told Jovanna about the incident, but Melanie never confessed. If you were Jovanna, would you have confronted Melanie or silently forgiven her, as Jovanna did?

8. Kyla found out that Angie had been abusive to Deidra. Consequently, it was difficult for Kyla to trust that Angie would not become abusive to her as well. Do you believe the concept of once an abuser, always an abuser? Do you believe that the threat of abuse was the only reason Kyla returned to Asia?

9. Although Asia forgave Kyla, she admitted that she wouldn't be surprised if Kyla cheated again. Knowing Kyla, do you think she will cheat again or remain loyal to Asia?

Notes

Notes

Notes

ORDER FORM
URBAN BOOKS, LLC
78 E. Industry Ct
Deer Park, NY 11729

Name: (please print):_____

Address: _____

City/State: _____

Zip: _____

QTY	TITLES	PRICE
	16 On The Block	$14.95
	A Girl From Flint	$14.95
	A Pimp's Life	$14.95
	Baltimore Chronicles	$14.95
	Baltimore Chronicles 2	$14.95
	Betrayal	$14.95
	Black Diamond	$14.95
	Black Diamond 2	$14.95
	Black Friday	$14.95
	Both Sides Of The Fence	$14.95
	Both Sides Of The Fence 2	$14.95
	California Connection	$14.95

Shipping and handling-add $3.50 for 1st book, then $1.75 for each additional book.

Please send a check payable to:

Urban Books, LLC

Please allow 4-6 weeks for delivery

ORDER FORM
URBAN BOOKS, LLC
78 E. Industry Ct
Deer Park, NY 11729

Name: (please print): _____

Address: _____

City/State: _____

Zip: _____

QTY	TITLES	PRICE
	California Connection 2	$14.95
	Cheesecake And Teardrops	$14.95
	Congratulations	$14.95
	Crazy In Love	$14.95
	Cyber Case	$14.95
	Denim Diaries	$14.95
	Diary Of A Mad First Lady	$14.95
	Diary Of A Stalker	$14.95
	Diary Of A Street Diva	$14.95
	Diary Of A Young Girl	$14.95
	Dirty Money	$14.95
	Dirty To The Grave	$14.95

Shipping and handling-add $3.50 for 1st book, then $1.75 for each additional book.
Please send a check payable to:
Urban Books, LLC
Please allow 4-6 weeks for delivery

ORDER FORM
URBAN BOOKS, LLC
78 E. Industry Ct
Deer Park, NY 11729

Name: (please print):_____

Address: _____

City/State: _____

Zip: _____

QTY	TITLES	PRICE
	Gunz And Roses	$14.95
	Happily Ever Now	$14.95
	Hell Has No Fury	$14.95
	Hush	$14.95
	If It Isn't love	$14.95
	Kiss Kiss Bang Bang	$14.95
	Last Breath	$14.95
	Little Black Girl Lost	$14.95
	Little Black Girl Lost 2	$14.95
	Little Black Girl Lost 3	$14.95
	Little Black Girl Lost 4	$14.95
	Little Black Girl Lost 5	$14.95

Shipping and handling-add $3.50 for 1st book, then $1.75 for each additional book.

Please send a check payable to:

Urban Books, LLC

Please allow 4-6 weeks for delivery

ORDER FORM
URBAN BOOKS, LLC
78 E. Industry Ct
Deer Park, NY 11729

Name: (please print):_____

Addre

City/S

Zip:

| QT |

Shipping and handling-add $3.50 for 1st book, then $1.75 for each additional book.
Please send a check payable to:
Urban Books, LLC
Please allow 4-6 weeks for delivery